"She's a ship, Miss Lambert.

"A seaworthy vessel, meant to sail to foreign ports. It would be sacrilege to use such a ship for nothing more than fancy tea parties."

"Is that how you see us, Captain?"

"What I see..." He wasn't even aware that his fingers had closed around her upper arm. Or that he had dragged her so close he could feel the sudden breath of air on his cheek as she looked up at him. His tone softened to a caress. "...is someone too grief stricken to think clearly."

"I assure you, Captain, my mind is perfectly clear on—"

Her words were abruptly cut off as he dragged her against him and covered her mouth with his.

He hadn't meant this. Hadn't meant to even touch her. But one look into those angry eyes and he'd felt the most amazing sexual jolt, which had him reaching out to take. To touch. To taste. And now, with his mouth on hers, he was free to indulge.

Dear Reader,

Have you ever been tempted to turn Mr. Wrong into Mr. Right? In each of our books this month, you'll delight in the ways these least-likely-to-marry men change their tune for the right woman!

USA Today bestselling author Ruth Langan brings us *The Sea Witch,* the first book in her brand-new miniseries, SIRENS OF THE SEA, which takes place in 1600s England and features three sisters who lose their father and brother and are forced to carry on the family tradition of serving the king as privateers. Lady Ambrosia Lambert and sea captain Riordan Spencer join forces to thwart a villain's plot to steal a cargo of gold bound for the king. With Riordan, Ambrosia faces many battles, but none more powerful than convincing him that their love can prevail...!

Mainstream historical author Bronwyn Williams returns to Harlequin—after nearly eight years—with *The Paper Marriage.* In this darling Americana story, a quirky matchmaker divines a marriage of convenience between her nephew, a steel-coated bachelor who needs help raising his adopted daughter, and a young widow in financial trouble. And in *Prince of Hearts* by debut author Katy Cooper, Edmund Tudor, the king of England's youngest brother, must choose between the woman he has fallen in love with and his duty to his brother's kingdom.

Be sure to look for *Prairie Bride* by talented newcomer Julianne MacLean. Here, a manly Kansas farmer, jilted by his fiancée, weds a mail-order bride out of necessity—and finds it frustrating when his secretive wife begins to soften his hardened heart!

Enjoy! And come back again next month for four more choices of the best in historical romance.

Sincerely,

Tracy Farrell,
Senior Editor

RUTH LANGAN

THE SEA WITCH

HARLEQUIN®

TORONTO · NEW YORK · LONDON
AMSTERDAM · PARIS · SYDNEY · HAMBURG
STOCKHOLM · ATHENS · TOKYO · MILAN · MADRID
PRAGUE · WARSAW · BUDAPEST · AUCKLAND

ISBN 0-373-29123-X

THE SEA WITCH

Copyright © 2000 by Ruth Ryan Langan

This edition published by arrangement with Harlequin Books S.A.

® and TM are trademarks of the publisher. Trademarks indicated with
® are registered in the United States Patent and Trademark Office, the
Canadian Trade Marks Office and in other countries.

Visit us at www.eHarlequin.com

Printed in U.S.A.

Please address questions and book requests to:
Harlequin Reader Service
U.S.: 3010 Walden Ave., P.O. Box 1325, Buffalo, NY 14269
Canadian: P.O. Box 609, Fort Erie, Ont. L2A 5X3

For Maggie Ryan Langan,
the newest link in our chain of love
And for her proud parents, Mary and Dennis
And siblings Caitlin, Bret, Ally, Taylor and Isabella

And for Tom
Who started it all in first grade.

Prologue

Land's End, Cornwall, 1665

"I bring a message from our mutual friend." Two figures huddled in the cabin of a ship that flew no flag. The candles had been snuffed. The only illumination came from the moonlight that filtered through the small porthole.

"I hope he sent gold with his message." The voice was raspy from years at sea.

There was the rattle of coin as the well-dressed man reached into his pocket and withdrew a sack. "You do as our friend asks and you'll be a wealthy man."

"Or a dead one." Work-roughened fingers grasped the sack. It disappeared from sight. "Now, tell me what it is he wants done."

"What he wants, what we all want, is for Charles to remain a weak monarch, so that, when the time is right, a certain mutual friend can step forward and claim the throne. That will seal our fortune. But for now it means assuring that certain shipments of gold bound for the king never reach London."

There was a low rumble of laughter. "My men and I have no problem with that. We were pirating these waters when the king was learning to walk."

"Times have changed now. Charles has his own privateers, who know a thing or two about fighting back. That's why our mutual friend paid you so well. If you have to, hire an army to ride with you." He produced a rolled parchment. "This is a list of some of the ships' captains who are loyal to the king and have agreed to stand with him. I'll have more names soon. See that they're destroyed."

"With pleasure."

A bottle was produced, ale poured. The two lifted their glasses.

"To England," the well-dressed man said. "And a new monarch."

The second man gave a raspy laugh. "To gold in my pocket. That's the only king I serve."

Chapter One

"Ambrosia." Bethany Lambert and her younger sister, Darcy, stepped into their oldest sister's room, then paused.

"Oh, don't you look pretty." Bethany eyed the red satin gown Ambrosia was wearing, admiring the low, rounded neckline and long tapered sleeves. "Isn't that from the bolt of satin Papa brought from Paris on his last voyage?"

"Aye." Ambrosia turned away from the window, where she'd been standing for the past half hour. In her entire ten and seven years, she'd never been concerned about her clothes. Nor was she today. She usually wore whatever their housekeeper, Mistress Coffey, made available to her. "There's no sign of the *Undaunted*."

Bethany, younger by a year, caught her hands and began pulling her toward the door. "It'll be here. If not tonight, then tomorrow. Don't worry. Papa and James will be home soon."

Darcy, the youngest at ten and five, couldn't hide her eagerness. "Grandpa and the others are already in the carriage."

The three sisters were as different in looks and personality as it was possible to be. Ambrosia was as tall and robust as most men, with long legs and a slender but decidedly feminine figure. Her hair was the color of a raven's wing. As oldest, she was the acknowledged leader. What's more, she was absolutely fearless.

Bethany had red hair, green eyes and a voluptuous figure that even the most modest of gowns couldn't hide. With a fiery nature to match her hair, she drew the eye of every man from cradle to coffin. Not that she minded. Her father claimed that she'd come into this world batting her lashes and twisting everyone around her finger.

Darcy was tiny, delicate, with blond hair and laughing blue eyes and a nature so sweet it was impossible not to love her. There was a shyness about her that was irresistible.

With reluctance, Ambrosia allowed herself to be led down the stairs and out the door.

Old Newton Findlay offered her a hand up into the carriage. "Ye're looking fine, Ambrosia."

"Thank you, Newt." She managed a smile for the old man, who had sailed with her grandfather and her father until he'd lost a leg to a shark. Now he hopped around in a strange, uneven gait caused by the wooden peg that served as a leg. Instead of sailing, he drove their carriage and helped around the grounds of the home they called MaryCastle, built on a spit of land that jutted into the Atlantic. The three young women had grown up hearing Newton's tales of his seagoing adventures.

Newton had put on a jacket over his usual sailor's garb to placate the housekeeper, Mistress Coffey, who believed in strict rules of propriety.

As Ambrosia settled herself beside her sisters, their housekeeper frowned. Mistress Coffey, a thin stick of a woman, had taken to wearing black when her husband died more than twenty years ago. Today's black gown had a high neck, long sleeves, and was starched so stiffly it threatened to crack when she moved. Not a single white hair was allowed to slip free of the perfect coil at the nape of her neck. "Hurry, Newton. We don't want to be late for Edwina's tea."

Ambrosia's head came up sharply. "I don't see why we should have to waste our time on Edwina's tea. Edwina Cannon is a silly, empty-headed twit."

"Ambrosia." Shocked and outraged, their ancient nurse, Miss Winifred Mellon, put a hand to her mouth. The old woman had been brought as nurse to the children of MaryCastle years ago, when Captain John Lambert's beloved wife, Mary, had died unexpectedly. But when the children were grown, and no longer needed a nurse, they'd learned that this sweet old woman had nowhere to go, and so they had simply kept her on. She spent her days reminding them of their duties as proper young ladies. Whenever their behavior was especially outrageous, she would have one of her fainting spells. Her spells occurred so frequently, no one seemed to notice anymore. Family and staff alike simply went about their business until she came around.

Because she was a maiden lady, and exceedingly proud of it, Winifred appeared only in white clothing. This day she was dressed in a gown of white wool. Over that she wore a heavy woolen shawl of purest white. Her white hair was as soft as a baby's, and fanned out around her pale face like cotton balls. She had even tied a white lace cap around her head, which Darcy thought looked like a sleeping cap.

"Calling Edwina names is beneath you, Ambrosia," Winifred said with that note of disapproval they had heard since childhood. "Your father would be shocked to hear his daughter speak in such a manner. And what would your brother say about such unladylike behavior?''

"James would agree with me, Winnie." Ambrosia's eyes flashed. "He escorted Edwina to a May Day picnic last year and said he couldn't detect a single thing in that empty little head of hers. All she cared about was her precious bonnet. Can you imagine wasting a whole day boasting of a bonnet? James is well rid of her.''

Winifred glanced at the housekeeper, and the two old women sighed. When it came to the defense of their older brother, James, the three Lambert sisters were as fierce as the king's soldiers. No woman would ever be good enough for him. As for their father, Captain John Lambert, his daughters were even more protective. Let no man speak ill of him. They adored him, and he returned their affection a hundredfold. Despite the fact that his duties as a ship's captain took him away from home for long periods of time, his daughters were devoted to him. Whenever he returned from the sea, their house rang with joyous laughter. His quick wit and charm made him a much loved leader in the tiny village of Land's End, as well as the rest of Cornwall.

There was no denying that theirs was a handsome family. The captain and his son were tall and muscular, their skin ruddy from their time spent at sea. Many a woman young and old hoped to snag the interest of John or James Lambert. As for the three sisters, perhaps because of the early death of their mother, and the long absences of their father and older brother, they had formed a special bond. At times they seemed to need no one but each other. They were their own best friends and confidantes. But their independence worried their nurse and housekeeper.

"You'd best learn to curb that tongue, Ambrosia," Winifred said sternly. When Bethany started to laugh, she turned on her. "And you'd best listen as well. Such impudence could become an impediment to making a proper marriage."

Ambrosia frowned. "If that be true, then I shall simply remain as I am. Alone, and enjoying my own company, Winnie. For I'll not forsake my independence for any man."

"Nor will I," Bethany echoed. "If a man can't love me for myself, he isn't worth the time of courtship."

Sweet Darcy nodded in agreement.

This had Mistress Coffey shaking her head in despair. "Then I'll remind you that you could find yourselves the only three spinsters in Land's End."

Seeing the shocked look in Winifred Mellon's eyes, the housekeeper's face flamed. To cover her lapse she sputtered, "At least you behave like a lady, Miss Mellon. What man would possibly want a wife who would rather sail than sew?"

From the driver's seat old Newton snickered. "A man's man, that's who. A man of the sea."

"See?" Geoffrey Lambert, dressed in his finest captain's coat and hat, cocked an ear toward Newton. "What did you see?"

Geoffrey had been one of England's finest sea captains until an accident with a misfired cannon had left him almost completely deaf. Now he spent his days regaling his granddaughters with tales of his adventures, and teaching them everything he could about survival at sea.

According to Mistress Coffey, he used his misfortune to hear only what he chose to hear.

"What I see is an old fool," she said under her breath. "Ah, here's the Cannon estate now. And look how many fine carriages are here ahead of us."

Ambrosia exchanged a look with her two sisters. Mistress Coffey detested being late.

"Now remember what I told you," the housekeeper lectured sternly. "Lord Silas Fenwick is a most important man in London. It's rumored that he's decided it's time to take a wife, and that he's come here to look over our eligible young maidens. Behave yourselves, and you may be able to snag a very wealthy husband."

As they filed inside, each sister took a deep breath, preparing for an hour of tedium.

"Ambrosia. Bethany. Darcy." Edwina Cannon's shrill voice assaulted them the minute they stepped into the parlor. "You must come meet Lord Silas Fenwick."

The three sisters studied the tall, elegantly dressed young man with sandy hair and a handsome, patrician face.

"Lord Fenwick, I'd like to present the Lambert sisters. Ambrosia, Bethany and Darcy."

"Ladies." He caught the hand of each in turn and, with a soulful look guaranteed to cause a flutter to young maidens' hearts, lifted it to his lips.

Edwina had her fingers locked around his arm in a death grip. "Lord Fenwick said he simply had to take tea with Mama and me, in order to see our lovely estate. You must come over here and let me tell you how we met."

"Must we?" Ambrosia saw the way his brow arched, but in truth, she didn't care. Not about Lord Silas Fenwick or Edwina Cannon, or how they'd happened to meet. All she could think about was that Papa might arrive home while they were out, and she would miss his homecoming.

"What a fine looking gentleman," Mistress Coffey was saying to Edwina's mother.

"He's been showing considerable interest since his arrival in Land's End. They make a lovely couple, don't you think?" Mistress Cannon saw the frown on the housekeeper's face and decided to drive home her point. "With Edwina's beauty and his wealth, they'd have such a fine life. Did I tell you that he said he'd insist that his wife keep a home in London?"

"How could anyone leave Cornwall for London?" Ambrosia remarked.

In the silence that fell over the room, Geoffrey Lambert held a hand to his ear. "Eh? What's done?"

"London, Grandpapa," Bethany shouted.

"Oh. London. Filthy place," the old man muttered.

Lord Silas Fenwick cleared his throat, striving to regain control of the festivities. "This is a lovely time of year in Cornwall. I noticed quite a few ships in the harbor."

Ambrosia accepted a cup of tea and a fancy pastry. "Our father's ship, the *Undaunted,* should be coming in any day now."

"I've heard of your father, Captain John Lambert. Your brother, James, is also aboard, isn't he?"

"Aye." Ambrosia's eyes lit with sudden pleasure. "Do you know them, Lord Fenwick?"

"I haven't met them. But my grandfather founded one of England's finest import businesses, which I've inherited. I've made it my business to know many of England's ships and their captains."

"Do you sail, Lord Fenwick?"

He smiled. "My interests lay more with business than sailing. But I do own a lovely ship, the *Sea Devil.* I've taken the king on several cruises along the Thames."

Edwina Cannon's eyes widened. "You mean you actually entertain the king of England, Silas?"

"Aye." He patted her hand, then smiled indulgently. "Perhaps someday I'll introduce you to him. I know he'll find you as charming as I do."

While Edwina giggled, Ambrosia set aside her tea with a clatter. "Oh, my, Mistress Coffey. I do believe we should be starting home."

"Home?" The housekeeper looked flustered. "But, Ambrosia, we just got here."

"I can see that Grandpapa is growing weary." She looked over at the old man, who was staring into space. "Grandpapa, are you ready to leave?"

"Sleeve?" He glanced down. "Is there something on my sleeve?"

"Leave, Grandpapa," Darcy shouted into his ear. "Would you like to leave?"

"Aye. Had my fill of sweets. Tea, too." He yawned. "Might take a nap before dinner."

Ambrosia leapt at the opportunity. Putting a hand under his elbow, she helped him to his feet.

Edwina stood and followed them to the door, towing Lord Fenwick with her. "But you haven't even heard how Silas and I met, Ambrosia. And I so wanted to tell you." She wrapped her hands around his arm again, staring up into his eyes.

Eyes, Ambrosia thought with sudden insight, that looked bored. As though he'd rather be anywhere than here with this silly female. The man must be desperate for a wife if he'd waste his time on Edwina Cannon.

She managed a smile. "You can save it for our next tea, Edwina. But Grandpapa's comfort must come first. You understand."

"I suppose so." Edwina offered her cheek, and the three sisters dutifully brushed their lips over skin that reeked of rosewater.

As they made their way to the waiting carriage, Silas watched with interest. Then, seeing Edwina's look, he turned to her with a sly smile. "A...colorful family."

"They're considered strange by everyone here in Land's End. The sailors say the three sisters can sail a boat as well as any man. And they've been known to handle weapons as well."

"Weapons? You jest."

"Nay. It's true. Ambrosia can wield a sword as well as any man. Bethany has been seen shooting a coin from the branch of a tree with her father's dueling pistol. And Darcy can bring down a bird in flight with the toss of her knife." As the carriage rolled out of sight, she sighed. "All in Land's End are convinced the three Lambert sisters are doomed to spinsterhood. What man would ever want a wife who'd rather brawl like a common sailor than sew and cook?"

"Ambrosia." Bethany and Darcy stepped out onto the widow's walk, the wide balcony that ran the length of the upper story of their house overlooking the sea.

The wind here was always brutal, gathering strength as it rolled across the endless miles of the Atlantic. Both young women drew their shawls around their shoulders as they faced into the breeze, hair flying wildly, skirts whipping about their legs. They made their way to where their oldest sister stood.

"Mistress Coffey says you're to come inside." Bethany's voice could hardly be heard above the roar of wind and waves. "Before you catch your death."

"Tell Mistress Coffey that I intend to stay here and watch for Papa."

Bethany shook her head. "Come inside, Ambrosia. Grandpapa is looking forward to your company at table."

Ambrosia turned and both her sisters could see the troubled look in the depths of those dark eyes. "Papa's ship should have been back days ago."

"Don't say that. It's bad luck." Bethany caught her sister's hand, as much to draw strength from her as to offer comfort. They were all concerned. But until now, none had dared speak the words aloud. "You know how it is when Papa and James put into some far-off port. There are goods to be bartered. Fresh crew to hire. And supplies to be loaded aboard ship for the return voyage."

Ambrosia's hands clenched at her sides. "Go and placate Mistress Coffey and Grandpapa. As for me, I'll stay here awhile, and hope to catch the first glimpse of the *Undaunted*'s masts."

The two younger sisters glanced at each other, then positioned themselves on either side of her. The warmth of the fire awaiting them inside was forgotten. As was the comfort of the meal their housekeeper had prepared.

"We'll all stay." Darcy's hand found its way into Ambrosia's.

"Aye. Together." On the other side of her, Bethany squeezed her fingers.

These three were determined to be, as they had been since childhood, a formidable wall of strength against the unknown. Whatever fear was in their hearts, they would face it together.

But it wasn't to be. It wasn't the cold that finally brought the three sisters indoors. It was old Newton, who came upon them in the fog that rolled in just before dusk. A fog so thick it blanketed the land, making it impossible to see beyond the railing of their porch.

Bellowing orders in that same voice he'd always used aboard their father's ship, he shouted, "Ye'll get indoors now, lasses. Or I'll carry ye in meself."

Without a word of protest they scurried inside, and followed him down the stairs. Nobody but Newton would dare to treat them in such a manner. But the old sailor had known them since their birth. It was he who had taught them how to haul sails, to climb to the top of a mast, and how to chart a course by reading the stars. Just as he'd taught their father years before them.

Now he shuffled in that strange, unsteady gait. At the door he turned. "Watchin' won't bring yer father and brother home. Now go and eat, before old Miss Mellon takes one of her spells."

"Winnie's spells only seem to come on whenever she thinks one of us is behaving in an unladylike manner," Bethany muttered.

"Aye. So go now. And behave yerselves like ladies."

Chastised, they nodded and left. But not without giggling over their old retired nurse, who now spent her days listening to Grandpapa repeat the tales of the sea he'd told a hundred times or more. And arguing with old Newton about the improprieties of teaching young ladies how to sail and handle weapons. All of which gave their housekeeper, the elderly Mistress Coffey, even more reason to complain about the three old people who seemed always underfoot when she and the servants were trying to do their work.

Now she clucked around the three brooding young women like a mother hen, trying to lift their spirits with silly, pointless gossip gleaned from Edwina's tea. "Have you heard about the gown Edwina Cannon has commissioned for the village ball? Cloth of gold, almost as fine as that worn by King Charles's mistress at his masque last year." Her voice rose as it always did when she was caught up in the excitement of the moment. "Think of the life Edwina will live in London if, as her mother hints, Lord Fenwick should propose marriage. And she's only," she added pointedly, "ten and six." Her gaze lingered a moment on Ambrosia, hoping to see a reaction.

When nobody spoke, she circled the table pouring tea. "Will you three be going to the vicarage tonight for the weekly psalm readings?"

Ambrosia glanced at her two sisters. "I suppose we must. Do you think the vicar would forgive us if we chose to decline?"

"He'd be bitterly disappointed." The housekeeper was reluctant to push too far. But she knew that the young deacon, Ian Welland, who had just come up from London two years previous, had eyes for Ambrosia. Mistress Coffey had often seen him, while the choir sang, or the old vicar, Thatcher Goodwin, was giving his sermon, turn to stare at Ambrosia as she sat with her sisters in the family pew. And though Ambrosia dismissed him as too soft and dull for her taste, Mistress Coffey harbored hope in her heart that all was not lost. After all, Ambrosia was getting on in years. Her own mother had been only ten and five when she'd come here as a bride. Perhaps when enough of Ambrosia's friends in the village found themselves husbands, and began to raise families of their own, she might be inclined to do the same. If she couldn't snag a wealthy London lord, what better catch could there be than a gentle man of the cloth, who would neither drink nor use vile language nor resort to violence against others?

The housekeeper looked up when she heard a knock on the door. "Now who would intrude at dinner hour?" She set down the teapot and hurried from the room.

Minutes later she came back looking highly agitated. Her skin had gone pale. She was clutching her hands together at her waist. "There is a stranger here. He has asked to see the three of you."

"Did he give a name, Mistress Coffey?" Ambrosia set aside her tea.

"A Captain Spencer. He said he brings news of your father and brother. And…" Her voice caught in her throat. Her lips trembled slightly as she realized the serious implications. "He is accompanied by the vicar and deacon."

"Here now." Though her own heart was pounding, Ambrosia took charge, dropping an arm around the old woman's shoulders, before leading the others into the parlor.

The old parson and his young assistant were seated on high-back chairs, nervously watching the door, their hands folded stiffly in their laps.

It was a strange parade as Geoffrey Lambert gathered his shawl around his shoulders and helped Miss Mellon, as white as a ghost, across the room. Old Newton planted himself firmly in the doorway, like an avenging angel, while Mistress Coffey took two steps inside the room, then stopped.

A man stood warming himself by the fire, staring thoughtfully into the flames.

When the three sisters stepped into the room, the parson cleared his throat. "Ladies, this gentleman is Captain Riordan Spencer."

The stranger turned. He was tall, with dark hair badly in need of a trim spilling over a forehead that was furrowed with concern. His face, tanned from wind and sun, might have been handsome were it not for the seething emotions that seemed to harden all his features. His hands, big and work worn, were fisted at his sides.

For a moment nobody spoke. Then Ambrosia stepped

forward and offered her hand. "Captain Spencer, I'm Ambrosia Lambert."

"Miss Lambert." He accepted her handshake, all the while staring into her eyes with a directness that was most unsettling.

She felt a jolt at his touch. Such strength. And so much tension. It fairly vibrated through him. Up close, his eyes were as gray as the Atlantic during a storm. Eyes that harbored pain and mystery.

"These are my sisters, Bethany and Darcy, and our grandfather, Geoffrey Lambert. Our nurse, Miss Winifred Mellon, our housekeeper, Mistress Coffey, and our friend, Newton Findlay."

The sea captain acknowledged the others, then turned back to Ambrosia. "I bring news of your father and brother."

For a moment she swayed slightly, and he reached out a hand to steady her. He could feel the slight trembling, and continued holding a hand to her shoulder a moment longer than necessary, as though to offer her a measure of strength for what was to come.

"Are they…?" She couldn't bring herself to say the words. For in that instant, she knew. Knew by the pain in his eyes. By the gruffness of his tone. By the fierce emotions that clouded his countenance.

"There was a…" he glanced toward the old people, who were staring at him, then turned back to her "…terrible storm. The worst we've ever encountered. We lost many men. Your father and your brother, James, among them."

"No. Oh, no." Bethany sank down in a chair and began to weep softly.

Darcy knelt at her feet and buried her face in her hands. Mistress Coffey fled the room in tears, while Miss

Mellon reached for her smelling salts to keep from fainting.

The others spoke not a word. But they continued staring at this stranger, their features tight, their eyes bleak.

Ambrosia clutched her hands together so tightly the skin was white. "Were you with them, Captain?"

He nodded, wishing he could offer something more than words. "My ship, the *Warrior,* went down. I brought your father's ship, the *Undaunted,* to its home port, along with the sailors who survived. It was Captain Lambert's last request."

Ambrosia could hear her two sisters weeping softly, but she dared not look at them. Not yet. She had to get through this.

"Their bodies...?"

He shook his head. "I'm sorry, Miss Lambert. But if it's any comfort to you, the sea holds them now."

"Aye. The sea. They loved it so." She bit her lip and turned away, unwilling to let this stranger see her grief. She swallowed hard, then assumed her role as hostess. "You've come a long way, Captain. You must be hungry."

"This isn't necessary, Miss Lambert." He seemed almost annoyed at her civility at such a time. "I'll take a meal at the tavern, before returning to the ship."

"You can't possibly return tonight." She glanced out the windows, seeing nothing but the fog that blanketed the countryside. "I marvel that you even made it to shore."

"It wasn't easy." He continued to stare at her in that direct manner. "But I couldn't allow you to wait until the morrow for such news. I knew you must be beside yourself with worry."

"We were. Thank you. That was most kind, to sacrifice your own safety and comfort for ours.'' She rang, and a minute later Mistress Coffey stopped in the doorway, holding a crisp handkerchief to her overflowing eyes.

''Please prepare a meal for Captain Spencer. And bring ale, to chase the chill.'' She turned to the vicar and his young deacon. ''Have you had your dinner?''

''Aye.'' Vicar Goodwin stepped forward and placed a hand on her shoulder, squeezing gently. ''We must get back to the vicarage in time for the Bible reading. But if you'd like, Ambrosia, we'll pray now for the souls of your father and brother. I'm certain 'twould give you and your family much comfort.''

She nodded, and signaled for her sisters to join her. The three gathered around their grandfather and elderly nurse, heads bowed, hands linked, as the old preacher intoned the prayers for the dead. When he had finished, he turned to the young deacon, who added his own prayers in a slightly more eloquent tone, hoping to impress his audience.

By this time Bethany and Darcy were sobbing outright. Ambrosia drew them close and pressed her lips to their cheeks. ''Go upstairs now. Take Grandpapa and Winnie with you. And when I'm finished here, I'll come to you.''

For a moment they hesitated, and she managed a weak smile. ''Go now. I'll be fine. I promise.''

While they fled up the stairs, she escorted the vicar and deacon to the door, where she offered her hand. ''Thank you both for your kindness.''

''You'll come to the vicarage tomorrow, Ambrosia,'' the old preacher said. ''Even without the…bodies of your father and brother, we must plan a proper funeral.''

''Aye.'' She endured the expression of sympathy from the deacon as well, before watching as the two men hurried out into the fog-shrouded night. Then she returned to the parlor.

Newton was gone. He would, she surmised, handle his grief alone in his quarters above the carriage house, with a flask of ale.

Their guest, she noted, had turned to stare into the flames. When the maid, Libby, entered with a tray and glasses, Ambrosia thanked her and sent her off to assist the housekeeper.

She poured a tumbler of ale and walked up beside him.

He turned and accepted it from her hand. ''Thank you.'' He nodded toward the tray. ''I wish you'd join me, Miss Lambert. I'm sure you can do with a bit of fortifying right now.''

''Aye.'' She filled a goblet, but instead of sipping, she merely stared into its depths, as though searching for answers.

''Here, Miss Lambert.'' With his hand under her elbow he directed her toward a pair of chairs drawn up near the fire.

Again she experienced that strange tingling when he touched her. As though all those raw emotions she was feeling were being felt by him as well. As though they shared some common bond of pain.

When she was seated, he settled himself across from her and stretched out his long legs toward the heat of the fire. ''I deeply regret the pain I've brought you and your sisters.''

When she said nothing, he sipped his ale in silence.

''Now that we're alone, tell me what happened, Captain. I need to know the details. Did you see my father and brother…die?''

He nodded. ''It happened right before my eyes. The ship staggered beneath the waves. They were swept overboard, as was half the crew. There was no way to save them. We were all fighting for our very lives, trying to keep the *Undaunted* from being split from stem to stern. Their bodies had to be abandoned to the sea."

She closed her eyes a moment, fighting an almost overwhelming sense of loss. She wanted, needed desperately, one more chance to look upon her beloved father's face and that of her brother. To see them, to touch them, to kiss them goodbye. But that was to be denied her. Instead, she would have to make do with memories. And oh, the flood of tender, loving memories were almost more than she could bear.

She opened her eyes to find Captain Spencer watching her. "And my father's ship? Has it sustained much damage?"

"Aye. When you view it by morning light, you'll see that we were fortunate to make it to home port. The hold is flooded. The bow is badly torn. But the hull is sturdy. She's still a fine, proud ship. But it will take some work to make her seaworthy."

The housekeeper stepped into the parlor. Her eyes were red and puffy from weeping, but she managed to say, "I have a meal prepared."

"Thank you, Mistress Coffey." Ambrosia stood and offered her hand. "I hope you'll understand that I must go to my family now, Captain. I hope that after you eat, you'll agree to spend the night."

He accepted her handshake. "I'd be honored, Miss Lambert."

She nodded. "When you've finished your meal, I'll have my housekeeper show you to my brother's room. I think you'll find everything you need for your comfort."

He continued to hold her hand. His voice lowered. "I want you to know this, Miss Lambert. Your father recognized the danger he was facing. While we fought the storm together he spoke of his three daughters. Of the pride he took in the three of you. Of his hopes for your future. And he asked a favor of me. One that I had hoped never to have to carry out, for I loved him as though he were my own father.'' His voice was gruff with emotion. ''Captain Lambert asked me, should I survive, to bring the *Undaunted* home, and tell you how very much he loved you, and was counting on you to carry on.''

She caught her breath. ''To carry on? He said that?''

''Aye.''

Tears swam in her eyes, but she blinked them away, desperate to get through this without breaking down. ''Thank you, Captain Spencer. For…everything.''

She turned and fled up the stairs, leaving Riordan Spencer alone with the housekeeper, who was weeping softly into her hands.

Chapter Two

Riordan sipped the strong hot tea Mistress Coffey had provided with supper. He couldn't recall a thing he'd eaten. Throughout his solitary meal, his mind had been cluttered with so many conflicting thoughts. And all of them centered on Ambrosia Lambert.

He'd come here expecting something quite different. He'd been bracing himself for an emotional scene, with young women fainting and needing to be helped to their beds. A house filled with helpless old people and hysterical servants, perhaps. Which was why he'd taken the time to engage the assistance of the village vicar.

Their grief had been deep. And sincere. That had been all too obvious. But the extraordinary strength in them, and especially in the eldest, Ambrosia, was remarkable.

She'd known. He could see it in her eyes when she'd first looked into his. She'd sensed at once why he was here. But he'd watched how stoically she had absorbed the blow and carried on. He'd had to fight an almost overpowering desire to take her in his arms and offer her solace. To whisper in her ear that somehow everything would be all right, though he knew, in her young life, nothing would ever be the same again.

He set down his cup with a clatter. It wasn't tea he wanted, but something stronger. As he shoved away from the table, the housekeeper entered.

"Would you like anything else before I show you to your room, Captain?"

"A bit of ale would be nice."

She nodded and rang for the maid. "I'll have it brought to you, Captain Spencer. If you'll follow me."

She led him up the wide, curving staircase to the second floor. As he passed a closed door, he heard the muted sound of women's voices. One was weeping. Another was speaking softly.

He frowned as he continued on until the housekeeper opened a door, then stepped aside.

"A servant will be along with your ale, Captain. I hope you find everything you need. If not, you have only to ask Libby."

"Thank you, Mistress Coffey."

She left and he glanced around. The bed linens had already been turned down. A fire blazed on the hearth. Steam still rose from the basin of warm water on the washstand. Despite their grief and shock, the Lambert family and servants had been able to efficiently handle the addition of an unexpected guest.

Along one wall stood a desk and chair. Atop the desk was a small framed miniature of a handsome young man and a beautiful woman and their four little children. Riordan picked it up and studied the faces. His eye was drawn immediately to the girl with dark hair and eyes. Even in early childhood, it would seem, Ambrosia had been a rare beauty.

At a knock on the door he called, "Come."

The maid entered and placed a tray on the night table. Like the housekeeper, the girl's eyes were red and puffy from weeping. "Will there be anything else, Captain Spencer?"

"Nothing, thank you, Libby."

She nodded and let herself out.

With a sigh he removed his jacket and stiff shirt before pouring a tumbler of ale. Then he walked to the fire and stared thoughtfully into the flames as he drank.

It had been a long and difficult voyage home. And this day had been a particularly harrowing one. The fog had come in without warning, leaving them sailing blind. When they'd finally lowered the anchor just offshore, it had taken more than half a dozen trips from the *Undaunted* before all the crew was deposited safely on dry land.

Riordan had taken the sailors to the village tavern, where he'd paid them their wages, and, as a bonus, had paid for their rooms and meals. By now they would have had their fill of fine English ale and even finer English wenches, and would be tucked up in their beds, snoring like beached whales. The thought made him smile for the first time in many days. He drained his glass and filled it a second time, setting it on the tray.

He sat on the edge of the bed and eased off his boots, then stripped naked and climbed between the covers. Plumping the pillows, he sat with one hand beneath his head, the other holding the ale to his lips. As he sipped, he found himself waiting for his mind and body to adjust to the unusual stillness of the house.

His first days home from sea were always the same. After the pitch and roll of a ship beneath his feet, and the sound of the waves lapping against the hull, there was something unsettling about the eerie quiet he experienced on land.

He forced himself to think about his future. He was a

captain in need of a ship and a crew. And he had both
here in Land's End. There was the *Undaunted*. After
some much-needed repairs, she would be as good as new.
And there was her crew. They'd proven themselves to be
hardworking and fiercely loyal to Captain Lambert. And
soon enough they'd be broke and restless and eager for
the next seagoing adventure. A man would be a fool not
to take them on. Especially a man who would be just as
restless for his own next challenge.

Ambrosia Lambert would be a challenge.

Her brother, James, had once confided to Riordan that
his sister could wield a sword like a man. At the time
Riordan had scoffed. Now, having seen her, he wasn't so
sure James hadn't spoken the truth. There was a quiet
strength in her. This was no weeping willow, bending
and blowing in the wind. She would be a majestic oak.
Standing tall, while those around her were swept away
by the storms that raged through life.

Any man would be fortunate to have a woman like
that by his side. She had that rare combination of beauty
and strength of will. There was intelligence in those dark
eyes as well. A man could search the world and never
find a woman to compare. He ought to know. Hadn't he
sailed the world and back, without ever once losing his
heart? In fact, he'd despaired of ever finding a woman
who could hold his interest for more than a night.

Perhaps, in Ambrosia Lambert, he'd met his match.

As the thought struck, he set aside his ale. Fool, he
berated himself. He'd spent less than an hour with the
woman, and he was already giving in to fantasies. It was
obvious that he'd been without the comforts of the flesh
for too long. Besides, everyone knew that a man in love
with the sea had no room in his heart for another.

He blew out the candle and closed his eyes, determined

to put his good friend's daughter out of his mind and get some much-needed sleep.

Unable to settle down, Ambrosia prowled her father's study, touching a hand to the objects that littered his desk. A ship's log that had belonged to his grandfather. His first sextant, which he'd used as a boy to chart a course around the coast of Cornwall. She picked it up and closed her eyes, trying desperately to feel the warmth of his touch. But all she felt was the coolness of the metal in her hand.

With a sigh she unrolled the map of the world, placing heavy objects on all four corners to keep it from curling. Then she lifted a candle to study the routes her father had traced across the ocean. She felt a heaviness around her heart as she read her father's precise script. He'd taken such pride in his work. And in the fact that he was doing his monarch's bidding.

Across the room she spotted the hooded cloak her father had always favored on his short visits home. She picked it up and buried her face in the folds, breathing him in.

"Oh, Father. I can't bear knowing I'll never see you and James again. I need you here. We all need you. Please don't leave us floundering in this storm, without a compass to guide us." The tears threatened, and she had to swallow hard to hold them back. Though it was difficult, she lifted her head and took in several deep breaths, struggling for composure. When she turned, she caught sight of a tall figure in the doorway and shrank back.

"Forgive me, Miss Lambert." Riordan stepped into the light. "I had forgotten to give you this earlier. I'd tucked it into the pocket of my coat, so that it wouldn't be lost.'' He handed her a thick book. ''This is the ship's log from the *Undaunted*. Your father wanted you to have it.'' He took a step back, annoyed with himself. ''It was never my intention to intrude upon your grief. I'll leave you now.''

''Nay, Captain.'' Ambrosia cradled the book to her chest, then straightened her shoulders. ''Please stay. I have a need to talk to someone about my father and my brother.''

He nodded. ''I understand.'' Rubbing his hands together, he glanced toward the fireplace. ''Would you like me to make a fire?''

''That would be nice. I'll fetch some tea. Or perhaps you'd prefer ale?''

''I would.''

She walked away and returned a short time later with a tray. For a moment she caught her breath at the sight of Riordan just straightening from the fireplace. With his jacket absent she could see that he was lean and muscled, and, like her father, his face and arms sun-kissed from his years at sea. Dark hair spilled over his forehead in a most appealing manner. He brushed it aside with his hand, then looked over to see her watching him.

''I'll take that.'' He crossed the room and took the tray from her hands. ''Where would you like it?''

''Over here.'' She indicated a round table set between two chairs drawn up before the fireplace.

When they were comfortably seated she poured him a tankard of ale and handed it to him before pouring herself a cup of tea.

She sipped, then said softly, ''My brother spoke of you, Captain. He held you in high esteem.'' She didn't bother to add that James had spoken of Riordan Spencer with a reverence usually reserved for heroes.

"I regarded James as a friend. And I loved your father as though he were my own. Our paths often crossed. And when we would put into port, we would share a tankard. Always, your father and brother spoke of their home, and the three lovely young women who held their hearts. And now that I've met you, I can see why."

"Tell me about Father's last day."

"I already did."

"Nay." She shook her head, sending black curls tumbling. "I want to hear everything. Everything he and James said. Everything they did. I have this desperate need to know, Captain. Do you understand?"

He stared at her for long moments, seeing the pain she was suffering. Her loss was so grievous. And yet she was so incredibly brave.

He nodded. And then, searching his mind for any detail that might ease her grief, he went through that last day, and the terrible storm that had followed. Through it all she remained silent. But in her expressive eyes he could read the torrent of emotions.

Her voice softened as she told him, "From the time he was just a little boy, James always wanted to follow Father to the sea. By the time he was ten and one, there was no stopping him. And so Father took him along on his first voyage, and when James came home with his tales of adventure, I was so jealous."

"I find that hard to believe, Miss Lambert."

"It's the truth. My sisters and I are accomplished sailors, Captain. There is nothing aboard ship we can't do as well as any member of a crew." She saw his look of surprise, before he covered it by turning to stare into the fire. "And often, when Father found himself shorthanded, he would permit my sisters and me to accompany him on short voyages around the coast. When I turned ten and one, I begged him to allow me to join his crew as James had done. And when he refused I was absolutely devastated.''

Riordan turned to look at her. ''Your father's work was dangerous. And often violent. That sometimes makes the men who engage in such work violent as well. I can understand why he wouldn't want his daughters involved.'' His tone rang with emotion. ''At times it's a dirty, thankless job. Certainly not for the faint of heart.''

She was on her feet, her eyes blazing. ''I assure you, Captain Spencer, my sisters and I are neither delicate nor faint of heart.''

He smiled as he stood, towering over her, and she realized how darkly handsome he was. Handsome, with a hint of danger.

''Forgive me, Miss Lambert. I wasn't speaking of you and your sisters. I was merely stating a fact of life at sea.''

Without realizing it he caught her arm. A mistake, he realized. For the mere touch of her caused a tingling in his hand that sent heat rushing through his veins.

Very carefully he released his hold on her and took a step back. ''I can see why your father took such pride in his children, Miss Lambert.''

''Did he say so?'' There was such hunger in her eyes. Hunger to know everything about the father who would never return to her.

''Aye. Often. He spoke of you the same way he spoke of his work.''

''And how was that?''

''With a fierceness that only a true sailor can understand.'' Riordan didn't realize that his own tone had taken on that same note of hushed intensity. ''Once a man has tasted life at sea, it steals his heart and plants a restlessness in his soul, until there's little room for anything else. The sea is his home, his refuge. His mistress, though she is often cruel and fickle.''

His words sent a thrill along her spine, for she'd often heard her father speak of his love of the sea in a similar manner. ''And what of you, Captain Spencer? Now that you've lost your ship and half your crew, will you return to the sea? Or have you had your fill of death and destruction at the hands of this fickle mistress?''

''I assure you, Miss Lambert, there is nothing that would cause me to turn my back on the sea.''

She nodded. ''I'd expected as much.''

As she started to turn away, he closed his fingers around her arm again. This time he steeled himself for the expected heat. ''Though I know this isn't the proper time, I would like to talk to you about the *Undaunted,* Miss Lambert.''

She struggled to ignore the splinters of fire and ice curling along her spine. What was it about this man's touch that caused such a startling reaction? ''What about my father's ship?''

''I would be happy to oversee the repairs, and make her seaworthy once more.''

''You would do that?'' She turned to him with wide eyes.

For the space of a heartbeat he couldn't find his voice. He was, quite simply, drowning in those eyes. ''My own ship is lost. The *Undaunted* can, with the proper repairs, be ready to set sail within a fortnight. And then, if you and your sisters are willing, I'd be happy to buy it from you.''

She shook her head. ''I thank you. But the *Undaunted* isn't for sale.''

''But Miss Lambert—''

"Not for any price, Captain Spencer."

"I don't understand. Will you keep it here, anchored like some sort of shrine to your father and brother?"

"Is that what you think? That my sisters and I have no use for the *Undaunted* except as a memory?"

"She's a ship, Miss Lambert. A seaworthy vessel, meant to sail to foreign ports. It would be a sacrilege to use such a ship for nothing more than fancy tea parties."

"Is that how you see us, Captain?"

"What I see…" He wasn't even aware of the fact that his fingers had closed around her upper arm once more. Or that he had dragged her so close he could feel the sudden breath of air on his cheek as she looked up at him. His tone softened. Lowered to a caress. "…is someone too grief stricken to think clearly."

"I assure you, Captain, my mind is perfectly clear on—"

Her words were abruptly cut off as he dragged her against him and covered her mouth with his.

He hadn't meant this. Hadn't meant to even touch her. But one look into those angry eyes and he'd felt the most amazing sexual jolt, one that had him reaching out to take. To touch. To taste. And now, with his mouth on hers, he was free to indulge himself.

Her lips were the sweetest he'd ever tasted. Cool, like the English mist, but with an unexpected fire that caught him by surprise. She tasted wild and sweet, like a meadow after a spring rain.

He swallowed her little gasp of shock and took the kiss deeper until she sighed and leaned into him.

His hands were in her hair, though he couldn't recall how they got there. And his mouth was whispering over her face, brushing soft kisses over her cheeks, her forehead, her nose, before returning to claim her lips.

Ambrosia had never in her life been caught so completely off guard. One minute she'd been coherent and expressing an opinion. The next, her mind was wiped clear of all thought. It was the most incredible feeling. As though some strong, unknown force had taken over her will.

Her lips heated and softened under his. Her skin warmed at his touch. Her blood seemed to slow and thicken, inching through her veins like molten lava. Her heart was pounding in her chest, her temples. And all she could do was hold on, while his hands, his lips, worked their incredible magic.

Riordan knew that he'd stepped over a line. Knew that he had no right to take advantage of her at such a vulnerable time in her life. He had to end this. But not yet. Not just yet. Not when her lips were so soft and willing. Not when her body was pressed just so to his, making him all the more aware of the desire that ran hot and fierce through his veins, taking over his will.

Her breath came out in a little sigh, and he pleasured himself a moment longer, lingering over her lips until he could find the strength to lift his head.

Calling on all his willpower, he took a step back, breaking contact. "I'll leave you now. We'll talk about the disposition of the *Undaunted* some other time."

"I've made my position clear. There's nothing more to talk about, Captain Spencer."

"Riordan." His smile was quick and dangerous. "After what we've just shared, 'Captain Spencer' seems far too formal, Ambrosia."

He turned away, needing to put some space between them. Those stormy eyes were still far too tempting. And those angry, pouting lips had his heart tripping over itself.

Ambrosia Lambert was, he realized, like the ocean on a fine summer day. All cool and calm on the surface. But underneath lay a raging whirlpool that, unleashed, could take a ship, or a man, down.

Chapter Three

Ambrosia climbed to the widow's walk and began to pace its length. She needed this release from the storm of emotions raging inside her. Emotions that had her reeling.

In her whole life she'd never been kissed like that. It had left her shattered. Riordan Spencer was unlike any man she'd ever known. There was such raw, seething passion in him. A passion that excited her, even while it frightened her. Perhaps that was what bothered her the most. Not the kiss, but her reaction to it. To the hint of danger and mystery of the man who had acted so boldly.

She thought of the deacon, Ian Welland, who had spent the past two years working up the courage to shake her hand after Sunday services. For permitting that, he considered her daring. What would he think if he knew that in the space of mere hours of meeting a stranger, she had permitted him to kiss her with such intimacy? Not only permitted it, but actively participated in it?

If the truth were known, she would probably be condemned as a harlot. But for some strange reason, she felt no remorse. All she felt was a sense of wonder. As though she'd just uncovered some rare, hidden part of herself that she'd kept buried for a lifetime.

She stopped her pacing to touch a finger to her lips. They felt different somehow. Softer. The taste of Riordan Spencer was still there. He'd tasted of the sea. All dark, swirling waters and the pull of deep, compelling tides. Exotic. And decidedly dangerous.

She'd always loved danger. In fact, like the rest of her family, she thrived on it.

She resumed her pacing. Determined to put Riordan Spencer from her mind, she gave in to other thoughts that she'd been avoiding.

It was time to face some hard facts. Her whole world would never again be as it had been. Her beloved father and brother were never coming back. On the morrow she must plan a fitting tribute to two men of the sea. In addition, she had a household to run. The future of her sisters to see to. Elderly family and servants who would depend upon her generosity to see them through a comfortable old age.

But how? She paused to stare up at the midnight sky, visible now that the fog had rolled out to sea. How was she to accomplish all these things, when all their father had left them was this house and his ship, the *Undaunted*?

They could get by, for now. With spring just blooming into summer here in Cornwall, they had a full larder, and a generous garden planted. They wouldn't soon go hungry. But she must come up with a plan that would take them through the winter, and all their winters to come.

She could make a good marriage, of course. With someone who would provide for her family and elderly retainers. It was what Mistress Coffey would advise. But the thought of marrying someone simply for security was repugnant to Ambrosia. She'd been privileged to witness the love between her father and mother. Until her mother's death, there had been a deep and abiding affection between them. Her mother's untimely demise had left a void in her father's life that no other woman could have filled.

Ambrosia closed her eyes, and for a moment all she could see was Riordan Spencer looking at her in that dark, unfathomable way that made her pulse race and her throat go dry. Nay. She would never marry any man simply for the sake of security. She wanted a man who would make her burn for him. A man who would speak to every deep, dark secret she'd ever harbored in the farthest recesses of her heart.

Numb with cold, and in need of rest from the thoughts that plagued her, she lifted her skirts and made her way to her room. Once there she slipped into her nightshift and brushed her hair, long and loose, in preparation for bed. Before she could settle herself between the covers, however, her gaze fell upon the ship's log, which she'd placed on her night table.

With a feeling of love she traced her fingers over the frayed leather cover. Then, as she opened the book, a thick envelope, bearing the royal seal, fell to the floor.

She bent and retrieved it, then began to read.

To some you are a privateer. But to me you are so much more. Because of your courage, my friend, England remains free. But unlike those nobles who are rewarded by their grateful king with tracts of land and glorious estates, men like you are forced to ply their trade in secret. Your only reward is this sealed missive from a grateful king, thanking you for your loyalty. And the knowledge that you have served your country with courage and honor, my friend.

For long minutes Ambrosia sat staring at the letter, feeling such love and pride and grief that it was almost overwhelming. Her father had not been a simple ship's captain, carrying cargo all over the world. He'd been a loyal and trusted friend to King Charles of England, putting his life on the line for the sake of crown and country. And at the request of that king, had become a privateer, a sailor who attacked those ships that sailed for countries considered the enemies of England.

She thought of all the fine silks and satins her father had brought home through the years. The fine ales, the crystal, the occasional silver and gold. That had been his only payment for risking his life for his country.

The answer to all her questions came as clearly as these words, written in the king's own hand. She and her sisters would, quite simply, carry on their father's noble work.

She tossed a shawl over her shift and hurried out to wake Bethany and Darcy. There was not a minute to waste.

"Then you agree?" Ambrosia had dragged Bethany from a sound sleep and hauled her into Darcy's room, where the three were now huddled in the middle of their youngest sister's big feather bed.

"Aye." Bethany nodded, sending fiery curls dancing around her cheeks. "Isn't that what Father meant when he sent word with Captain Spencer that we must carry on?"

Darcy smiled. "Father wouldn't have taught us to handle the *Undaunted* unless he wanted us to take up where he left off. Nobody is more qualified to sail her than we are. But will the crew follow our orders? You know how they feel about a woman aboard ship.''

"I've thought of that." Ambrosia lowered her voice. "We need a ship's captain. Someone strong enough to take command of the crew, but still committed to carry out our orders. And I believe Father has sent him to us in our hour of need."

"Captain Spencer?" Bethany looked at her sister with new interest. "But we don't know anything about him. What if he should prove to have some...unsavory traits?''

Ambrosia shrugged. "We'll do as Papa always did when hiring on his crew. We'll rely on our own instincts. Right now I believe he had a genuine love for Papa and James. Besides, I've heard James speak of him. He held him in the highest regard."

"All right." Bethany relaxed. "Do you think he'll stay?"

"He's in need of a ship and a crew. We can provide him with both. But only if he's willing to accept the fact that we are part of the offer."

"And how will you get him to do that?"

Ambrosia bit her lip. "I don't know. I haven't thought that far yet. I needed to know that both of you agreed with me first."

"I think he'll do it," Darcy said softly.

The other two looked at her.

"Why?" Bethany asked.

"Because you told us that he loved Father and James. I think, Ambrosia, if you appeal to his goodness and decency and his loyalty to them, he'll have no choice but to agree."

Ambrosia frowned. "I'll be taking unfair advantage."

"Aye." Darcy laughed, and after a moment the other two joined in the laughter.

"Exactly." Bethany leaned over to kiss her little sister's cheek, before turning to her older sister. "You'll appeal to his seaman's code of honor, Ambrosia. He won't be able to refuse."

Her eyes narrowed. "You're both cunning."

"Aye. And devious and clever. All the things we'll need if we're to carry on Father's legacy of ruling the seas."

"Not to mention duplicitous." Bethany's laughter suddenly faded as a new thought intruded. "You do realize, don't you, that we'll be forced to lead two lives? For we must not only be pirates by night, but fine, upstanding citizens of Land's End by day."

"How can we accomplish that?" Darcy looked from one sister to the other.

Ambrosia thought a moment. "It's possible. But it will take some doing. We'll each have to take our turn. While one of us goes to sea, the other two will be here at home to carry on as always."

"We'll have to take someone into our confidence." Bethany looked troubled. "It won't be possible to carry out our plans without the help of the servants."

"We can trust Newton."

"He'll put up a terrible fuss," Darcy said.

"Aye." Ambrosia smiled. "But in the end, he'll stand with us. The old pirate's never lost his love of the sea. And Grandpapa. We are his only hope of carrying on the family tradition. Now Libby…"

Darcy shook her head. "She's too much of a chatterbox. The first time she runs out of gossip down at the wharf, she's apt to tell everyone."

Ambrosia and Bethany nodded agreement.

"But what of Winnie and Mistress Coffey? I don't see how we can manage this without their assistance."

"Winnie's as timid as a mouse." Bethany shook her head. "She'll either faint or take her leave of us, telling all who'll listen that we've lost our sanity."

"And Mistress Coffey will strongly disapprove. It goes against everything she's ever believed a lady should be." Darcy looked from one sister to the other.

"You may be right." Ambrosia slid off the bed and started toward the door. "For now, we'll keep Winnie and Mistress Coffey in the dark, and bring them into our confidence only if necessary. I'll tell Newton my plans after we return from the vicarage this afternoon." She straightened her shoulders and drew in a deep breath. "Let's get some rest now before we meet with the vicar and deacon, and plan a proper seaman's ceremony for Father and James."

"What about Captain Spencer?" Darcy asked.

Ambrosia shrugged. "I'll just have to wait and see. And when the time is right, I'll present our offer."

As she stepped out of Darcy's room, she came face-to-face with the man they'd just been discussing.

"Good morrow, Ambrosia." Riordan paused to stare in surprise. Bare toes peeked from beneath the hem of her nightshift. The shawl she'd carelessly tossed over her shoulders couldn't hide the lithe young body clearly outlined through the sheer fabric. Dark hair spilled in a glorious tangle to below her waist.

Remembering the softness of that hair caused him to clench a hand at his side to keep from reaching out to it. "You're up early."

"I might say the same of you, Captain."

"Riordan." He flashed her a smile, then had to tear his gaze from the dark cleft visible at the neckline of her gown. "Aboard ship, I'm used to rising at dawn. I thought I'd go down to the shore and row out to the *Undaunted.*"

"I'd like to go with you."

He was surprised. And more pleased than he cared to admit. "I'll be below stairs. I thought, since the servants aren't awake yet, I'd fix something to take with me to eat aboard ship."

"Make enough for two. I'll be dressed in no time." Ambrosia turned away, aware as she did that he was standing very still, watching her by the light of the flickering sconces along the walls. As she hurried to her room she could feel the tingle of nerves along her spine.

Once inside her room she let out the breath she'd been unconsciously holding. She was going to have to get over these strange feelings she experienced whenever she got too close to Riordan Spencer. After all, if he accepted her plan, they would be forced to work in very close quarters. Work that would require each to trust the other completely. There would be no room for doubt, awkwardness or tension. Their very lives would depend upon absolute trust.

She dressed quickly in an ivory chemise. After a few moments of hesitation she decided to discard the layers of petticoats. Mistress Coffey would be shocked, of course, but they were simply too bulky. She pulled on a cotton shirtwaist and long navy skirt, then laced up leather boots. Finally she twisted her hair into a knot at her nape. Instead of a shawl, she decided to fetch her father's hooded cloak. It was warmer and much more practical.

When she stepped from her father's study, Riordan was waiting, with a basket over his arm. "You're as good as your word. I've only just finished with the food." He cast her an admiring glance before opening the door. "The cloak was a good choice. The wind may be brisk this morrow."

He led the way across the rock-strewed beach to where the big wooden skiff lay waiting—the same skiff that had carried the sailors from the *Undaunted* to shore.

"Careful." Riordan offered his hand, and Ambrosia felt a quick thrill as he helped her aboard.

She settled herself in the prow and watched as he discarded his jacket, then picked up the oars and began rowing. His shirt couldn't hide the ripple of muscle along his back and shoulders with each movement. She couldn't tear her gaze from him as he moved the oars through the water with effortless grace.

With each pull of those oars, they drew closer to the *Undaunted,* which lay several hundred yards offshore. Because of the excessive water in the hold, it rode low in the water.

Riordan dropped anchor, then took hold of the rope ladder that dangled over the side. "Shall I carry you up, Ambrosia?"

She couldn't hide her little prickle of annoyance. "I can take myself up, thank you. I've been climbing aboard the *Undaunted* since I was able to walk."

He bit back a smile. "Suit yourself. I'll hold the ladder steady while you climb."

She set her foot on the first rung, silently cursing the long skirt that impeded her movements. She noted that Riordan Spencer seemed to be enjoying the view of her foot and ankle, as well as a good bit of leg.

Despite her clothing, she climbed quickly, and pulled herself over the rail. When she looked down, Riordan was right behind her, carrying the basket of food over his arm.

He stepped aboard the ship, then held back while Ambrosia began to walk around the deck. On her face was a look of sorrow mixed with pain. He watched her pause to run a hand over the wheel, before moving on to test the lines that held the sails. Then without a word she went below, and he knew she was headed for the captain's cabin.

Silently he set down the basket, then decided to busy himself elsewhere, so that Ambrosia could have some time alone.

In her father's cabin, Ambrosia stood very still, filling herself with the familiar sights, sounds and smells. The creaking of timbers as the ship pitched and rolled in the ocean swells. The sound of water lapping against the hull. From a table anchored to the floor she picked up her father's pipe, inhaling the sweet smell of tobacco. She sat down in her father's chair. After all these years, it bore the imprint of his body. In a series of small cubbyholes on the wall were the neatly rolled maps that her father had often consulted on his voyages. Across the room was the small bunk, secured to the floor and wall. Above it, the small round porthole.

Ambrosia closed her eyes, imagining her father just waking, and peering out that window to see the progress his ship had made in the night.

Suddenly, without warning, she found herself weeping. All the grief that she'd kept locked up inside her came rushing out. She rushed across the room and curled up on her father's bunk, allowing the tears to flow until there were none left.

Ambrosia had no idea how much time had passed since they'd first boarded ship. She'd been locked in grief, unaware of anything except the deep, bone-jarring pain around her heart. Now, feeling more composed, she made her way across the deck in search of Riordan. She found his boots and shirt in a heap beside the ladder that led down into the hold.

Peering down, she cupped her hands to her mouth. "Hello down there."

When there was no answer, she felt a moment of panic. Had he drowned? Fallen overboard?

"Riordan." Without thinking she hiked up her skirts and started down the ladder.

It was dark down here and she could barely make out the shape of objects floating on the blackened water. The rancid odor of death and decay was all around. She couldn't control the shivers that raced through her as something brushed past her ankle.

Just as she was about to step lower something bobbed to the surface, sending up a spray of water. For a moment she froze. Then she let out a long, slow breath. "Riordan."

"Ambrosia. You shouldn't be down here."

"I...was worried about you. I called out, and when you didn't answer, I came looking for you."

"I'm fine. I just wanted to check the hull. Go above."

He swam toward the ladder and watched as she scooted up and out of the way. Minutes later he followed her. When he was once more on deck, she couldn't help but stare.

He was naked to the waist. His black breeches were soaked, and molded to him like a second skin. Water sheeted from his torso. He tossed his head, sending a spray of water around him.

For the space of a moment Ambrosia couldn't seem to catch her breath. He was the most magnificent man she'd ever seen, all powerful sculpted muscle and sleek sinew. Like some ancient Greek god rising from the sea.

"Here." Seeing the gooseflesh on his arms, she removed her father's cloak and handed it to him.

"Thanks." He slipped it on, grateful for its warmth. Then he bent and rolled up his wet pants before sliding his feet into his boots.

"Have you eaten anything yet, Riordan?"

He shook his head. "I was waiting for you."

"Then we'll eat. It'll help warm you."

While she retrieved the basket, he started a fire in a small cooking brazier. Within minutes they were seated on either side of it, warm, snug and eating their fill of thin slices of roast beef and thick slabs of bread spread with some of Mistress Coffey's gooseberry preserves.

Ambrosia looked up. "Now that you've had time to assess the damage, what do you think? Can the *Undaunted* be repaired quickly?"

"Aye. I think so. I checked the hull. There don't appear to be any leaks. What water there is in the hold was the result of the waves from the storm."

Ambrosia glanced around. "The deck seems to have taken a beating. What's that?" She stood and examined the charred wood of the rail. "Was there a fire aboard the *Undaunted*?"

He ducked his head. "Probably the result of an overturned brazier during the storm."

"It looks more like…" She peered over the side. Glanced back at him. "Is that a hole?"

He walked over to stand beside her. "We may have hit some…shoals in the fog."

"Shoals? A brazier fire?" She glanced beyond him. "And over there at the bow. More charred wood. What do you suppose caused that?"

When he said nothing she put her hands on her hips. "Now, Riordan, I think it's time you told me the truth."

"I don't know what you mean."

"You know exactly what I mean. The damage in the hold may have been caused by a storm. But this damage was caused by something far different." Her voice lowered. "Could this be the result of cannon fire?"

"Why would you even consider such a thing?"

"Because of a missive I found inside the cover of the ship's log. A missive from the king, thanking my father for his service to England as a privateer. Now you'll tell me, Riordan. I need to know the truth. Was the *Undaunted* struck by cannon fire?"

Instead of answering, he posed a question of his own. "Would it make any difference to you and your sisters how your father and brother died?"

Ambrosia took a deep breath, preparing herself for what was to come. "I must know the truth. No matter how painful. Now that I know my father was engaged in a dangerous task for his country, I must surmise, from this damage, that the *Undaunted* was engaged in a battle."

Riordan paused for just a moment. What an amazing young woman she was. Even in her grief, her mind was sharp, overlooking nothing. He realized at once that, however reluctant he might be, he had no choice but to trust her with the truth, for he owed her that much.

"Aye. A fierce battle. It was with a rogue ship. As you may know, there are ships that lie in wait for cargo ships. They're called rogues because their allegiance is not to any king or country, but only to themselves. They take what they want by any means necessary."

He waited for her reaction.

When she merely nodded, he said, "They came out of

a fog bank, flying the flag of England. But it was a disguise. They were prepared for us.''

''Us?'' She held up a hand to halt his narrative. ''You were sailing with my father and brother?''

''Aye. We had left the port in Wales together, for the voyage home. Then my ship, the *Warrior,* encountered the rogue and faced an attack. What I didn't know was that they had cannons undercover, and more than a hundred soldiers, all armed. I had less than two score men. When my vessel was hit with fire, and beginning to sink, your father brought his ship around and rescued us.''

Riordan paused to stare into the distance, seeing in his mind's eye the ferocious fighting that ensued. ''At first the tide of battle was in our favor. We launched some cannon fire of our own. From our decks we could see that the rogue ship couldn't put out the flames. She was listing badly. That's when we came around her stern and boarded her, expecting to make quick work of her. Your father and brother, rest their souls, fought bravely. But they were surprised by a contingent of more soldiers concealed belowdecks. We finally managed to subdue the lot of them. But by then the storm struck and we feared that the *Undaunted* would break in two unless we cut her loose. We took our dead and wounded and fled, setting sail for home.''

''Were my father and brother already...dead when the storm struck?''

He nodded. ''They'd put up a courageous fight. I ordered their bodies carried aboard their ship. But when the storm grew too fierce, the bodies were swept overboard. There was no way to retrieve them. They had to be abandoned to the sea.''

She closed her eyes, fighting tears.

''I know you wanted to see them. I tried my best to

bring them home to you. If it's any comfort to you, they died heroes, Ambrosia."

She looked away. "All who fight for England are heroes."

"Aye. But you don't understand." He put a hand under her chin, forcing her to look at him. His eyes were bleak. "If they hadn't come back for me and my men, they'd have been home with you and your sisters days ago. The fight wasn't theirs. It was mine. And because of me, they're now dead." His voice was filled with despair. "And I'm the one who must go on, knowing I cost the lives of my two dearest friends."

Ambrosia wanted to comfort him. But the pain around her own heart was too deep. She forced herself to speak over the lump in her throat that was threatening to choke her. "What was the name of the rogue ship and its captain?"

"The *Skull*. Captain Eli Sledge. Why do you ask?"

She sucked in a breath. It was time to state her position and force Riordan Spencer's hand. And he had just given her the weapon. She dared not think of his pain now. She must, instead, consider the task that lay ahead for her and her sisters. "Then I swear this vow. As soon as you have made your repairs to the *Undaunted,* she will not rest in port until the *Skull* and its captain and crew have gone to a watery grave."

He regarded her with an air of suspicion. "You've changed your mind? You'll sell the *Undaunted* to me?"

"Nay, Riordan. You misunderstand. With you as captain, my sisters and I will avenge the death of our father and brother. We have agreed to carry on our family's proud tradition."

"As sailors?"

"Aye. As sailors of the cargo ship the *Undaunted*. And more. As privateers, in service to our king."

Chapter Four

Riordan gave Ambrosia a look of complete disbelief. "What is this foolishness?"

"Call it what you will." At the look in his eyes she turned and flounced away, putting as much distance between them as possible. "My sisters and I have already agreed. We send a missive to King Charles in London this very day." She ignored the little flutter in the pit of her stomach and decided to quell her nerves with a bluff. "If you refuse our offer to captain the *Undaunted,* we'll find someone who will."

"No sailor would be foolish enough to trust his life to three empty-headed females."

She whirled, eyes blazing. "Do you suggest that our gender determines our brains?"

"Of course not, but—"

"Or that, because we are female, we cannot wield a weapon with the same skill as a man?"

"Skill, perhaps. But your size—"

"I'm as tall as many men, Riordan. And a sword in my hand makes up for whatever I may lack in physical strength. Would you care to test me?"

"Test you?" For a moment he was taken aback. Then

he began to laugh. "There aren't many men who could best me in a swordfight. I doubt the woman lives who could."

"Very well." She turned away and began packing up the remains of their meal. When the basket was loaded she looked up. "I have a meeting with the vicar. Afterward, we'll agree upon a place where we can test our skill."

He caught her by the arm. "You can't be serious."

She pulled herself from his grasp and stood facing him. "I am deadly serious."

He swore under his breath. Then, to keep from throttling her, he handed her the cloak and turned away with a muttered, "We'll see about that."

When he'd pulled on his shirt and jacket and made his way to the rope ladder, he discovered that she'd already climbed down and was waiting in the small skiff.

Without a word he picked up the oars, grateful for the chance to work off some of his anger. What sort of woman made plans to meet with a man of the church, to discuss the funeral of her father and brother, and then planned a swordfight afterward?

When they reached the shore, he stepped into the water and beached the skiff, then caught her hand to help her out.

He decided to give her one more chance. He kept his voice deliberately soft, persuasive. "I ask you, Ambrosia, to give up this foolishness."

She struggled to ignore the little thrill caused by his simple touch. "Call it what you will, Riordan. My sisters and I have made our decision." She started to turn away.

"Little fool. What do I have to do to convince you?" Without realizing it, he closed his hands roughly around her upper arms, dragging her against him.

"Take your hands off—"

Her words were cut off by a punishing kiss. For the space of a moment they both seemed consumed by such fierce emotions, they came together like two warriors in the heat of battle, all flash and fire and desperation. He dragged her against him, she pushed fiercely away, until, by sheer force of his size and strength, he managed to dominate.

At her little cry of distress he realized what he'd done. As if to atone, he released her at once and took a step back. But it was too late. Without knowing how, she curled her fingers into the front of his shirt, drawing him back to her. Her cry became a whimper as her mouth found his.

And then he was lost. Whatever regrets he had momentarily suffered for his hasty actions were now forgotten. His arms closed around her, drawing her firmly against him. His lips moved over hers, taking the kiss deeper.

Riordan felt himself becoming caught in a riptide. Needs, fierce and demanding, tugged at him, dragging him down into some dark place in his mind. And though it was now full morning, and they were standing on the beach in view of any who chose to look, it felt as though they were alone in the universe. The thought of taking her here, now, had his blood running hot with desire.

Despite the wind that whipped their hair and clothing, heat poured between them. Heat that had their breath backing up in their lungs until they were both gasping.

Finally, as if awakening from a drugged sleep, they came to their senses and stepped apart, eyes wide, chests heaving.

Ambrosia struggled to calm her ragged breathing.

Shame washed over her when she realized what she'd just done. For this had been as much her choice as his.

She had a sudden desperate need to prove that the passion they'd just shared meant nothing to her. In a voice that was little more than a whisper, she threw down the words with all the force of a gauntlet. "When I return from the vicarage, meet me in Father's study. And bring your weapon."

"Ambrosia. For the sake of all that's holy, give this up."

"Never."

She stormed away, her skirts flattened against her legs, her dark hair streaming wildly in the wind.

He stared after her, his thoughts as gloomy as the clouds that hovered over the waves. This damnably obstinate little female would have to be taught a lesson. And though he was loath to actually harm her, he would have to inflict enough pain that she came to her senses and gave up this foolish notion of becoming a privateer and fighting alongside hardened sailors.

Riordan was in the garden when the carriage bearing Ambrosia and her sisters returned from the vicarage. He could tell by their pallor and their strained expressions that it had been a difficult and emotional scene. He could imagine the vicar and his young deacon dredging up every heart-wrenching prayer and hymn, while the three young women fought back their tears and struggled to put up a brave front.

Newton helped the three young women down from the carriage, then drove the team toward the carriage house. Ambrosia paused for the space of a moment, glancing at the tall figure in the garden. Then, head high, chin jutting, she gripped her sisters' hands and the three made their way indoors.

Riordan waited, giving Ambrosia time for the tea Mistress Coffey had prepared. He knew that the old people lay in wait for their return. Their grandfather, their old nurse and their housekeeper would need to hear every detail of the planned service. The grief she'd buried would have to surface once again.

An hour later he made his way to her father's study, hoping against hope that she had come to her senses and would excuse herself.

When the door opened she was staring into the flames of the fire, lost in thought. He lifted his head and watched as she carefully closed the door and set the brace. Then she crossed the room. In her hand was a sword.

"What's the matter, Ambrosia? Afraid you might change your mind and run away?"

She glanced at the locked door. "I did that to insure that no one hears the sound of swordplay and comes to investigate."

"If you think of this as swordplay, you're sadly mistaken." He picked up his own sword and brandished it menacingly, hoping to put fear in her heart. "There's but one reason to take up a weapon. And that's to use it against another. Do you understand?"

"Aye." She wiped her hands on her skirt, then lifted her own sword and faced him.

To Riordan it seemed incongruous that this tall, elegant young woman, in her perfectly coiffed hair and modest, fashionable gown, would even consider going up against him in a fight. But he had thought this through. If this was what it took to make her face the futility of her decision, so be it.

He touched his blade to hers, all the while holding her

gaze. "Since the challenge is yours, Ambrosia, make the first move."

She smiled. "How gallant."

"I'm only trying to be fair."

"Fair, is it?"

In the blink of an eye, she managed to send her blade slashing against his, nearly knocking his sword from his hands.

Stunned, he took a moment to recover. He'd been cautioning himself not to hurt her. And all the time, she'd come here determined to best him. Not only to best him, but to humiliate him.

Ambrosia used that moment of confusion to back him against the wall, where she pressed the tip of her blade to his shoulder.

"If this were a true fight, you would already be wounded, Riordan. Your blood would be flowing down your sleeve, causing you grave pain."

"Aye. How very kind of you to spare me, Ambrosia." His eyes narrowed as he brought his sword crashing against hers with such force he knew her hand, as well as her entire arm, had to be vibrating from the blow.

"And if this were a true fight," he said with an exaggerated smile, "and not merely an exercise in foolishness, I would have used enough strength to relieve you of your weapon."

Her eyes widened. But to her credit she managed to continue holding her sword, even though she could no longer feel her fingers. They had gone completely numb.

To cover her confusion, she danced nimbly out of reach of his blade. He charged forward, and she was forced to duck to one side, nearly losing her footing. At the last moment she retained her balance and spun to face him.

Their blades sang through the air, meeting, clashing. With each thrust of Riordan's blade, Ambrosia felt her own strength beginning to wane. While he'd spent months aboard the *Warrior* working from sunup to sundown, she'd done nothing more strenuous than lift a teacup entertaining her neighbors from Land's End. Such activities had left her ill-suited to the task before her.

"Tired, Ambrosia?"

She slashed out, shredding the sleeve of his shirt. "I'm feeling as refreshed as a newborn."

"And about as dangerous." With a knowing look he wielded his sword with such skill she was forced to retreat until she felt the wall at her back.

"Now what will you do, Ambrosia?" His smile was quick and dangerous.

The sword in her hand moved with lightning speed, just missing his fingers.

"So." He shot her a look of admiration. "You hope to draw blood, do you?" He lunged.

Just as nimbly, she ducked and came up swinging. This time her blade tip pierced his arm. He felt the pain, white-hot, and then the sticky warmth as blood oozed from the wound.

She appeared stunned. "Forgive me, Riordan. I didn't mean—"

He cut her off. "Of course you did. We both know this isn't play." He was almost grateful for the pain. It reminded him that he'd been holding back, trying desperately to disarm her without causing her harm.

Now he slashed out, taking care to concentrate only on her blade, so that he wouldn't wound her tender flesh.

At first Ambrosia returned the attack with a smile. She could see that he'd been surprised by her skill, and more than a little impressed. But soon, as they exchanged thrust for thrust, parry for parry, she found her breath coming harder and faster. Her smile disappeared as she struggled to keep one step ahead of the man who wielded his sword as he did everything else—effortlessly.

They moved across the floor, Riordan on the attack, Ambrosia defending. With each step he took, she managed one in retreat until, too late, she noticed that she was directly in front of the fireplace. With the flames crackling at her back, a large settle to her left, a pair of high-back chairs to her right, there was no place left to go.

Riordan saw her eyes narrow at the sudden realization that she was trapped.

"Do you yield, Ambrosia?"

"Nay." Gritting her teeth, she lashed out with her weapon, only to find he'd anticipated the move. The tip of his sword caught her sleeve. It was only his superior skill that had him drawing away before his blade could pierce her tender flesh.

She thrust again, and once more his blade was there first, slicing across her fingers lightly enough to hurt, but draw no blood.

With a cry of pain she nearly dropped her sword. At the last minute she regained her hold on the hilt and drew her arm back. At the same instant he pressed the tip of his sword to her chest. "Yield, Ambrosia. For God's sake, yield before you're hurt."

"Never." It was her intention to grasp her sword in both hands and lift it over her head. But before she could do so, he snagged her roughly by the arm. Caught by surprise, she found her weapon clattering to the floor.

He twisted her around and dragged her roughly against him, then pressed the blade of his sword to her throat. His voice held an edge of frustration. "Now, Ambrosia, if I were your enemy, your pretty throat would be slit, and your life would be over.''

She was aware of the deeply coiled tension that he seemed to be holding by a tenuous thread. For several seconds she didn't move. Finally, when she felt him take a deep breath and release his hold on her, she whirled. In her hand was a very small, very deadly knife.

He looked from the knife to her eyes, glittering in the firelight. ''Where did you get that?''

''From my waist. I was warned to never go into battle with but one weapon. It was one of the first lessons my grandpapa taught me. And if I were truly your enemy, Riordan, this would have already found its way to your heart.''

For the first time he smiled. ''I'll give you high marks for that. And for the way you handled your sword.''

She arched a brow. ''A compliment? From the arrogant Captain Riordan Spencer?''

''Aye. When it's warranted. But I'll remind you, Ambrosia. The knife is too little, too late. In a real fight, you'd have already been dead, or at least mortally wounded.''

''So you would like to think. But I saved this knife for last, knowing you wouldn't be expecting it. Admit it. You were caught unawares.''

''Aye.'' He never took his gaze from hers as his hand swept in a wide arc, knocking the knife from her grasp. It clattered to the floor.

In the silence that followed his voice was a low rasp of anger. ''Now what will you do? Yield?''

''Never. If I have to, I'll fight with my nails. With my teeth. Shall I show you what damage I can inflict?''

''There's no need. But I'll remind you of this, Ambrosia. Nails and teeth might wound, but they will never kill.

And one other word of warning. Your father's study is a small, confined space.''

''As are many of the quarters aboard ship.''

''That may be true belowdecks. But above there's plenty of space for an enemy to run, to duck, to hide. And while you're trying to keep up, the surface below your boots is moving, tilting, swaying. And often slick with salt spray and blood. It isn't enough to be able to wield a sword or a knife. You must be fleet of foot, agile of limb and always one step ahead of your opponent.'' He retrieved her sword and knife. Instead of handing them to her, he placed them just out of her reach beside his own weapon.

He fixed her with a look. ''I was wrong about you, Ambrosia. You're a far better swordsman than I'd expected.''

She put a hand to her heart in mock astonishment. ''Careful, Captain. Before you know it I'll be overwhelmed with your sweet words.''

''Don't let my words fool you. Though your skill comes as a surprise, I still think you have no business aboard ship. What you and your sisters intend is foolhardy. And extremely dangerous.''

She waited, hearing something in his tone she hadn't heard before. Could it be grudging acceptance?

She decided to risk everything. ''You don't have to be a part of this, Riordan. If you think me foolish, you can walk away. My sisters and I will bear you no hard feelings, even though you claim to have loved our father like your own.'' She offered her hand. ''Give me your answer. Will we seal the bargain? Or would you rather turn away?''

He stared down at her hand for a long silent moment. Annoyed at her foolishness, Ambrosia felt her heart stop.

She should have waited awhile longer, to give him time to consider. Now she'd pushed too hard, too quickly.

Hadn't Father warned her that it had always been one of her shortcomings?

Riordan looked up into her eyes and reached out a hand. But instead of shaking hers, he used it to pull her close, until their faces were inches apart.

"Little witch. It's already too late for me to turn away, and you know it."

She let out the breath she'd been unconsciously holding and started to smile. It was as Darcy had said. She'd used whatever weapons necessary to win him over.

His next words had her eyes going wide with surprise. "But we'll seal the bargain my way." Before she could react, he dragged her into his arms.

"Nay." She pushed against his chest, but realized once again that her strength was no match for his. Especially now, with the heat of battle still pumping through his veins. And the slow, simmering passion still seething in his soul.

"Aye." With one hand holding her still, he plunged his other hand into her hair and dragged her head back, all the while staring into her eyes. "You know exactly what you're doing, don't you, Ambrosia?"

"I don't know—" she had to draw in a quick breath "—what you mean."

"Oh, I think you do." With his eyes steady on hers he framed her face with his big hands and lowered his mouth to hers.

She tried to draw back, but he anticipated her move and held her firmly. When she tried to turn her face away he tightened his grasp. She looked up to see that dangerous light in his eyes. The same light she'd seen during their duel. This was, she realized, a similar duel. One he was just as determined to win.

As his mouth lowered to hers, she kept her eyes open, watching for a way to escape. With a wicked smile he surprised her by simply brushing his lips over hers in the merest whisper of a kiss.

At the first touch of his lips on hers, the heat was so incredible she could feel it clogging her throat, bringing a flush to her skin. And as he gradually deepened the kiss, she was helpless to fight him. All she could do was wrap her arms around his waist and hold on as she felt the floor beneath her feet begin to tilt and sway.

His lips continued whispering over hers, nibbling, teasing, until she sighed and offered more. Instead, he confounded her by brushing soft little kisses over her cheek, her jaw, the corner of her mouth.

Frustrated, she clutched at the front of his shirt and dragged him close, offering her lips. She wanted, needed, the feel of his mouth on hers again.

"Do you yield now, Ambrosia?"

"Yield?" At that hated word she suddenly froze. "No, Riordan Spencer. I'll never yield."

"Then I'll simply have to claim victory and take what I want." This time there was nothing gentle about the kiss as his mouth moved over hers, taking, taking, until she could feel the breath in her lungs straining to be free. For a moment, as his mouth plundered, she thought he would devour her. And though she would never admit it, even to herself, she wanted him to.

She heard a sound, and realized it was her own voice, rough with need. Against her will she wrapped her arms around his neck and opened to him, giving him all that he wanted and more.

It was a kiss unlike anything she'd ever known. A kiss

that left her breathless and trembling with need. As his mouth took her higher, his hands moved along her back, her sides, until they encountered the soft swell of her breasts.

She flinched and tried to pull away, but once again he'd anticipated her. He took the kiss deeper until her head was spinning and she couldn't hold a single coherent thought. All she knew was that she wanted him to go on holding her like this, kissing her like this, touching her like this, and never, ever stop.

When his hands moved along her sides a second time, she had no will to fight him. His thumbs found her nipples and stroked until her sighs of pleasure became a whimper of need.

Riordan knew he had to stop. He'd intended only to teach her a lesson. But somewhere along the way the line of reason had blurred, until now all he could do was absorb the pleasure, without fear of the consequences. All he wanted was to take her. Here. Now.

The thought was so tempting that he lingered a moment longer, pleasuring himself with the taste of her lips, the press of her body to his. Finally, calling on all his willpower, he managed to lift his head.

"Let that be a lesson to you, Ambrosia. There's a time to fight. And a time to yield."

"I yield to no man, Riordan Spencer. And especially not to you."

"Aye." He took a step back, breaking contact. Because the need to touch her was still so compelling, he picked up her sword and knife and held them out to her. "I could tell by that kiss that you wanted no part of it."

She blushed. He'd hit too close to the mark. To cover her embarrassment she snatched her weapons from his hand, and prayed he wouldn't notice the way her own were trembling.

She flounced to the door on legs that felt like rubber. After throwing the latch she turned. "Shall I tell Mistress Coffey that you'll be staying on with us?"

"Aye." At her little flash of triumph he couldn't help adding, "At least until the *Undaunted* is seaworthy once more."

"We have a bargain. One you sealed."

"And one I hope you'll relieve me of, when you've come to your senses. For that alone, I'll stay. I owe your father that much."

He could see, by the look she gave him, that his arrow had found its mark. She fled the room, slamming the door behind her.

When he was alone, Riordan stalked to the fireplace, where he stood staring down into the flames. Desire still vibrated through him, leaving his chest burning, his limbs more than a little unsteady.

What was he getting himself into here? Between now and the time the repairs to the *Undaunted* were completed, he had to find a way to convince Ambrosia and her sisters that their plan was impossible.

As if that weren't enough, he would have to find a way to keep his distance from that infuriating little female. Each time he got too close, sparks flew. And one of these times, unless he exerted a great deal more self-control, they were both going to get burned.

Chapter Five

Ambrosia sat between her two sisters in the carriage. Across from her sat her grandfather, who had withdrawn inside himself. He was, after all, saying goodbye to his son and grandson this day. Could there be a fate more cruel than that for a man?

Beside him sat Riordan Spencer, looking as stern, dark and grim as the angel of death. After her first glance Ambrosia kept her gaze averted, refusing to look at him.

As old Newton guided the team along the road to the village, Ambrosia stared out across the rolling hills dotted with sheep. She'd always loved this countryside. The mere sight of the green, verdant land, the wild, rock-strewn beach and the endless ocean never failed to stir her heart. But this day her poor heart was too heavy. This day she and her sisters would have to face the reality of their loss in front of the entire village of Land's End.

The carriage rolled up to the church, where dozens of other carriages were already parked. In the doorway the vicar and deacon, in their somber robes, stood waiting.

Riordan stepped from the carriage, then offered his hand to the young women. When Ambrosia tucked her hand in his, he steeled himself not to flinch.

Since that scene in her father's study, they hadn't spoken. He'd managed to avoid her at supper by taking himself off to the village tavern, where he'd lifted a few with the crew from the *Undaunted*. By the time he'd returned to his room, she and the others were already asleep.

This morning, while they'd dressed for the funeral, he'd walked along the beach, filling his lungs with brisk, salty air and preparing himself for what was to come.

Now he followed Ambrosia and her family inside the church and up the center aisle, where he could overhear the murmurs and whispers from the crowd.

"Such a waste," a young woman was saying. "James could have made a fine match here in Land's End. But what woman had a chance, when he'd already given his heart to the sea?"

"And what of his father?" an older woman whispered loudly. "Without a wife for all these years. But he never considered marrying again. And all because of those daughters of his. What woman stood a chance to win John Lambert with those three around?"

"They've always thought they were better than anyone else," said Edwina Cannon, in a bonnet far too frivolous for a funeral, watching their progress with a pout on her lips. "When we were girls, they never wanted to play with the rest of us. They were always too busy sailing with their father, or swordfighting with their brother."

Riordan's eyes narrowed, hoping Ambrosia and her sisters hadn't overheard. He looked around and was astounded to see that the church was filled to overflowing. There were even sailors standing in the back, their hats in their hands, their heads bowed respectfully.

At Ambrosia's insistence, the front rows in church had been reserved not only for the family but also for the household staff and the crew of the *Undaunted*. These people, many of whom had worked for the Lambert family for a lifetime, were touched by her kindness. Hardened sailors walked grim-faced into church and took their places of honor beside cooks and scullery maids.

As the bells tolled, the parson and his young assistant ascended the altar and began the ageless tribute to the dead. The words of the familiar prayers were a soothing balm to Ambrosia's wounded heart. She closed her eyes and allowed them to pour over her. But when the entire congregation stood and began to sing the ancient hymns, she found she couldn't swallow the lump in her throat.

Beside her, Bethany's hand slipped into hers. From the other side, Darcy closed her fingers over Ambrosia's and squeezed. The three stood, too overcome with grief to join in. For all they could see, in their mind's eye, was the vision of their father and brother singing these same hymns with such fierce enthusiasm on those rare occasions when they'd been home from the sea and were able to attend services with their family.

Behind them, Riordan watched the three young women cling to one another, struggling with their emotions. He wished he could offer some comfort. But, he reminded himself, they didn't need him. They didn't need anyone except each other this day.

As the service went on, the parson gave a glowing tribute to Captain John Lambert and his son. With each word, Ambrosia felt her jaw tighten and her spine stiffen, knowing those assembled would be watching. Whatever grief she felt would be held inside, to be expressed only in the privacy of her own home. Here, in front of the entire village, there was no room for anything that might invite pity.

When the service finally ended, Ambrosia and her sisters led the way down the aisle, with their grandfather proudly among them. The ship's crew and the household staff followed. Once outside, the villagers surged forward, grateful for the opportunity to finally convey their condolences.

Riordan stood a little away, watching and listening.

"Oh, you poor dears." A little birdlike woman leaned on her white-haired daughter's arm and pushed her way through the crush. The others moved aside respectfully, for she was the oldest woman in the village.

She grasped Ambrosia's hand. "Whatever will you do now? What a pity, to leave no sons to care for three helpless women. But it's always been the way of the sea."

"We aren't helpless, Mistress Clay." Ambrosia pushed aside her grief and anxiety and accepted the old woman's sympathy, if not her meaning. It seemed pointless to argue, since the next one to rush up to her was already crying loudly enough for the entire village to overhear.

"What a terrible loss. Terrible, terrible loss. Will you be selling that fine big house, Ambrosia?"

"Certainly not." She turned in time to see her younger sister, Bethany, about to explode with anger.

"But who will see to your future?"

"We shall see to our own, Mistress Heathrow."

"Oh. Aye. Of course. I only meant…" The old woman swallowed and tried again. "If only you had some men to look after you."

"We'll not be needing men. We'll look after ourselves, Mistress Heathrow."

"Ambrosia. Bethany. Darcy." Riordan watched as the young woman with the fancy bonnet shoved her way through the crowd.

"Edwina." Ambrosia gritted her teeth as the young

woman sank her fingernails into her arm and held on. Knowing how Edwina craved attention, she was prepared for almost anything.

"I'm so sorry for your loss." Edwina's voice carried above the others. "And I'm so sorry that my betrothed had to leave before the service ended. You did know that Silas Fenwick and I are to be wed?"

"Nay. But now that you've chosen this moment to announce it, I'm sure the entire village of Land's End wishes you well."

"I thank you, Ambrosia. Silas wanted you to know that he sends his condolences as well."

"How very kind of him." Ambrosia could see that Edwina Cannon intended to wear her conquest like a badge of honor.

"He said it is a personal loss, since his import company depends upon every ship that sails for England." She lowered her voice. "He also knows a good deal about the man who sailed your father's ship home."

"Riordan Spencer?" Ambrosia glanced to where he stood alone, then returned her attention to Edwina.

"Indeed."

Riordan heard his name spoken. And could see a frown on Ambrosia's face. A frown that seemed to deepen with every word spoken by Edwina, whose head was bent in earnest conversation.

"Silas told me that you should beware Riordan Spencer. He is the eldest son of a very wealthy lord who has vast estates outside London."

At Darcy's gasp of surprise, Edwina puffed herself up, loving the fact that she seemed to know more about this mystery man than his hostesses. "As eldest, Riordan should have inherited great wealth when his father died. But before his death, his father disapproved of Riordan's chosen activities and disinherited him, leaving everything to Riordan's younger wastrel brother.''

Ambrosia's tone frosted over. ''Thank you for your concern, Edwina. It would seem that the loss of our father and brother is nothing compared with the petty gossip from London.''

''Petty gossip?'' The young woman's cheeks turned bright pink. ''Mama and I simply thought, now that you have neither father nor brother to look out for your welfare, that you ought to be warned about the sort of man you've taken into your home.''

''At least you recognize that it is still our home, Edwina. If you'll excuse us.'' Ambrosia caught her sisters' hands and turned away. ''We have a great many *friends* waiting to offer their sympathy.'' She turned her back on the woman, who could do nothing more than slink back into the crowd.

The three sisters stood in the churchyard for nearly an hour, accepting the sympathy of the villagers. When at last most of the citizens of Land's End had returned to their homes, Ambrosia led a procession of carriages back to MaryCastle. There the servants and crew were rowed out to where the *Undaunted* lay at anchor. When they had clambered aboard ship, those members of the crew who had sailed with Captain John Lambert for many years were asked to say a few words.

Afterward, while the sailors sang some of John and James Lambert's favorite songs, Ambrosia, Bethany and Darcy tossed flowers onto the waves and watched them drift away. Then they made their way to where their grandfather stood alone, staring out to sea, and hugged him fiercely.

Standing at the bow of the ship, Riordan found himself deeply moved. Unlike the church service, which had seemed stiff and formal, the words spoken here came from the heart. The tears of the sailors were also heartfelt, being shed without embarrassment. Winifred Mellon, Mistress Coffey and old Newton stood side by side, wiping away tears and squinting into the sunlight reflected off the water.

It occurred to Riordan that Captain John Lambert and his son, James, were fortunate to have such loyal, loving friends and family. A man could search the world over and never find a treasure as rare and priceless as this. And as the last of the songs washed over him, he realized that there was no way he could walk away from this family in their time of need.

Despite the fact that all around him hearts seemed to be mending, his own heart felt shattered beyond repair. He might tell Ambrosia Lambert that he merely wanted a ship to sail. In truth, what he wanted wasn't healing but revenge. Against the man who had cost him his ship. The man who had taken his best friends. The man who had left three lovely young women alone, and desperate enough to plan something far too risky for their own good.

"Are you coming, Riordan?"

Lost in thought, he nearly jumped out of his skin when Ambrosia touched a hand to his arm. "Sorry." He glanced over to see the last of the crew climbing down to the waiting skiff. Many of the servants were already ashore and heading toward the house in the distance. "Maybe you could send Newton back for me when everyone has been taken care of."

"All right." She left him staring out to sea and made her way to the railing. Minutes later she turned.

Riordan was still standing where she'd left him, lost in thought once more.

Was he thinking about his father's fortune that had been denied him? Was he wishing he could be anywhere but here?

She turned away, mentally cursing Edwina Cannon and her hateful gossip. Ambrosia would give anything not to know about Riordan's past. But now that she knew, she couldn't help wondering. Had he accepted her offer because he truly wanted what she wanted? Or because he'd been left with no other choice?

It didn't matter, she told herself. Nothing did. Not Riordan Spencer. Not silly Edwina Cannon, nor the gossip she was spreading. All that mattered to Ambrosia now was that she find a way to keep on going, no matter how much her heart was breaking.

She made her way belowdecks, needing to see and touch the things her father had loved. As she entered his cabin she paused, half expecting to hear his deep voice, his booming laughter. Instead, all she heard was the creak of the old ship and the slap of water against its hull. She breathed in the sea air and felt again the knife twist to her heart.

"I'll find the ship responsible for this, Papa. And the men. And when I do, they'll pay. I promise you."

She thought of her brother, and the anger and jealousy she'd felt when her father had allowed him to go to sea. How she'd begged and pleaded to be allowed to join him.

"I'm sorry, James. I thought we'd have years ahead of us. Years to laugh together, to grow old together. And what little time we had was wasted." A big wet tear rolled down her cheek. "Wasted because I was too busy wanting what you had." She drew her arms around herself, feeling suddenly cold and miserably alone. "And oh, how I wish I could have you back. I'd give anything..." The tears came harder now. Faster. "...anything in the world if I could just have you back with me."

"Ambrosia, the skiff is..." Riordan stopped in the doorway of the cabin.

She stood with her back to him, arms hugged tightly to her, her whole body shaking with sobs. It occurred to him that she might resent his presence. But at the moment he didn't care. He had to offer her what comfort he could.

He walked to her and drew her into the circle of his arms.

For the space of a heartbeat she held herself stiffly. "I don't need—"

"Aye. You do, Ambrosia. Sometimes we all need to just let the tears flow."

His words seemed to unlock a door. For just a few moments she would allow herself this weakness. Would allow him to be strong for both of them.

She crumpled against him. And then she wept until there were no tears left.

Ambrosia lifted her head. "I'm...fine now."

Without a word Riordan handed her a clean linen handkerchief. She wiped her tears, then took a step back. "Thank you."

He knew what those words cost her. She'd accepted these few moments of grief in his arms, but she would still consider it a momentary weakness. "Are you ready to go back?"

"Aye." Her spine stiff, she nodded and followed him out of the cabin and up the ladder to the deck. She was surprised to see that the sun had already made its arc across the sky and dusk was settling over the land. The whole day had been spent in grieving.

"Newton's waiting." He led her across the deck to the rope ladder hanging over the side of the *Undaunted*.

She climbed down, with Riordan following. When they were both settled in the skiff, old Newton began rowing.

"Good night to be on the water." The old sailor glanced at Ambrosia's red eyes, then looked away.

"Dead calm," Riordan remarked.

"Aye." The old man noted that, although the two were seated side by side, they were taking great pains not to touch. Something's going on, he thought, though he wasn't certain just what. His first thought was that it was a shame they disliked each other so intensely.

"Think it'll rain on the morrow, Newt?"

The old sailor glanced skyward. "Nay. Going to be warmer, though."

"Good. I'll be able to get started on those repairs."

"You're going to work on the *Undaunted*?"

Riordan nodded. "I've offered to put together a crew and make the necessary repairs."

"If you don't mind, I'd like to help."

Riordan smiled. "I'd like that. As long as it doesn't take you away from your other duties."

"It won't." The old man brought the boat smoothly to shore, then climbed out in that strange, unsteady gait before helping Riordan drag it onto the beach.

"Thanks, Newt. I'll look for you on the morrow." Riordan offered a hand to Ambrosia, who stepped out of the boat.

As soon as she was on dry land, she pulled her hand away as though it burned. "Good night, Newt."

"'Night, lass." The old man watched as the two made their way to the house. His eyes were narrowed in thought. He'd known Ambrosia Lambert since before she'd taken her first steps. She'd always been the most fearless female ever born. But something had her as skittish as a school of fish being circled by a hungry shark. And since he'd never before seen her back away from a fight, he was beginning to think it was something other than dislike that had her acting so strange. In fact, maybe what had her worried was the fact that she liked this newcomer a bit too much for her own good.

Newton smiled. Aye. That would frighten the lass. She'd never been one for filling her head with female notions. Feelings for a man would be unsettling for a lass like Ambrosia. Especially a man like Riordan Spencer, who seemed to be her equal in both strength and daring.

Newton touched a hand to the small, deadly knife he kept tucked beneath the waistband of his breeches, a throwback to his days at sea. Maybe he'd just keep an eye on Riordan Spencer. If this newcomer had anything other than Ambrosia's best interest in mind, he'd answer to Newton's blade.

Chapter Six

"Not smooth enough." Riordan ran a hand over the board being offered by one of the seamen hired on to help with the repairs. "Newt?" He turned to search for the old man, who had been put in charge of a crew. "Where's Newt?"

"He said he had a chore to see to this morrow, Cap'n," one of the seamen shouted.

Riordan gave a sigh of disgust. "Have this one planed again. And we'll need more hot pitch to seal those seams."

"Aye, Cap'n." The seaman repeated the command, and the sailors laid the plank across several rocks and began smoothing and planing it.

Another crewman, stripped to the waist, applied hot pitch to the hull of the *Undaunted*.

Like the others, Riordan had stripped off his shirt, baring his torso to the sun. The weather had grown steadily warmer, as spring turned into summer in Cornwall.

Riordan had no trouble finding men willing to work. Most of the sailors were eager to help with the repairs. The sooner the ship became seaworthy, the sooner they could return to their first love. Weeks spent on land had them itching to feel the deck of a ship beneath their feet and the sting of salt spray against their faces.

Riordan lifted a hand to mop the sweat from his brow and paused to stare at the small boat just sailing into his line of vision. It was much smaller than the *Undaunted*. But a tidy craft, with its sails unfurled and billowing in the fresh breeze. As he watched, one of the crew climbed the mast and unsnagged a line, then swung down to the deck with all the grace of a dancer.

A second crewman stood at the helm, guiding the boat through the shallows. It took a master sailor to maneuver the submerged rocks hidden along the Cornish coast. Many a ship's captain had discovered too late that his hull had been ripped from stem to stern by such dangers.

While Riordan watched, two sailors climbed the rigging and began lowering the sails. The sight of it stirred his heart.

With its sails trimmed, the sleek craft slowed, then headed toward the shore of a private cove a few hundred yards distant.

As it passed, Riordan blinked, then found himself staring in openmouthed surprise.

The three crewmen were dressed like any other sailors, in tight-fitting breeches tucked into tall boots, hair tied back with colorful scarves, the sleeves of their shirts billowing in the breeze. And though the men around him seemed to take no notice as they continued to work, Riordan became acutely aware that these were unlike any sailors he'd ever seen. For one thing, they were small. Smaller than the two white-haired men seen standing on the deck. For another, the breeze flattened their shirts against their bodies, revealing curves where there should be none.

After shouting orders to continue working, Riordan began running along the shore. By the time he reached the secluded cove where the boat had anchored, the crew had already leapt over the rail to trudge through the shallows to the beach.

"I thought as much." With his arms crossed over his chest, he watched as Ambrosia offered a hand to Darcy, who had been tugged to her knees in the surf.

"Riordan." The two women paused and glanced at each other in consternation.

His gaze was fixed on Ambrosia. Her clothes were thoroughly soaked, and plastered to her like a second skin. Despite the coarse shirt, her breasts were clearly visible, drawing his gaze against his will. Her face was sun-kissed and smudged with dirt. Her hands were callused from holding the wheel against the pull of the waves. For it had been Ambrosia who had guided the boat through the dangerous shallows. With a skill he was forced to admire, no matter how grudgingly.

Bethany, coming up behind them, tossed an armload of weapons into the sand and came to an abrupt halt.

He stared down at the weapons, then up at the faces of the three women. "What's this?"

"Work." Old Newton trudged through the water and dropped to his knees in the sand. "If they're going to take on the family business, they need to prepare themselves."

"The family business." Riordan nearly laughed. "Did you think a morning's sail would be enough preparation?"

Ambrosia lifted her chin, unwilling to respond to his sarcasm.

Geoffrey Lambert was the last to reach shore. Huffing from exertion, he sat down in the sun-warmed sand. When he caught his breath, he said, "They were a bit out of practice. But I think, by the time the *Undaunted*'s ready, they will be as well.''

''You think?'' Riordan's smile was wiped away, replaced with a ferocious scowl. ''And what if they aren't ready? Will we have another funeral in the village church? Will we mourn a few more of the Lamberts? I would have thought you of all people, Geoffrey Lambert, would be honest enough to tell these three females that what they're planning is nothing more than a foolish, empty-headed scheme.''

Ambrosia's eyes blazed. ''I'll remind you, Captain, that you remain here at the invitation of three foolish, empty-headed females.''

He pointed a finger in her face. ''And I'll remind you, Ambrosia Lambert, that I am here by choice. And I will remain here only so long as I choose.''

Old Newton stepped between them. ''Now is not the time, Cap'n. The lass's blood is still hot from the fighting. She's had quite a challenge this morning.'' He turned to Ambrosia. ''As for you, lass, you're keeping the cap'n from his work aboard the *Undaunted*.''

When she started to open her mouth, the old man shook his head and gave her a look she'd recognized since childhood.

Without a word she clamped her mouth shut and turned away to retrieve her sword. Then, with her sisters following, she trudged through the sand toward the house.

Riordan stood watching. But though anger still made his blood run hot, he couldn't help wondering if it was further fueled by the sight of her backside in tight-fitting breeches. She was, by far, the most beautiful sailor he'd ever seen.

When he turned back, he saw two old men watching him. Without a word he turned and stalked away.

"Where is Ambrosia, Mistress Coffey?" Fresh from a bath, Riordan was prepared to try once more to talk some sense into one very obstinate female.

"She's in the parlor, Captain."

"Thank you. Would you mind sending Libby in with some ale?"

"I'm not sure ale would be appropriate, Captain. They're having tea. You might want to…"

She swallowed back her protest, since he was already striding away. With a shrug she rang for the maid. He'd find out soon enough that Ambrosia wasn't alone.

Riordan stepped into the parlor, pausing on the threshold when he realized that Ambrosia and her sisters were entertaining guests.

"Excuse me, ladies. I didn't realize you weren't alone."

Ambrosia glowered at him for a moment. Then, seeing the way Edwina Cannon's face lit up at his arrival, she decided to have some fun.

"Riordan. Come in. I'm sure our guests would love to visit with someone who has been to so many fascinating places."

"I wouldn't dream of intruding on your…" He turned and realized that Libby was right behind him, bearing a tray with a pitcher and tumbler.

"Here's your ale, Captain Spencer." She brushed past him and placed it on a side table.

Seeing his uncertainty, Ambrosia crossed the room and took his arm. "Riordan Spencer, may I present Edwina Cannon and her mother."

He gritted his teeth while managing a smile. "Miss

Cannon. Mistress Cannon.'' He recognized the younger woman as the one at the church who'd been attempting to draw as much attention to herself as possible.

"So, Captain.'' Edwina patted the place beside her on the chaise. "Come and tell us about all those fascinating places you've seen.''

He pretended not to notice her invitation. Pouring himself a tumbler of ale, he stood by the fireplace. "Most of my journeys have been rather dull.''

"Nothing could be as dull as life in Land's End.'' Edwina's mouth turned into a pout. "Please, Captain. Tell us about the world beyond Cornwall.'' She held out a hand and he had no choice but to accept it and take a seat between her and her mother. "Have you seen India?''

"Aye.'' He sipped his ale and decided to go along with this little charade. Especially since Ambrosia was wearing such a smug look on that pretty face.

She looked the picture of a proper lady, in a gown of palest pink, her hair tied to one side in fat sausage curls that fell over her shoulder and spilled across her breast. In her hand was a cup of tea.

Tea. It made him want to laugh out loud. Those same hands had earlier held a ship's wheel.

Ambrosia's sisters were equally fetching. Not at all the wet, tired, dirty urchins that had tumbled from their boat on the beach that morning.

He wondered how much effort it had cost them to prepare for this little visit. From the looks on their faces, they'd been caught unawares and had been forced to work quickly to make themselves presentable.

He turned his attention to Edwina. "You'd find India fascinating, Miss Cannon. It's a land of such contrasts. Rajahs, as wealthy as any king, being carried through the streets. Vendors selling delicacies. The scents of rich spices wafting from the bazaars. Dazzling women hidden behind veils.''

"Oh, how I envy you, Captain.'' Edwina gave him one of her sweetest smiles. "Have you been to the New World, as well?''

"Aye.'' He leaned back, stretching out his long legs, crossing his feet at the ankles.

Edwina moved closer until her shoulder brushed his. When he saw the way Ambrosia's eyes narrowed, he merely smiled. If it was revenge she wanted, he could do the same. And use this situation to his own advantage.

"In fact, I was in the naval attack against the Dutch when we captured New Netherland and claimed it for England, renaming it New York.''

"You were, Captain?'' Even her mother was caught up in the excitement.

Across the room, Ambrosia sat up straighter. Why had he never told her this? Perhaps, she realized with a twinge of regret, because she'd never bothered to ask. She'd been so wrapped up in her own problems, she'd never given a thought to Riordan Spencer and the life he'd lived.

Edwina touched a hand to his. "How wonderful. What did you think of the New World?''

"It's a splendid land. Savage and quite beautiful. I'd like to return one day. I think, given time, it could rival England and France.''

"You must be joking, Captain. I've heard it's completely uncivilized.''

"Aye. But as more people make their way to its shores, they'll bring their cultures with them. It could become unlike any other country we know. Think of it. French, English, Spanish, all living under the same rule, swearing allegiance to the same country. A country without a monarch. Where the laws will be made by the people themselves.''

Edwina closed a hand over his and looked into his eyes. ''Please, Captain, tell us more. You must have so many interesting stories to tell about the places you've been and the people you've seen.''

He forced a smile. In truth, though he enjoyed the look of annoyance on Ambrosia's face, he'd had enough of Edwina Cannon. The sound of her voice set his teeth on edge. The sweet, cloying fragrance of rosewater was so strong even the scent of ale couldn't hide it. He much preferred a low, breathy voice. And the faintest hint of wildflowers.

He extricated himself from her clutches and crossed to the tray, where he poured himself more ale. ''I'm afraid, Miss Cannon, that I haven't led the life of excitement you might expect.''

''That's not what my fiancé, Lord Silas Fenwick, had to say. He said your life has been nothing but colorful, Captain Spencer.''

Riordan studied her with new interest. ''You're betrothed to Silas Fenwick?''

''They're to be wed in London,'' her mother announced proudly.

''And when is this momentous event to take place?'' Riordan sipped his ale, hoping it would cover the bad taste that had suddenly materialized.

''Silas thought we might be wise to wait until winter, when all his important friends will have returned from the country.''

''A wise decision.'' Riordan glanced beyond the guests to where Ambrosia sat in silence.

Edwina followed his glance. ''I was telling Ambrosia

and her sisters that Silas knows your family, Captain. It's a pity about your inheritance.''

Riordan went very still.

Seeing it, Ambrosia felt a wave of regret. She'd trapped him into staying in the parlor because she was tired of Edwina's silly prattle. But she hadn't intended this.

She jumped in, hoping to steer the conversation to a more comfortable topic. ''I'm sure Riordan would much rather talk about his travels than discuss his private affairs.''

''Not so private, I assure you.'' Edwina covered her mouth with her hand and giggled. ''Silas says everyone in London knows about it.''

''That may be true, Edwina.'' Ambrosia set her cup down with a clatter and got to her feet. ''But I assure you, most would have the good sense not to discuss it in Riordan's presence.'' She caught the young woman by the elbow, nearly lifting her out of her seat. ''I do believe we'll have to end this visit, as lovely as it has been. Mistress Coffey needs our help in the dining room.''

Edwina pulled herself free of Ambrosia's grasp and turned to Riordan. ''Goodbye, Captain Spencer. I'm so glad I had this opportunity to meet a man of such mystery.''

He glanced down at her outstretched hand and lifted it to his lips. ''The pleasure was mine, Miss Cannon. It would seem that Silas Fenwick has found…the perfect partner.''

She was still giggling as she followed her mother and the others out of the parlor. As soon as they were gone, Riordan drained his glass and poured another. When Ambrosia returned minutes later she found him standing in front of the fire, staring into the flames. On his face was a dark, shuttered look.

"I'm sorry, Riordan. I didn't intend any of that."

"No need to apologize, Ambrosia. This wasn't your fault."

"But it was. I wanted to get even for that little scene at the beach. And I thought…" She shrugged. "I can't think of anything worse than being forced to make conversation with Edwina Cannon. But I never dreamed that even Edwina could be that thoughtless."

"No harm done. Whatever she's told you, it's probably the truth. The life I've chosen to live was considered disgraceful by my family. And I've no one to blame but myself." He turned away and set his glass on the tray. Then he looked over at her. "Tell Mistress Coffey that I won't be taking dinner with you and the others."

"Where are you going?" She hated the bleak look in his eyes. And hated even more the thought that it was her carelessness that had put it there.

"I believe I'll walk to the village. Maybe chat with the crew."

He walked from the parlor. A minute later she heard the front door open and close.

It was her turn to stare into the fire. And wonder why her little revenge tasted like ashes in her mouth. She tried to tell herself that it was merely because she was too tenderhearted to cause harm to anyone, even if it had been unintentional. But there was a nagging little fear that it went deeper than that.

Was she beginning to care too much for Riordan Spencer? She sincerely hoped not. For if he were to discover such a weakness in her, he might use it against her. After all, he'd made no secret of his dislike for this plan of hers. If all it took were a few sweet words and stolen kisses, a man of his reputation wouldn't be above using such tactics to dissuade her. Especially since it would mean that he'd get to captain the *Undaunted* without the interference of others.

Chapter Seven

The days passed in a blur of work. For Riordan the clear, sunny skies over the Cornish coast meant that he and the seamen could work from sunup to sundown without interruption. Within days the charred wood had been replaced with fresh sturdy beams. The hold of the *Undaunted* had been bailed out, and a crew had been put to work sealing the cracks with hot pitch. All the rips in the sails had been mended, and they now lay bleaching in the sun while the mast and riggings were checked for damage.

Newton slid down the mast after having carefully examined everything. His lips split into a wide smile. "She's better than new, Cap'n."

"I think you're right, Newt. From the looks of her, she's ready to set sail."

The old sailor squinted into the setting sun and watched as the *Sea Challenge* sailed into view. "The *Undaunted*'s not the only one ready, Cap'n. The lasses are, too."

Riordan gave him a level look. "You can't mean that, old man."

"Aye. I do. They've honed their skills until they're as able as any sailor I know."

"Seagoing skills, perhaps." He watched as Ambrosia brought the sleek craft through the shallows. He would give her this much—she could pilot a ship as well as anyone he knew. "But you and I know that the *Undaunted* isn't just a merchant ship. How can three women possibly survive in battle?"

"Ye've had a taste of Ambrosia's skill with a sword."

"I held back, Newt. I didn't want to hurt her."

"She claims to have done the same." When he saw Riordan's look of disdain, he added, "And she's even better now, Cap'n. Their grandfather and I have been working the lasses with sword, knife and pistol. I'd put them up against anyone, even the king's own soldiers." He started in the direction of the cove where the *Sea Challenge* was just setting anchor. "I promised to give the lasses a hand when they docked."

"You mean they can't manage by themselves?"

Riordan's sarcastic tone had Newton turning. "They took their grandfather along. Geoffrey Lambert needs a bit of help getting to shore is all."

At once Riordan regretted his comment. Reluctantly he joined the old man. When Newton looked over, Riordan gave him a wry smile. "I've grown a bit fond of the old fellow myself. Wouldn't want to see him fall overboard."

When they reached the small craft, the three sisters had already lowered the sails and were busy gathering up their weapons. Ambrosia was helping her grandfather over the side of the rail.

Before he could drop into the water, Riordan caught him and assisted him to shore, where he helped him to sit in the warm sand.

Ambrosia, Bethany and Darcy waded through the water behind him.

As Newton took the weapons from their hands he asked, "How'd it go today, lasses?"

Ambrosia nodded toward her grandfather, who was wearing a smile that stretched from ear to ear. "You'd better ask Grandpapa."

Riordan leaned close, shouting into his ear, "Do you think your granddaughters are ready for life at sea, Geoffrey?"

The old man cupped a hand to his ear. "Tea? Aye. I'd like that."

"Sailing, Geoffrey." Riordan was shouting louder. "Aboard the *Undaunted.*"

"Eh? What is it you wanted?"

Defeated, Riordan shook his head. "Nothing, Geoffrey." He turned to Ambrosia, who was stifling a chuckle. "I think I quite agree with Mistress Coffey. He hears only what he chooses to hear."

"You should have seen my granddaughters," Geoffrey suddenly blurted. "I don't believe there's a man in England who could best them at handling a ship or handling a weapon."

The three young women beamed with pride. But Riordan turned away with a look of disbelief.

"Are you coming in for tea?" Darcy called as he started to walk away.

He turned and saw that all three sisters were smiling. "Dinnertime will be soon enough. Until then, I believe I'll just check the repairs again."

"Is the *Undaunted* finished, Riordan?" Ambrosia's voice held a note of contained excitement.

"It appears so."

"How soon can she take an assignment?"

"I've received word that there's an English ship, the *Dover,* aground up the coast, carrying tea and spices from India."

"Where is she bound?"

"She's bound for here, actually. Land's End. She's asking for help before her weakness is discovered by a rogue ship that might claim right of salvage. It should be a simple run. No more than a day or two. I thought it would give me a chance to see how the *Undaunted* handles after her repairs."

"Excellent," Ambrosia cried. "When do we leave?"

The sound of "we" grated on his nerves, even though he'd expected it. "I thought I'd leave on the morrow. At dawn."

Ambrosia nodded. "Then I'll be sailing with you. My sisters and I drew straws. I drew the long one. Mine's the first run."

He wouldn't be surprised to learn that she'd rigged the draw. It would be like Ambrosia to make certain she had the first chance at it.

He glanced from her to the two old men who stood beside her, grinning like fools. Maybe they were, Riordan thought. A couple of old fools, and a few young ones as well. All thinking this was some sort of lark.

"Fine. Well, I'd like Newt to accompany you."

The old man's eyes lit up like a child's. "You mean it, Cap'n?"

"I do. Someone's got to watch out for her." He saw Ambrosia's sudden frown and added, "Tell Mistress Coffey I won't be here for dinner."

"Where will you eat?"

"At the tavern. While I sign on the crew." He started away, then turned back. "We leave at first light. If you're late, Ambrosia, the *Undaunted* will sail without you."

"I'll remind you that I'm the owner, Riordan."

"And I'll remind you that I'm the captain. What I say goes."

Ambrosia was still frowning as he strode away. Then she turned and trailed after her sisters toward the house. So it was to be a contest of wills, was it? It was time Riordan Spencer learned that she had no intention of losing. Or of missing her first chance at a sea voyage.

Riordan packed his seabag and pulled on his jacket, then paused in front of the window overlooking the beach. The sky was still dark. Too dark to make out the ship anchored just offshore. But he sensed its presence and felt the quick tug at his heart. It had always been this way. Whenever he was about to embark on a voyage, he needed no reminder to awaken. Needed no food to fuel his body. This hunger for adventure, this thirst for the sea, were all-consuming.

He blew out the candle before leaving the bedroom. As he strode past Ambrosia's door, he paused a moment to listen for any sound that might alert him that she was awake. Hearing nothing, he smiled and moved on. Perhaps he'd been given a reprieve. Perhaps she would oversleep, and the *Undaunted* would sail without her.

His smile grew as he descended the stairs and let himself out the door. He'd hate to be around when she awoke and discovered that they'd left without her. Knowing Ambrosia, she'd be hissing and spitting like a sack of wet kittens.

He strode along the beach, his bag over his shoulder. When he reached the skiff, Newton was already seated inside, holding aloft a lantern and waiting to pilot him out to his ship.

"Good morrow, Newt. Have you seen Ambrosia?"

"Nay, Cap'n. But I wouldn't worry. The lass is too excited to miss her first voyage."

"So you say." Riordan tossed his bag on the seat, then nudged the old man aside. "Let me row, Newt. I need the release."

As he moved the oars through the water, the old man grinned at him, showing white teeth in the darkness. "Excited, are you, Cap'n?"

"Aye. I've been ashore too long. My blood's hot for the sea, Newt."

"As is mine." The old sailor glanced at the black water, gilded here and there by ribbons of moonlight. "She's calm this morrow. We're in for some fine weather. At least on the first leg of our journey."

"I hope you're right. If so, it should be an easy run up the coast and back."

He lifted his oars and they drifted close to the waiting ship. When they came alongside the rope ladder, Riordan hefted his seabag. "You'll bring the crew out when they get here?"

"Aye, Cap'n. I see the line of their lanterns coming down the shore now. We'll be along shortly." He handed over the lantern and took up the oars.

Before Riordan had even made it over the rail, the skiff had disappeared into the darkness. All that could be heard was the splash of oars in the water.

Riordan stood for a long time breathing deeply, enjoying the pitch and roll of the deck beneath his feet. He watched as the skiff, now aglow with lantern light, began another run toward the *Undaunted.* Then he picked up the lantern and his bag and headed for the cabin below-decks.

He threw open the door and strode inside, setting the lantern on the table before stowing his bag in the closet.

Then he withdrew a rolled map from one of the small cubbyholes along the wall and unrolled it, using the lantern to anchor one side. As he bent to the map he heard a sound behind him and turned. When he caught sight of a figure sitting up in his bunk, he reached for the knife at his waist. In the blink of an eye he had the figure pinned, and was holding the blade at a throat.

"Stop, Riordan."

At the sound of that husky voice he froze, then slowly lifted his hand away. "Ambrosia. What are you...?"

He took a step back, staring at her in alarm.

She looked like a gypsy he'd once seen. Dark hair tumbling about in wild tangles. Eyes still heavy-lidded from sleep. A crimson shirt falling off one shoulder in the most provocative manner.

He felt a rush of heat and blamed it on the fact that he'd been caught by surprise.

"I spent the night aboard the *Undaunted*."

"So I see." He sucked in a breath, unsure whether to throttle her or kiss her. He wanted both in equal measure. "Afraid you'd oversleep?"

She smiled. "Perhaps I was afraid you might leave before the appointed hour."

"It had occurred to me. But there was the crew to consider. I dare not leave without them. Otherwise, I must confess, I would be more than a little tempted."

"You won't be sorry I came along, Riordan."

"Nay. But you might be. Some of the sailors are superstitious. They won't like sailing with a female aboard."

"It can't be helped, for most of these men have known me since I was a child. There's no way to hide the truth. Still..." She tossed aside the blanket and got to her feet. She was wearing men's breeches tucked into boots. She pulled on a vest, covering more evidence of her gender. Then she began twisting a piece of black cloth around her head. When she was finished, her hair was completely covered. "Aboard ship I'll just be Seaman Lambert."

Seeing the way his jaw dropped, she gave a sly smile. "Admit it, Riordan. If you didn't know better, you'd never guess, would you?"

He gave a grudging shake of his head. It wouldn't do to mention the fact that her face was too beautiful to ever be mistaken for a man's. "All right. You might be able to get away with this charade. But remember, Ambrosia. Every sailor aboard the *Undaunted* will be expected to carry his share of the workload."

"That doesn't worry me. There's nothing aboard ship I can't do."

"We'll see about that." He turned away and bent over the map. "If you're finished dressing, you can get started hoisting the sails. We've no time to waste."

She felt the sting of dismissal, and for a moment considered reminding him whose ship he was commanding. Then she realized the futility of it. Until they returned to shore, Riordan Spencer was captain of the *Undaunted*. A law unto himself. Whether she liked it or not.

"Newt, take the wheel."

"Aye, Cap'n." The old man stepped up, and Riordan left him to walk to the rail.

With the sails lowered and most of the crew already asleep belowdecks, he was free to look back on their first day. It had gone smoothly, without incident. They'd enjoyed fine weather and a brisk wind that filled their sails and carried them smartly along the coast of Cornwall.

Now, with a skeleton crew on deck, they would drift on the tide until first light. With a good breeze on the morrow they ought to make their destination, the small village of Bretton, by midafternoon. They would salvage the cargo of teas and spices, and head back to Land's End, arriving the following evening.

It had proven to be a perfect trial of the *Undaunted*. Riordan smiled in the darkness. She was a fine ship. Sleek, sturdy. And proving to be better than ever, since her repairs.

Out of the corner of his eye he saw a shadow move on deck. He turned. And caught his breath.

Ambrosia stood with her face to the stars, breathing in the fresh sea air. Now that darkness covered her, she had removed the scarf and vest she'd worn throughout the heat of the day.

"I should think you'd be sound asleep by now. You've put in quite a day." He felt a twinge of regret. He'd worked her hard. Harder than the other sailors, he now admitted. And only because he was so determined to prove her unfit to be in their company.

"Aye. I am tired. But it's a good tired."

He moved closer and lowered his voice. "I'm sorry, Ambrosia."

She turned to look at him. "For what, Riordan?"

"For…singling you out for so much duty. I should have been more impartial."

"I didn't mind the work."

He saw the glint of starlight reflected in her eyes and felt a sudden tug of desire. "But it was unfair. I was testing you. Trying to push you beyond your limits."

"I know." She didn't bother to add that her anger had been the fuel that kept her working when her muscles protested and her body craved rest. "I'd expected as much."

He touched a hand to her arm and felt the rush of heat.

It was impossible to be close to her and not be aroused. "You must think me a cruel taskmaster."

She turned, so that her mouth was mere inches from his. Her breath was warm against his face and he breathed her in. For one brief moment he thought about kissing her. Then he remembered that Newton was just across the deck, holding the wheel. Though the old man couldn't hear their words, he could surely see them.

She smiled in the darkness, and Riordan felt his lips curve in response. And then she spoke, and the smile died.

"Nay, Riordan. You were simply being a man. And no more cruel than any other. None of you can bear to imagine a woman doing what you do. Enjoying what you enjoy. Wanting what you want. But I'll expect an apology when I've proved you wrong."

She turned and walked across the deck.

Before she could descend the ladder, he came up behind her and caught her arm in a painful grasp. "Where do you think you're going?"

"Belowdecks to my bunk."

His eyes narrowed. "With the sailors?"

"Aye. With the sailors. Isn't that what I am? Isn't that what you were so determined to prove to me all day?"

"Perhaps. But you forget how you look." He caught a handful of her hair and for the space of a heartbeat felt all the air leave his lungs. He wanted, more than anything in the world, to plunge his hands into these glorious tangles and kiss her mouth until they were both breathless. He actually leaned toward her and tempted himself with the thought of how she would taste. Salty from the sea air, lips still warmed from the sun. Wickedly wild and gloriously feminine.

His fingers tightened on her shoulder, and he drew her

close. "You might try to deny it, Ambrosia. But you're a woman. A beautiful, desirable woman. One look at you and a man might forget everything he's ever learned, including how to be civilized."

"All except you? Is that what you're saying, Riordan? I'm sure a leader such as yourself would have no trouble remembering who he was."

Temper had him tugging her head back more viciously than he'd intended. "I'm only warning you that once you fall asleep you'll be helpless. You wouldn't stand a chance against all those men."

"Wouldn't I?"

He was stunned to feel the cold steel of her knife against his throat. "The first one who touches me will pay with his life. After that, I doubt there will be any others wanting to risk the same fate. Don't you agree…Captain?"

"Aye." Eyes narrowed, he released her and took a step back.

"Now I'll bid you good-night."

With a hiss of annoyance he watched as she descended the ladder into the darkness below.

As he returned to take the wheel, he felt a grudging respect. He hadn't seen her reach for her knife. Yet there it was, close enough to slit his throat if she'd so desired.

As he approached, old Newton called, "I see you had a few words with the lass."

"Words?" He stood beside the old man, willing his heartbeat to return to normal. "It isn't possible to exchange words with Ambrosia Lambert. 'Twould be easier to exchange blows."

"She's always been a fierce scrapper." The old sailor smiled in the darkness. "But I've a feeling when the lass gives her heart, it will be equally fierce. The man lucky enough to win Ambrosia Lambert will possess something greater than any earthly treasure. He'll have love and loyalty that will last a lifetime."

"Aye." As he reached for the wheel, Riordan touched a hand to his throat. Though she hadn't broken the skin, he'd felt the press of that razor-sharp blade. And had seen the determination in those eyes. "Providing she doesn't kill him first."

Chapter Eight

The second day of their voyage was nothing like the first. The sun disappeared behind a bank of angry clouds. The wind came up, out of the north, whipping the sea into dark, churning waves that rolled across the deck of the *Undaunted*, making it impossible for sailors to cross from one side to the other without the use of ropes to keep from being swept overboard. And then came the rain. A strong, steady downpour, punctuated with heart-stopping rumbles of thunder, and lightning that danced across the sky in blinding flashes.

By the time they'd managed to ride out the storm, the *Undaunted* had been blown far off its charted course. It would take hours to make up for what they'd lost.

"Seaman Lambert." From his position behind the wheel Riordan bellowed a command. His heart went out to Ambrosia. She'd been valiantly battling the weather for hours alongside the other sailors. Like them, her clothes were soaked clean through, plastered to her skin. It was no longer possible to hide her gender. Those who hadn't known before could surely see, by the breasts clearly visible beneath her wet shirt, that there was a female in their midst. But all had accepted her as one of their own, for she was willing to work twice as hard.

"Aye, Captain?" Ambrosia looked up from her task of swabbing the deck.

"Fielding needs help belowdecks preparing the food." It would give her a rare chance to change into dry clothes and even drink some hot tea while she helped with the meal.

Ambrosia's eyes blazed. "Do I look like a cook? Let someone else help Fielding."

Riordan's mouth clamped into a hard, tight line. Why must she always be so damnably stubborn? "Are you questioning my command?"

"Nay, Captain." She spat the words from between clenched teeth. "But I'd rather swing from the rigging during a lightning strike than be stuck belowdecks with Fielding."

Several of the other seamen chuckled. It was well known that Fielding spent most of his time eating, while ordering his assistants about like a monarch. But most of the sailors didn't mind galley duty. It gave them a chance to be dry and well fed.

"Very well." Riordan turned to a young lad no more than ten and three. "Brandon, go below and help Fielding." He turned to Ambrosia with a look that dared her to argue. "Seaman Lambert, you have your wish. Climb that rigging with young Randolph and begin unfurling the sails. We need to make up for the time lost."

Ambrosia heard the laughter of the other sailors, and saw the relief on their faces that they'd been spared such an order. Lifting her chin, she took hold of a rope and began to climb hand over hand.

The waves were so fierce they sent a wall of stinging salt spray spilling over the rail, nearly swamping her. She was grateful when she'd climbed high enough to avoid the waves. Still, the ropes were stiff and wet, burning her hands until they bled. And to add to her misery, each time she looked up she was forced to close her eyes against the rain that fell directly into her face.

From his position on deck Riordan watched her progress with a sense of self-loathing. Once again she'd managed to light the short fuse of his temper, causing him to push harder than he'd intended. The last thing he wanted was to order her to take such a risk. But she seemed determined to force his hand at every turn.

He glanced at Newton, who also seemed concerned as Ambrosia clung to the ropes with one hand while with the other she worked the sails. The young seaman who worked across from her seemed to be having a bit of trouble with snarled lines. Seeing it, Ambrosia swung hand over hand until she was beside him. Together they worked the ropes until the knot was free. Then Ambrosia swung back in a graceful arc, catching another rope in her hands and easily returning to her position.

As she and young Randolph started down, Riordan let out the breath he'd been unconsciously holding. He glanced at Newton. The old man winked, then turned away and continued swabbing the deck.

Minutes later Ambrosia paused beside Riordan. "Is there anything else you'd like done before I go below-decks and eat, Captain?"

Because there were several sailors close enough to overhear, he merely shrugged. "Nothing, Seaman Lambert. For now." As she started away he added in a low tone, "You and Randolph did a fine job."

She never even bothered to acknowledge his remark as she stalked off in silence.

* * *

"There she is, Cap'n." Newton pointed through the dusk of evening to the ship that lay battered and broken a few hundred yards offshore.

"Hoist our flag, Newt. Let her know we're fellow countrymen."

"Aye, Cap'n." The old man unfurled the English flag and began to pull the ropes until it flew at the very top of the mast, above the sails.

Within minutes a sailor aboard the crippled ship climbed to the top of the mast and began waving a lantern.

"She's signaling us to come aboard, Cap'n." Newton stood beside Riordan, who was turning the *Undaunted* toward shore. "Ye'd best watch these shallows. They're treacherous. Ye wouldn't want to share the fate of that one."

"You're right, Newt. Send a couple of sailors topside and have them watch for hazards."

"Aye, Cap'n." The old man shouted for several sailors to climb the rigging. Satisfied, he glanced at Riordan. "Ye might want to turn the wheel over to the lass. She's familiar with these shores. Been sailing them since she was no bigger'n a wee babe."

"What's the matter, Newt? Losing faith in me?"

"Nay, Cap'n. But we've already lost too much time. I'd hate to lose even more when we're this close to our goal."

"We'll make it, Newt." He steadied the wheel. "But summon Seaman Lambert. No harm in having a second pair of eyes."

"Aye, sir." The old man shuffled away and returned a short time later with Ambrosia trailing.

"You sent for me, Captain?"

He kept his gaze on the water directly in front of them.

It wouldn't do to allow any distractions now. And Ambrosia was definitely a distraction.

"Newt tells me you know these waters."

"I do."

"Then I'd like you beside me. If you see that we're heading into trouble, I want you to shout a warning immediately."

"Aye, Captain."

She stood beside him, staring intently at the waves. But she couldn't ignore the presence of the man beside her. There was such strength in him, such a sense of power. Except for her father, she'd never known a man so sure of himself.

"This is the worst possible time to navigate such waters. With the sunlight faded, it's impossible to see every hidden danger. Did you know that more ships have run aground along this coastline than almost any other in all of England?"

"Aye." He kept his gaze unwavering, loving the sound of her voice, so low and breathy. "I know."

"Careful. There's a shoal up ahead, and in high seas like this many an unsuspecting ship has been carried onto it and left high and dry."

"And unable to defend itself against the many pirates who operate in these waters, I'm told." He nodded toward the rotting hulls of abandoned ships that were as numerous as the rocks, and gave silent testimony to the hazards involved in navigating the wicked shoreline of Cornwall.

"Rocks dead ahead, Captain," she called, even before the seamen who were high in the rigging had spotted them.

As Riordan turned the wheel, the shout came from

above, confirming what Ambrosia had just calmly told him.

He shot her an admiring look. "Well done, Seaman Lambert."

She actually smiled. "Thank you, Captain."

The *Undaunted* inched slowly toward the crippled ship. With Ambrosia's words of warning to guide him, Riordan brought them alongside.

"Ahoy the *Dover*," he shouted. "This is the *Undaunted*. Come to rescue your crew and deliver your cargo."

"Ahoy the *Undaunted*. Come aboard."

Riordan turned the wheel over to Newton. "Ambrosia, stay here with Newt. I'll take a couple of sailors with me and determine the size of the cargo and the number of men needed."

"I can carry my share, Riordan," she said before she could stop herself.

"Aye." He halted her with a look. "Of that I have no doubt. But the decision is mine to make. And I want you here."

He walked away, overhearing her mutter in an aside to Newton that she was once again being treated differently.

"Leave it, lass," the old man said tiredly. "The cap'n's doing his best for all of us."

She turned to him with a look of surprise. "Are you taking his side, Newt?"

"Nay, lass." He patted her arm. "There's no side here. Neither his nor yours. There's just what's best for all. But ye've got to learn that when ye push too hard, ye force him to push back. And when that happens, neither of ye likes the outcome."

Though she was inwardly seething, she managed to

keep her thoughts to herself. But she had no intention of letting up. Riordan Spencer needed to be reminded that she was as good as any other sailor aboard the *Undaunted.*

On board the *Dover,* Riordan greeted the captain and looked around the nearly empty ship in surprise. "Where are your sailors, Captain?"

"My crew has been taken to shore and given shelter," Captain Williams explained. "I kept only enough men to see that the *Dover* wasn't claimed for salvage until the cargo could be transferred to an English ship."

Riordan surveyed the damage. "I doubt she can be of any use even as salvage, Captain. Why would anyone try to claim her? She seems to be breaking up."

"Aye." The bearded man's eyes were bleak as he studied the toppled mast, the torn sails, many of which were floating nearby. The *Dover* was listing badly, her hold flooded, her hull breaking apart.

Riordan pointed to the cargo, which had been brought above deck to keep it from floating away. "Let's get this loaded aboard the *Undaunted* at once."

The sailors began the task of carting the heavy wooden casks containing tea and spices from one ship to the other, and storing them in the hold. By the time they'd completed the transfer, darkness had settled over the land.

"Thank you, Captain Spencer." The bearded man offered his hand.

"You're welcome, Captain Williams. I wish you good fortune with the *Dover,*" Riordan replied, clasping it firmly.

"And you with the *Undaunted.*" Captain Williams looked up at a sky so dark not even a hint of moonlight or starlight could be seen. "It's not a night for sailing, Captain Spencer."

"Aye. I thought we'd wait here for morning."

Captain Williams beckoned him away from the others. In a voice hardly more than a whisper, he said, "I must give you a word of warning. You'd best use the cover of darkness to put as much distance as possible between us."

At the urgency in the man's tone, Riordan tensed. "Are you trying to warn me of danger, Captain?"

Williams nodded. "My men spotted a rogue ship in the area. Even when it came within shouting distance, it hoisted no flag. It's what drove us to this. We had to get as close to shore as possible. I believe the only thing that kept them from coming in for our cargo was the many fishermen from Bretton circling our ship, offering to ferry our sailors to land. But once the captain of the rogue spots your sails, he'll know where you've come from and what you carry."

"I doubt a rogue ship would be interested in tea and spices, Captain."

"It's true. They wouldn't be. But if the casks marked tea and spices actually contained something much more valuable, they'd be willing to do whatever necessary to steal it."

Riordan's eyes narrowed. "Just what are we carrying, Captain?" At Williams's hesitation, he added, "I have a right to know what danger I may be bringing to my ship and crew."

"It's gold, Captain Spencer. To be delivered to the king's own representative in Land's End, who will arrange to have it taken overland to London."

"Gold?" Riordan stared at him in surprise. "Why all this secrecy?"

"King Charles has need of gold. But there are those

who would steal it, in order to weaken his position and see him lose favor with the people.''

"And yet you've taken me into your confidence." Riordan studied the man's eyes. "Why?"

"I was told you are a personal friend of His Majesty."

"That's not for others to know, Captain Williams."

"Aye, sir. I understand. Your secret is safe with me."

Riordan glanced around, to be certain no one was close enough to overhear. "Did your sailors not know what you carried?"

"Nay. If they did, they might have wanted to help themselves to some of the cargo when the ship ran aground. It's why I agreed to allow them to go ashore. I kept only those I could trust. And even then, I watched them as though I couldn't trust them." He smiled. "I'd advise you to keep this knowledge to yourself as well, Captain. Trust no one. For someone out there has knowledge of this cargo. Someone who will do whatever necessary to relieve you of it."

"What is the name of this man I must contact in Land's End?"

"His name is Barclay Stuart."

"Thank you, Captain." Riordan shook his hand again, then returned to his own ship.

"Newton," he shouted. "Have the sailors hoist the sails."

"We're leaving now, Cap'n? Before light?"

"Aye, Newt. We leave immediately."

For a minute the old man's eyes narrowed. Whatever information had been exchanged between the two captains, it meant some sort of trouble. Why else would a man of the sea risk the lives of himself and his crew on such a perilous undertaking? And all for the sake of simple cargo?

For the next hour, while they traversed the same dangerous path they'd so recently followed, no one spoke. All eyes were focused on the black water that lay ahead. All thoughts were centered on making it out to the deep without incident.

"Ship just off the stern, Cap'n." Newton's voice bellowed down from the rigging, where he'd climbed just before dawn.

"Can we outrun her, Newt?" Riordan called.

"She's bearing down hard. Running light. No cargo. She'll be upon us within the hour, I'd say."

At once a dozen sailors raced to the rear of the ship and strained for a glimpse of sails. As soon as they were spotted, the men began mumbling among themselves, until the mutterings became a roar.

"She's a rogue, Captain. She flies no flag."

From above came a shout. "Cannon, Cap'n. On the port side."

"Prepare to defend yourselves, men," Riordan shouted.

Though there was an air of expectancy about them, there was no sense of panic. These seamen had spent a lifetime doing battle against just such ships.

Several cannons were uncovered and braziers of fire were prepared on deck to arm them. Scabbards were strapped on, swords unsheathed. Knives glinted at waists or were tucked into boots. Several of the men carried dueling pistols.

As the rogue ship drew closer, many of the men stripped down for battle, removing jackets, hats, even shirts.

Ambrosia peeled away her heavy jacket and tossed it aside. She cursed the billowing sleeves of her shirt, but knew that they wouldn't impede her ability to fight. Since she couldn't discard her shirt, she would simply ignore it. She checked the knife at her waist, and rejected the offer of a fellow seaman's scabbard.

"I have no need. The sword will be in my hand, not tucked away out of sight."

"Ye might be sorry, lass," the old seaman said. "Most of these pirates go after the armed sailors first. Those of us who don't show our weapons stand a better chance of surviving."

"Armed or unarmed, once they see I'm a woman, they'll try to take me."

"Aye, alive if possible," the old seaman said.

She felt a sudden chill at the implication. "I'll survive." Her fingers closed around the hilt of the sword, and she lifted it, testing its weight. "If you'd like, I'll stay close and keep you safe as well."

The old seaman smiled. "Ye're a feisty one, lass. I'll hear what ye have to say when the fighting's over."

"I'd rather let my sword do my talking."

"Get down," someone shouted.

Ambrosia saw a stream of fire and heard a tremendous roar as a cannonball struck the side of the *Undaunted*. There was the sound of wood splintering as the deck beneath their feet trembled and shook. Almost at once it was answered by a volley of cannonfire from aboard their own ship. With a burst of deafening noise and a tail of fire that shot straight up in the air, two cannonballs struck the hull of the approaching vessel. It seemed to shudder, then continued on its course, heading directly into their path.

The *Undaunted* absorbed a second cannonball attack that had flames streaking across the bow.

Ambrosia felt a momentary rush of fear as the rogue

ship pulled alongside, casting a dark shadow over the deck where she stood. Her fear deepened as its crew let out a wave of bloodcurdling screams before leaping across the rail and challenging any sailor in their path.

And then there was no time for fear as Ambrosia was thrust into battle. And what a battle. At first it was almost impossible to hear over the roar of cannons and the screaming of the attacking sailors.

These sailors were unlike any she'd ever known. Filthy. Some with feet bared; others with rags tied about their feet in place of boots. Their clothes torn and dirty. Hair matted and streaming down their backs. While they fought with swords and knives, they cursed and swore and screeched like madmen.

With each victory they let out whoops of pure glee. They were, Ambrosia realized, enjoying the killing. Each dead Englishman was a trophy to be displayed. They called to one another and actually laughed as they pointed to another victim.

A sailor came at her waving his sword. She dispatched him with a single thrust, then turned to face two more. Out of the corner of her eye she noted that the old sailor was crouched behind her, cowering beside a burning brazier. She managed to run through the first attacker, but the second ducked her thrust, then came up swinging. Before he could pin her she danced, turned and caught his shoulder with a powerful blow. Giving him no time to recover, she ran him through with her sword.

She looked up to see Riordan facing two swordsmen, with another coming up on his flank.

"Behind you, Riordan."

He turned, evading the man's sword, and managed to run him through before returning his attention to the first two.

"Watch yourself, lass."

At the old man's shout, she turned and found herself facing a line of advancing pirates, all wielding swords.

She managed to fight off three of them before the old sailor finally came to her aid, unsheathing his sword and protecting her back. Just as she fought off the last of them there was a tremendous explosion as another cannonball smashed into the side of the *Undaunted*. The ship shuddered beneath her feet. Smoke billowed, and flames could be seen coming from belowdecks.

Choking in the thick black smoke, Ambrosia struggled to make her way toward the rail. Just as she got there and leaned far over to fill her lungs with fresh air, she felt the sharp sting of a blade and a sticky warmth as blood streamed down her arm. She turned. But before she could lift her sword in defense, she saw Riordan's blade run the man through.

Dazed, she managed to say, "I...didn't see him."

"Luckily, I did." He turned and took out two more swordsmen, but before he could take out a third, Ambrosia moved in, sending the man over the rail.

"Newt!" At her cry, Riordan turned and saw the old man fighting off a score of swordsmen.

Both Riordan and Ambrosia leapt to his defense. The three stood back to back, swords flashing, blades slicing, making quick work of the last of the rogue sailors.

When there was a lull in the fighting, Riordan turned to her. Suddenly his eyes narrowed. "You've been wounded."

She touched a hand to the warmth that soaked her sleeve. "It's nothing."

"Nothing?" He strode forward.

Just then there was a cry and they looked up to see the lad, Brandon, facing a bearded swordsman who, though wounded, had backed him against the rail, which was tilting precariously.

"Nay!" With a shout, Ambrosia charged the man, her sword lifted in challenge.

The man turned and met her with his sword upraised. Before the others could intervene, their blades slashed viciously, again and again. And though Ambrosia was skilled, this swordsman was bigger and stronger. With each thrust of his blade, he drove her closer and closer to the rail. Seeing what he planned, she danced out of the way, refusing to be pinned. But the movement cost her. His sword pierced her shoulder, opening another wound.

"Ambrosia." With a cry of outrage Riordan charged across the distance that separated them.

Before he could reach her, she slipped on a puddle of blood. Her feet flew out from under her. And before anybody could save her, she slipped over the rail and fell into the sea.

Desperate, Riordan ran the man through, then tossed his sword aside and leapt overboard.

As he hit the water, he felt his heart plummet.

Ambrosia was nowhere to be seen.

Chapter Nine

The water was choked with debris. Bodies. Splinters of wood from the two damaged ships. Gunpowder, which turned the waves inky black.

In a panic, Riordan swam underwater until his lungs screamed for air. But there was no sign of Ambrosia. He surfaced, shoving aside each barrier, desperate for the slightest movement that would indicate someone alive and struggling.

"Ambrosia!" He cupped his hands to his mouth and shouted into the mist that had settled over the ocean. Where was the morning sunlight? he wondered. Why had it failed him when he most needed it?

"Ambrosia!" He swam between two bodies, feeling a wave of such despair he was nearly overcome with it. He wouldn't allow this to be her fate. He couldn't.

"Riordan."

At the faint sound of her voice, he turned. She was nearly the length of the ship away, clinging to a piece of wood and drifting farther away with each pull of the tide.

With strong, powerful strokes he reached her and wrapped his arms around her. "Oh, Ambrosia. I was so afraid."

''Were you?'' With a trace of wonder she touched a hand to his face and closed her eyes, struggling to remain conscious.

''Cap'n.'' From the bow of the *Undaunted,* he heard Newton's voice.

''Here, Newt. Over here. Throw us a line.''

The sailors were already lining the rail, peering through the mist. When one of them located the darkened shadows clinging to the piece of wood, there was a roar from the deck of the ship. Minutes later a rope snaked across the water, and Riordan tied it around his waist. As he held fast to Ambrosia, the sailors hauled him in.

When they came alongside the *Undaunted,* a rope ladder was lowered and Riordan climbed it, cradling Ambrosia to his chest.

''Ye've found her, Cap'n.''

''Aye.''

''Is she…?'' Old Newton's face was almost as pale as Ambrosia's.

''She's alive, Newt. That's all I know for now.'' As Riordan headed across the deck, he shouted, ''Any of the rogue sailors left alive?''

''None, Cap'n.''

''And our sailors?''

''None dead. But more'n half a dozen wounded. None too serious.''

''Good. That's very good. And the fires?''

''We've put them out. We'll need to do a bit of mending. Our ship's listing to port. It's what had the lass tumbling over the rail. But we should be able to set sail by midafternoon.''

''That's good news, Newt. I'll leave you in charge while I see to Ambrosia.'' Riordan descended the stairs and carried her to his cabin. Inside he gently laid her on the bunk.

Working quickly, he tugged off her boots, then used his knife to cut away her clothes. There was a deep gash in her shoulder, a second in her arm. He poured a generous amount of ale over the wounds, then bound them with clean cloth, before wrapping her in a dry blanket. As he did he caught sight of her hands. The flesh of her palms was torn and bloody. This couldn't have come from holding a sword. And then he remembered. The climb up the rigging. The stiff, wet ropes had torn her tender flesh and left it raw. He felt a wave of remorse, knowing it had been his orders that had caused her unnecessary pain. And even with these raw, torn hands, she'd managed to wield a sword with the best of them.

She was so still it tore at his heart. He touched a hand to the bump on the back of her head. It worried him more than the sword wounds. She'd taken a terrible fall. He'd seen sailors who never recovered from such a blow.

His hands shaking, he filled a tumbler with ale and downed it in one long swallow. Then he changed into dry clothes and pulled a chair up beside the bunk. He wasn't leaving until she regained consciousness.

Though he didn't consider himself a religious man, he found himself praying. She had to recover. If she didn't, he'd never forgive himself.

Ambrosia lay very still, wondering at the strange silence. Except for the gentle slap of water nearby, there was no sound. The slow, easy rocking motion was soothing.

Was the battle over? Had she died? She moved her head and felt a quick stab of pain. Nay, not dead. She must be alive if she could hurt so badly. Very slowly she opened her eyes. Wonder of wonders, she was in her father's cabin, aboard the *Undaunted,* though she couldn't recall how she'd gotten there.

Father. He'd come back. She smiled and tried to sit up. At once she was swamped with pain. Her head. Her shoulder. Her arm. She moaned and fell back weakly.

"Ambrosia. Praise heaven, you're awake."

She looked over to see Riordan Spencer sitting beside the bunk. His eyes looked red rimmed and weary. A growth of stubble darkened his chin.

His voice seemed unusually tender as he asked, "Can you see me?"

"Aye." What a strange question, she thought.

"Can you see how many fingers I'm holding up?"

An even stranger question. Did he think her an imbecile? She gave him a most indignant look. "Four."

She heard him sigh, and wondered at the sound. "Was I…sleeping?" She couldn't seem to make her mouth work. She knew the words, but they wouldn't come out.

He nodded. "All day."

She glanced at the lantern, burning on a table. "Is it…night?"

"Aye. We've lowered the sails until morning. We should make port tomorrow evening."

"The rogues?"

"Dead. Their ship crippled and sunk below the waves by now. We boarded her and took what meager bounty there was. Then we made what repairs we could to the *Undaunted,* and sailed until darkness forced us to stop."

"The lad? Brandon?"

"He's fine, thanks to you." And so was he now, Riordan realized. Until this moment, he hadn't realized how very afraid he'd been. For a while there, he'd thought his heart might never beat again. But Ambrosia was alive.

And awake. And apparently unharmed by the bump to her head. He took in a long, deep breath, then touched a hand to her forehead. "Would you like something for the pain?"

"In...a moment. Tell me about...battle. Did we lose any sailors?"

"Nay. Some wounded, but none dead."

"Ah." She closed her eyes a moment. When she opened them, he was seated next to her on the bunk, holding up a glass. He lifted her head and held the glass to her lips.

After a single sip she coughed and made a terrible face before pushing his hand away. "That's dreadful. What is it?"

"Ale. Like none you've ever tasted. It's what the sailors drink to chase the cold Atlantic from their bones." He pressed the glass to her lips. "Drink. It will ease the pain. Or at least make you drunk enough that you won't care about it."

He held the glass until she drained it. Then he laid her gently back down. "Can you feel it working?"

"Aye." She smiled dreamily. "And you're right about...warmth. I believe my insides have caught fire."

He laughed, feeling better than he could ever remember. "Oh, Ambrosia. You don't know how happy you've made me."

"Happy?"

"I was so worried. I feared you might have sustained some serious injuries." He brushed a lock of her hair from her eye. "I couldn't bear it if you did. But you're fine now. Out of harm's way." He stopped talking when he realized she had already fallen asleep.

He felt such a wave of tenderness. After passing word to the crew that Seaman Lambert was doing nicely, he returned to his cabin. Draping a blanket around his shoulders, he sat down in the chair, propping his feet on the bunk. With a smile on his face he joined her in sleep.

Ambrosia was having the sweetest dream. A handsome stranger had sailed into Land's End. Dark and mysterious he was, causing the whole village to speculate that he was a pirate. When the vicar demanded answers, the stranger refused to comply, saying only that he'd come for Ambrosia Lambert, and he wouldn't leave until she agreed to sail with him for the rest of her life.

"Aye," she whispered in her sleep. "I'll sail with you. For it's what I want as well."

This dark handsome stranger smiled then and gathered her close, pressing his mouth to hers and commanding her to kiss him back.

She wrapped her arms around his neck and offered her lips.

"Ambrosia." A voice broke through her dream. A deep voice that calmed, even while it sent a thrill of excitement through her.

"Aye." She pursed her lips, waiting for that moment when he would take what she offered.

"Ambrosia." The deep voice was right beside her ear. She felt lips pressed against her temple. Heat spiraled through her and she came instantly awake.

"Riordan. I was…dreaming."

"Aye. A sweet one, I'll wager." He was sitting on the bunk, cradling her against his chest. The press of his arms around her caused the most amazing feelings. Feelings like none she'd ever known.

"You won't leave me alone, will you, Riordan?"

"Not if you don't want me to."

"I don't." She lifted a hand to his cheek in an achingly sweet gesture that had his heart leaping to his throat.

"Then I'll stay. And hold you." He stretched out beside her and then wrapped his arms around her once more. "There now. Is this better?"

"Aye." She closed her eyes and snuggled close against his chest, listening to the steady beat of his heart. She didn't know whether or not the sweet dream would return. But this would certainly help her forget her pain.

As she drifted back to sleep, Riordan studied her in the path of moonlight drifting through the porthole above the bunk. She was so beautiful she took his breath away. Hair as black as a midnight sky. Eyes that gleamed with the light of the stars. Skin as milky white as the sand bleached by the sun along the cliffs at Dover. And such lips. He felt the quick rush of desire as he studied them, pursed into a little moue of pleasure. Lips made to be kissed.

How could one woman—one obstinate, headstrong woman—have such an effect on his life? She had no regard for his orders. She deliberately flaunted the rules in order to test him. She took foolish risks, put herself in harm's way and nearly got herself killed.

And he loved her. Hopelessly. Desperately. And had, long before he'd ever met her. From the first time he'd heard James Lambert talk about his vexing little sister, Ambrosia, and her skill with a sword. From the first time he'd seen her likeness on the locket her father wore around his neck. From the first time he'd heard John Lambert speak with such passion about his daughters. It had only been worse when he'd met her in the flesh.

Flesh. He studied the darkened cleft visible beneath the blanket. The sight of her when he'd cut away her clothes had given him a jolt. She was even more perfect than he'd dreamed. But then he'd been so worried about her wounds, he couldn't really appreciate her beauty. Now, while she was mending and asleep in his arms, he was free to indulge himself. She was, quite simply, the most beautiful creature he'd ever met.

She sighed in her sleep and tensed in his arms. He pressed his lips to her temple. At once she settled back, relaxing once more. And as dawn light streaked the sky, he allowed himself to be lulled by the knowledge that the woman he loved was healing. And her sleek ship, the *Undaunted,* would soon be home.

"Riordan." Ambrosia awoke to sunlight streaming in the small round window. But it wasn't the sunlight that was causing this heat. It was the warmth of the man beside her. A man who was sharing her bed. And staring at her with such intensity, she felt her cheeks grow hot. "What are you doing?"

"Watching you. I've been watching you ever since I awoke."

"But what are you doing in my bed?"

"You forget, Ambrosia. It's my bed. And you invited me. In fact, you insisted that I not leave. Have you forgotten?"

She looked away, embarrassed. "Aye. I do remember now. But it was probably the ale."

"Was it?" He smiled. "What a shame. I'd hoped it was what you wanted, too."

"I did. I...do. But if you don't mind, now that I'm fully recovered, I think it best if you leave."

"Fully recovered?" He glanced at the bruise that darkened her pretty cheek and the bump that still stuck out like an egg at the back of her head. "I'd say you're far from recovered yet."

"And I say I am." She struggled to sit up, then scrunched down when she realized she was naked under the blanket. "Where are my clothes?"

"I'll have Newt fetch them. Fielding hung them from the rigging to dry."

She shot him an indignant look. "My breeches and chemise were hanging for all the crew to see?"

"Only your breeches, I'm afraid. I had to cut off your bloody shirt and chemise and toss them away. They're beyond repair."

"You cut..." She looked away, her face flaming.

Seeing her embarrassment, he lowered his voice. "I had no choice, Ambrosia. You were bleeding. I had to examine your wounds."

"Oh, I'll wager you did." She sat up, holding the blanket around her like a shield. "Next you'll probably tell me you didn't look."

He couldn't help smiling. "I see no point in lying. Not only did I look, I admired. My only regret is that I was so preoccupied with your wounds, I didn't get to really appreciate your beauty."

"My...beauty?" She sat up and the blanket fell off one shoulder.

Before she could pull it up, he closed a hand around her upper arm and dragged her close. Though the smile remained on his lips, there was a dangerous glint in his eyes. "Don't pretend you don't know you're beautiful, Ambrosia."

He saw the way her eyes widened at his words. And it occurred to him that she had never really thought about the way she looked. That only made her all the more amazing in his eyes.

He lowered his mouth, until it hovered just above hers. His hands at her shoulders tightened, and he drew her fractionally closer. "You're the most beautiful, desirable sailor I've ever had aboard my ship. And after a day and night of watching you, and worrying over you, I'm going to have to kiss you."

"You..." She pulled back. "You worried about me?"

"Aye. When you fell overboard, I thought my heart would surely stop beating until I found you." He began to draw her close once more. "And then when I found you, you were bleeding, and nearly unconscious, and it was another blow to my heart."

She touched a hand to his chest. "Such a poor, battered heart."

"Aye." He caught her hand in his and lifted it to his lips. "And then when I saw these..." he caught both her hands and held them, palms up "...saw what my cruel order had caused, I felt such remorse, Ambrosia." Very tenderly he pressed a kiss to each palm, sending heat curling deep inside her.

He drew her closer. "Will you forgive me for ordering you to climb the rigging?"

"Oh, Riordan." She touched a hand to his cheek, then allowed it to remain there while she looked up into his eyes. "It was my own fault, for goading you."

"Nay. I feel like a monster for what I did to you."

"But you were only—"

Before she could frame a reply, he covered her mouth with his in a kiss that was so hot, so hungry, it left them both trembling.

The blanket slipped away. Ambrosia was too caught up in the kiss to notice. But Riordan did, and felt a rush of need that had his breath backing up in his throat.

He pressed her against the bunk and ran nibbling kisses across her face, her cheeks, her jaw. Then he brought his mouth lower, to the soft column of her throat.

She made a sound that could have been a protest or a sigh. She knew they were sailing in dangerous waters, but she couldn't gather the will to stop him. His lips, his hands, were bringing such pleasure.

"Then I'm forgiven?" He whispered the words against her throat.

"Aye. At the moment I'd forgive you anything."

"Ambrosia." His mouth moved lower, finding the swell of her breast.

As his tongue circled her erect nipple, feelings jolted through her. Feelings unlike anything she'd ever known. Her whole body seemed on fire. She felt a curl of desire deep inside, and a warmth that even the fresh sea air couldn't cool. She found herself wanting things that until this moment she'd never even thought of. Things that frightened and alarmed her.

"Nay, Riordan." She pushed him away and sat up, gathering the edges of the blanket around her.

"You don't mean that, Ambrosia. You want this as much as I." His eyes narrowed. His breath was coming hard and fast. He hadn't realized just how close to the edge he'd come. And just how desperately he wanted her.

"I thought I did." She was far too honest to deny it. "But I…I need some time. I need to think."

With as much steadiness as he could manage, he got to his feet. "Then I'll leave you to your thoughts."

She glanced down at herself and gave a wry smile. "I certainly hope you can get me a shirt from someone in the crew. Or was it your plan to keep me confined to your cabin until the voyage is over?"

His smile returned. "I think I can manage one shirt." He opened his seabag and handed her a shirt of white linen. "I'm certain of one thing. It will look far better on you than it ever could on me."

He gave her one long final glance, then walked from the cabin and closed the door. When he was gone Ambrosia struggled out of the bunk and was forced to grasp the back of the chair to keep herself from falling. This momentary weakness was unsettling. In her whole life she'd never been ill. Had never been forced to take to her bed.

She shook her head to clear the fuzziness, then proceeded to dress. By the time she was ready to take her leave of the cabin, she was feeling stronger. The last thing she wanted was to embarrass herself by showing any sign of weakness in front of the others.

"Land's End, Cap'n." Newton pointed. "There's MaryCastle dead ahead."

"Aye. I see it, Newt." Riordan was grateful for the sea air that had helped to clear his head. But nothing would lessen this need for Ambrosia. If anything, it had grown deeper.

She had emerged from his cabin looking cool and beautiful in his white shirt and her black breeches, tucked into tall black boots.

He turned to glance at her now, loving the way she planted her feet on the deck. Like a born sailor. The thought struck him, and he couldn't help but smile. She had her face lifted, as though breathing in the salt air. Without the scarf, her dark hair streamed behind her, tossed by the wind.

He held the wheel steady as they drew near the shallows.

"I'd be careful if I were you, Cap'n." Newton's voice had him returning his thoughts to the work at hand. "For the next hour ye'd best not let yer attention veer. Many a ship's captain made the mistake of thinking he was home free, only to find his vessel sunk by the rocks lurking just below the water's edge here at Land's End.''

"Aye, Newt. I'll remember."

The old man moved closer, so that none of the crew could overhear. "It's easy enough to be distracted by a face as pretty as that, eh, Cap'n?"

"Aye, Newt." He frowned. "She is a distraction. A most pleasant one at the moment."

He ignored the surprised look on the old man's face and turned, shouting, "Seaman Lambert."

She made her way across the deck to stand in front of him. "Aye, Captain?"

"I'd like you to take the wheel."

He saw her eyes widen before she carefully composed her features. "Aye, Captain."

As she moved in front of him and took over the navigation of the ship, he took a step back, remaining directly behind her.

"Why are you doing this, Riordan?" She kept her tone low, so that the other sailors wouldn't overhear.

"I thought your grandfather and sisters ought to have the pleasure of watching you bring the *Undaunted* in. She's your ship, after all."

His words warmed her as nothing else could have.

"Look." He pointed. "Up there."

She gazed toward where he was pointing, and saw her family watching from the widow's walk.

He watched as she carefully navigated the hidden rocks, the sudden drop-offs and shallows, and brought the ship to their cove for anchor.

It was only when the anchor was lowered that he noticed how she favored one arm. His smile faded. "You're in pain."

"It's nothing." She rubbed her shoulder. "Just a little tender."

Knowing the others were watching, he managed not to touch her. But his voice, so close to her, was fierce with concern. "You should have told me, Ambrosia. I don't want you straining that wound."

He turned to Newton. "Order the skiff lowered, Newt. I must go to Land's End and meet with the king's representative, and arrange for him to claim our cargo." He turned to Ambrosia. "You're coming with me."

"To Land's End?"

"Nay. To shore."

"Shouldn't I stay here with the crew?"

"They're capable of standing watch until I return. As for you, I intend to ask Mistress Coffey to prepare a hot bath and a warm meal for you at once."

Ambrosia lay a hand over Riordan's and lowered her voice. "You know that I will refuse any special treatment."

He smiled, in that way that always caused her heart to tumble in her chest. "Indulge me, Ambrosia. I spent too many hours worrying about you. And now that we're home, I want to know that you're being cared for properly."

She swallowed. "Aye, Captain."

When the skiff was lowered, they descended the rope ladder and settled themselves inside.

Minutes later, as they landed on the beach, Riordan held out his hand and helped her from the boat.

She hesitated. "Will I see you for dinner?"

"Aye." He smiled. "As soon as our cargo is turned over to the king's representative in Land's End, my job is done."

"I'll tell Mistress Coffey to expect you."

Riordan watched as she walked across the beach. Then, leaving Newton beside the skiff, he started toward the village, content that his first voyage as captain of the *Undaunted* had ended well, despite some setbacks.

He was looking forward to a long hot bath himself. And perhaps a few minutes alone with Ambrosia, to take up where they'd left off aboard ship.

Chapter Ten

Riordan strode through the village of Land's End, eager to finish this business and get back to MaryCastle. He couldn't begin to relax until the gold was removed from the *Undaunted* and turned over to the proper authorities.

Then he smiled to himself. He would find some time alone with Ambrosia. He might even admit to her that she'd done a fine job aboard the *Undaunted*. Much finer than he'd expected. She'd worked harder than any other sailor. She'd pushed herself to the limit to prove to him, to the others and probably to herself, that she was up to the task. His smile grew. Aye, she was more than up to the task of sailing. And even in battle she'd done herself proud. If not for the unexpected fall, there'd be not a blemish on her record. And that fall could have happened to any one of them. What made it all the more remarkable was the fact that she'd rushed to the aid of young Brandon before the others had even noticed his predicament.

She was an amazing woman. And he intended to tell her that. Right after he kissed her full on the mouth. Because the truth was, he'd been thinking about that mouth ever since he'd first kissed it. And if he didn't taste her again, and soon, he'd go mad.

After inquiring at the tavern, he was told where he could find Barclay Stuart. His place of business looked out over the harbor filled with ships at anchor. It was a sight that stirred Riordan's heart as nothing else could.

He pushed open the door and stepped inside, closing it behind him. The walls were lined with maps of the world, the trade routes clearly marked. Every inch of space was cluttered with things much loved by seamen. Rope. Oars. Anchors. A ship's sextant sat atop the desk, which was littered with papers.

It would seem that Mr. Stuart wasn't a neat man. The papers even spilled over onto the floor.

Seeing no one at the desk, Riordan called out, "Mr. Stuart?"

His greeting was met with silence.

"Barclay Stuart?" Seeing a door ajar across the room, he stepped closer, then froze in midstride.

A pair of booted feet, twisted at an odd angle, lay in the doorway. Riordan hurried across and shoved open the door. A man lay in a pool of blood. From the looks of him, he'd been bludgeoned. A bloody wooden oar lay on the floor next to the body.

Though he knew it was a futile gesture, Riordan knelt and touched a hand to the man's throat. There was no sign of a pulse. Nor had he expected one.

Now Riordan realized why the desk was so disorderly. Someone had been searching for something, and had scattered Stuart's papers in the process.

At the implication, he felt a prickling along his scalp, and knew that there was no time to waste. He had to return to the *Undaunted* immediately.

Riordan always trusted his instincts. And right now he felt certain that he and his men were in serious danger. It stood to reason that Barclay Stuart would have kept a record of the actual cargo being carried by the *Dover*. If the murderer found that document, he would come looking for the gold. It was only a matter of time until word leaked out that it was the crew of the *Undaunted* that had salvaged the king's precious gold.

Now Riordan was more convinced than ever that the attack by the rogue ship hadn't been a random act. They had known. That meant others knew as well. There wasn't a moment to waste.

The *Undaunted* and her crew would be at the mercy of every pirate ship in the Atlantic.

"Newt." Riordan's greeting was abrupt. "We won't be unloading the cargo. Nor will the crew be departing for shore."

"Trouble, Cap'n?" The old man could see the worry in his eyes.

"Aye. We'll need supplies for a voyage, Newt. And soon."

"How soon?"

Riordan glanced at the sun, already hovering low on the water. "Before dark, so we can navigate the shallows." He stared intently at the old sailor. "Think you can do it?"

"Aye, Cap'n. I'll send some men to Land's End to replenish our supplies."

"They're not to speak of this. To anyone."

Newton nodded, though he felt uneasy at the urgency in Riordan's tone. "I'll see to it." He cast a glance toward the house. "What about the lass? Have ye told her?"

Riordan turned away. "That's to be my next stop."

He turned and strode toward MaryCastle, wishing he didn't have to be the bearer of such unhappy news.

Before he could even climb the steps the door was thrown wide and Ambrosia was standing there looking cool and regal in a gown of lemon yellow, her hair swept up in a mass of curls that danced beguilingly around a face made even more beautiful by the kiss of sunshine from her sea voyage.

"Riordan." She stood aside, allowing him to enter, then closed the door and caught his arm. "Come. My grandfather and sisters are in the parlor. They're eager to hear all about our adventure."

"Ambrosia." He tried to dig in his heels, but the sheer force of her energy swept him along. "We must talk."

"Aye. And we shall. But first..." She opened the parlor door. "Look who's here. Just in time to add to my tale."

"Captain Spencer." Bethany and Darcy leapt up and caught his hands, dragging him close to where their grandfather sat. "Ambrosia has just been telling us about the voyage." Bethany exchanged a smile with Darcy. "Was it as delightful as she claims?"

"Delightful?" He marveled at her choice of words. "It was...eventful."

Darcy's eyes were wide with excitement. "She said the *Undaunted* was attacked by a rogue ship."

"Aye."

Bethany had a hand to her throat. "And she was swept overboard."

"True enough."

"And you saved her," Darcy said with a note of drama.

He kept his tone dry. "Someone had to. Otherwise your sister would have drowned."

"Crowned?" Geoffrey Lambert had listened to the entire exchange, turning his head from one to the other. "Who's been crowned? Is Charles no longer king?"

"Aye, Grandpapa." Ambrosia nodded her head vigorously. "Have no fear. Your beloved young king hasn't faced the same fate as his father."

"Yet," Riordan said to himself.

Ambrosia's eyes narrowed. "What did you say?"

He shrugged. There was no point in saying more than necessary. He'd come here wondering how to broach the subject of taking Ambrosia along on another sea voyage, so soon after her return home. But now that he'd had a chance to see her, his mind was made up. She belonged here at MaryCastle, living the life of a country gentlewoman. Just seeing her in this beautiful gown, surrounded by her loving family, made him realize how unsuited she was to a life at sea. Those few days aboard ship had made him forget how gentle her life was here in Cornwall. Why should she sacrifice something this grand for the life of a lowly sailor?

Ambrosia handed him a goblet of ale. "What's wrong, Riordan? You seem distracted."

"Aye." He emptied the goblet in one long swallow, then turned to include the others. "There's been some trouble in the village."

"Trouble?" Ambrosia glanced at her sisters. "What sort of trouble?"

"The king's representative, Barclay Stuart, won't be taking our cargo off our hands."

"Why not?" Ambrosia settled herself on a chaise beside her grandfather, fanning out her skirts as she did. She was hoping she made a pretty picture for Riordan. One that might have him thinking about kissing her again. And maybe holding her and...other things. She felt her face flame at the naughty thoughts that were dancing through her mind.

"Because he's dead. Murdered."

"Murdered?" She leapt up, her face draining of all color. "Here in Land's End? How can you be certain it was murder?"

"Because I saw him lying in a pool of his own blood, with the weapon used against him tossed carelessly aside." Seeing her pallor, Riordan put a hand on her arm. "Listen to me, Ambrosia. You must send one of your servants to town to alert the authorities."

"You didn't see to that yourself?"

He shook his head. "There wasn't time." He was wasting even more right now. But they deserved the truth. He took a deep breath. "The cargo we salvaged from the *Dover* is bound for King Charles."

"The king desires tea and spices? "

"Listen to me." He touched a finger to her mouth. Determined to get through this without allowing his feelings to get in the way, he took a step back. It was dangerous being too close to this woman. "The cargo is not what you think. That's the reason we were attacked by the rogue ship. And the reason Barclay Stuart has been killed. Someone took great pains to find out what the cargo was, and who now has it. It's only a matter of time until one of the sailors aboard the *Dover* will disclose the name of our ship. And by the time that happens, I intend to have the *Undaunted* safely in port in London, and the cargo personally delivered to the king. I've already ordered Newton to see that fresh supplies are brought aboard at once. We leave within the hour."

Ambrosia and her sisters were, he realized, taking this shocking news better than he'd expected. While Bethany was relaying the news into her grandfather's ear, Darcy watched and listened without emotion.

Ambrosia nodded. "You're right, of course, Riordan. That's the wisest course of action." She started toward the door. "Very well. I'll just change and be ready to leave within the hour."

"Wait." He caught her by the arm, then cursed himself for his lapse when he was forced to endure another jolt to his already overcharged system. "You won't be going this time."

She smiled. "Bethany and Darcy will have their turns, I assure you. But this is actually part of the original voyage. And so I claim the right to continue until it's run its course."

"You don't understand, Ambrosia." He was making a determined effort to keep his voice calm and reasonable. "This is no ordinary sea voyage. A man has been murdered. A king's ransom sits in the hold of the *Undaunted*." Out of the corner of his eye he saw Bethany and Darcy clap their hands over their mouths at this news. He realized he hadn't yet told them what the cargo was. And it was best if he left it that way. "I have no doubt that before this journey ends, the crew will face grave peril. I can't permit you to be in harm's way."

"Permit?" Ambrosia's eyes went wide. She put her hands on her hips and faced him. "You won't permit? Since when were you appointed my lord and master, Riordan Spencer?"

His temper slipped a notch. "Be sensible, Ambrosia. I simply cannot, in good conscience, allow you to take this sort of risk."

"Allow? There's that word again." Her eyes grew dark and stormy. "I'll remind you, Riordan, that you are not my keeper."

"Perhaps that's what you need." He took a step closer, his own eyes narrowing. "Hell and damnation, woman. I'm trying to spare you pain and suffering."

"Nay. What you're trying to do is run my life. And nobody, least of all you, Riordan Spencer, can tell me what to do."

He realized his temper was completely out of control now, but he no longer cared. This emotional, unreasonable woman was going to be the death of him. "I simply cannot afford to be looking out for both of us during such a perilous journey."

"Fine. Look out for yourself, Riordan. And I'll do the same."

"Don't you understand?" He no longer cared that her grandfather and sisters were staring at him as if he'd lost his mind. And maybe he had, he thought. If not his mind, at least his temper. It was full blown, and about to explode. "You're a bloody distraction I can't afford, Ambrosia."

"A bloody distraction? Is that how you see me? A bloody distraction? Then I'll remind you, Captain, to keep your mind on your business, and I assure you I'll do the same."

"I fully intend to. For the sake of my life and that of my crew, I'm forbidding you to come."

"Forbid? You forbid me aboard my own ship?"

"Aye. That's what I said." He was shouting so loud, he knew the entire household could hear. It no longer mattered. Nothing had gone as he'd planned. And all because of this obstinate, infuriating female. Once again she'd twisted his words and made him sound like some kind of monster. When all he was doing was looking out for her welfare. "I forbid you to board the *Undaunted.* And every member of the crew will be given orders to that effect. If you should try to sneak aboard, I'll have you brought back in chains." He closed a hand around her wrist and dragged her close. "Is that understood?"

"Oh, I understand. I understand that you are a spineless, brainless goat masquerading as a man. Now you understand this, Riordan Spencer. When you return from London—"

"*If* I return," he shouted. "What we are about to do might cost us all our lives."

"Aye. *If* you return from London, you will be relieved of your duties aboard the *Undaunted.*"

His eyes narrowed. "You'd do that?"

"Aye. That and more. You can go to a watery grave. You can even go to hell and back, Riordan Spencer. I'll not shed a tear. Now leave me."

She wrenched free of his grasp and fled up the stairs, leaving him to stare after her.

He turned back to see her grandfather and sisters staring at him with matching expressions of disbelief.

"Forgive me. There simply is no more time for civilized explanations." He turned and strode out, slamming the door behind him.

Damn the woman, he thought. And damn his own quick temper, which had only made things worse.

Didn't she understand that he couldn't bear to see her harmed? Why couldn't she see that her very presence aboard ship would leave him weak and vulnerable to his enemies?

As he trudged across the beach toward the waiting skiff, he filled the air with a string of vicious oaths. He'd made his decision. There was no turning back. Now he would simply have to find a way to put Ambrosia Lambert out of his mind. For whatever they'd almost had together was, for now and all time, irretrievably lost.

* * *

Within the hour the *Undaunted* had set sail. Riordan was determined to see his ship and crew safely through the shallows before darkness overtook the land.

Once out to sea he ordered seamen to be posted in the riggings day and night, two fore, two aft. At least if they were attacked by rogue ships, they'd be warned in time to prepare a defense.

On board were two cannons and enough weapons to arm every man aboard ship.

Every man. Riordan stood at the wheel, watching clouds scudding across the moon. He felt an ache around his heart. Now that he'd had time to think it through, he realized he'd handled the scene with Ambrosia badly. He'd hurt her. Caused her embarrassment in front of those she loved.

He should have prepared himself better. But there'd been no time.

Time. Would there ever be time to mend this rift between them? How could she ever forgive a man who had torn her pride to shreds in front of her family? If only he could take back all those hateful words. But it was too late. Too late.

"Would ye like some relief, Cap'n?"

He turned to find Newton standing just behind him. It was a reminder of just how deeply he'd been affected by thoughts of Ambrosia. If the old sailor had been an enemy, he'd have found an easy mark in a man this distracted.

"Thanks, Newt. But I'd prefer to keep my hands busy." If only he could do the same for his mind.

"Whatever ye say, Cap'n."

The old man ambled to the rail, just as a shout went

up from the lookout in the rigging. "Ship bearing down on us fast, Captain. On the port side."

"Sound the alarm," Riordan shouted.

Newton gave a shout that had sailors dashing topside and taking up arms.

It took nearly an hour before the ship was close enough to hail in the darkness.

"Ahoy, the *Undaunted,*" came the sound of a decidedly feminine voice.

"That's Ambrosia," Newton shouted. "I'd know the lass's voice anywhere."

Riordan's eyes narrowed. He'd recognized it as well. "Newt," he called. "Take the wheel."

The old man did as he was ordered, and watched as Riordan fisted his hands at his sides, peering through the darkness as the *Sea Challenge* approached at top speed.

The lass had done it now, Newton thought. From the murderous look in the cap'n's eyes, she'd best be prepared to defend herself. Or she might find herself swimming all the way back to Cornwall.

Chapter Eleven

When the *Sea Challenge* drew alongside, Riordan stared in openmouthed surprise at the figures clearly outlined by lantern light.

Not only had Ambrosia brought her two sisters along, but her grandfather as well. The old man stood on deck, feet planted wide apart, a grin splitting his lips from ear to ear. In place of the shawl he usually wore around his shoulders, he was now proudly sporting the heavy woolen coat of a ship's captain.

Like Ambrosia, Bethany and Darcy wore the garb of sailors. Brightly colored shirts with billowing sleeves. Breeches tucked into tall boots. Hair tied back with scarves.

And then, while he watched in total disbelief, the dour housekeeper, Mistress Coffey, and the timid old nurse, Miss Winifred Mellon, appeared on deck. They looked for all the world as if they were out for a carriage ride.

"Permission to come aboard the *Undaunted*." Ambrosia's voice held not a trace of her earlier anger. In fact, she sounded absolutely elated about something.

Riordan's eyes narrowed. What was this new game she played? No matter. He was not going to allow himself to be caught up in any more hysterics. ''Permission denied.''

As he turned away from the rail he heard the thud of feet against the deck. He turned back to see that Ambrosia had ignored his words and had swung aboard. In full view of the entire crew.

''You would disobey a sea captain's command?'' He rounded on her, determined to put a stop to this insubordination at once. ''Seaman Lambert, you could find yourself in irons.''

''Aye, Captain. It's a chance I must take. But first you must listen to what I have to say. I believe my plan is worth the risk.''

''I've already heard you. There's nothing more to say.''

''Please, Captain.'' She lowered her voice. ''Could we speak privately in your cabin?''

It was on the tip of his tongue to refuse. But she'd risked so much, taking the little ship through the dangerous shallows at night. Even exposing her entire family to the danger. He'd listen. And then he'd send her packing.

''All right, Seaman Lambert. I'll give you one minute of my time. No more. We have no time to waste on foolishness.''

He allowed her to precede him to the stairs that led belowdecks. As he passed the crew, he saw many of them smiling. That only had him strengthening his resolve. He would not be persuaded to change his mind and take her aboard the *Undaunted*. Not after that ugly scene in the parlor.

In his cabin he closed the door and leaned against it, determined not to touch her. In fact, it would be better if he didn't look at her. That way, there would be no chance of weakening his resolve.

"One minute, Ambrosia."

She took a deep breath, wishing her heart wouldn't betray her like this. She'd come here determined to deal with Riordan Spencer as she would any man. But Riordan wasn't like any other man she'd ever met. Even when his cruel words cut her to the quick, she couldn't hate him, no matter how she tried. And oh, how she tried.

"After you left, my grandfather and sisters and I discussed your plight. We all agreed that what you do is noble. But there is a flaw in your plan."

His head came up sharply. "A flaw?"

"Aye. If, as you say, Barclay Stuart was murdered because someone is determined to learn of the cargo the *Undaunted* now carries, then it stands to reason that the murderer must now go forward and see his plan through. No matter what the cost."

"Aye. So, what is this flaw?"

"The *Undaunted*. She is bound to become a target."

"Of that I have no doubt. But we're prepared. She is fortified with cannon and weapons and men willing to give their last breath to keep her cargo safe."

"As I said, Riordan, what you do is noble. But also flawed. Once it is learned that the *Undaunted* defended herself against a rogue ship, do you believe her enemies will send another?"

"Aye. Don't you?"

"Nay. They'll send an armada. And though you and your men will fight nobly, you will, in the end, give up your lives and your cargo."

His eyes narrowed. "Are you suggesting that we merely give up our cargo without a fight?"

"If you think that, Riordan, then you don't know me

at all. Papa always told us that if we can't outfight our enemy, we must outwit him.''

"And how do you propose to do that?"

"By doing something completely unexpected. Your enemy expects you to arm yourselves and fight to the death. Instead, why not let them chase the *Undaunted,* and when the odds are too great, yield without a fight?"

"Yield?" He threw back his head and laughed. "This from a woman who doesn't know the meaning of the word? Now I know you jest. If you were drawing your last breath you would yield to no man, Ambrosia.''

"You're wrong, Riordan. Perhaps I would yield." She gave a sly smile. "If I had much to gain and nothing to lose."

"You call the king's gold nothing?"

She gave a gasp of surprise. "Is that truly what the *Undaunted* carries? Gold for the king?''

"Aye." He clenched a hand at his side. What a clever wench she was. She'd just caused him to reveal a secret he'd sworn never to repeat.

"Then we have no time to lose. Our plan is simple. Transfer the cargo to the *Sea Challenge.*''

"Are you daft? That little craft couldn't accommodate even half our crew. And even if she could, she's no warship. She'd be at the mercy of every rogue ship in the ocean.''

"You miss the point, Riordan. We wouldn't have a crew. Just us. Think about it. What rogue would waste time with a small, sleek sailing vessel out for a family picnic, when they can catch the prize of the *Undaunted*?''

As her words sank in, he stared at her in surprise. "You'd use the *Undaunted* as a decoy?"

She nodded.

As he mulled over her plan, he began to see the wisdom of it. When the *Sea Challenge* pulled alongside, with all its lanterns glowing, it had looked like nothing more than a floating parlor. A gentleman's ship, with nothing of value aboard except perhaps some fine ale. Still...

"What about the two old women aboard? Do you think it fair to dupe them into thinking they're just out for a harmless sailing trip?"

"Do you think I'd do such a thing, Riordan? Though we were uncertain of their reaction, my sisters and I took them into our confidence. And were amazed to learn that they'd already surmised what we were about. I suppose it's difficult to keep secrets in a family such as ours. Once they heard our plans, they were eager to join our party."

"But do they understand the danger?"

"Aye. There's no holding them back. Now, as to the *Undaunted*..."

He nodded. "Without the cargo to slow her down, the *Undaunted* could lead a fleet of rogue ships on a merry chase. It could take days to overtake her. And then the crew could yield and allow the enemy to board her. It could avoid needless death. Their lives might be spared if no cargo is found. But it's still a risk."

"The crew already agreed to risk their lives for the cargo. If there's a chance they might not have to fight to the death, I'd say it's worth the gamble."

He gave her a level look. "You'll be leaving the *Undaunted* vulnerable. She could be claimed for salvage. If so, you'll never see your father's ship again."

She swallowed hard. "I've thought of that. But our first thought must be for King Charles and his cargo. If that's the price I must pay, then so be it."

He studied her with new respect. He could see how heavily this weighed on her heart. She loved the *Undaunted*. Not only because it had been her father's, but because it was her heritage. Yet she was willing to give it up if necessary, for king and country.

"What about you, Riordan? Are you willing to put aside your notions about women at sea and trust us with your precious cargo?"

It took him less than a moment to realize that she'd just offered him the best chance they had of succeeding.

"Aye, Ambrosia. It's a brilliant plan." He turned away, afraid that if he didn't escape this minute, he'd have to drag her into his arms and kiss those lovely, pouting lips. "I'll have the crew begin the transfer at once."

When he strode away Ambrosia stood a moment, feeling the most amazing sense of elation. He'd actually agreed to her plan. And had even called it brilliant.

Maybe she was dreaming. She shook her head and forced herself into action. Perhaps, if they were able to carry this off, he might one day be able to forget that little scene in the parlor. She lifted her chin a fraction. Though she never would.

"That's the last of it, Cap'n." Newton watched as the sailors swung back to the deck of the *Undaunted*.

The *Sea Challenge* bobbed beside the larger, sturdier ship. The gold, stacked neatly belowdecks, had been covered with fancy quilts and made to resemble trunks.

Riordan took Newton to his cabin and closed the door. "Newt, what do you think of young Randolph?"

"A fine sailor, Cap'n. I've learned that his father and grandfather were seamen. Had their own ships until they were lost to rogues. The lad will one day have his own as well, I'm sure. He handles the *Undaunted* with great care."

"Do you think, if he were to captain her, he'd treat her like his own?"

The old man arched a brow. "Aye. I'm sure of it."

"Then send him to my cabin at once. I have some orders for him."

Puzzled, the old man left and returned minutes later with the young seaman.

"Randolph," Riordan said without preamble. "I'm about to ask your help."

"Aye, sir."

"I'm appointing you captain of the *Undaunted*. Now sit down, lad. There are some things we have to go over."

While Newton watched and listened, Riordan gave the young man very careful instructions. Then the two shook hands, and Riordan picked up his seabag and led the way above deck.

Newton followed on his heels. "What's all this about, Cap'n?"

Instead of an answer, Riordan gave him a mysterious smile. "Newt, how do you feel about family picnics?"

"Picnics?" The old sailor scratched his head. "Can't say I've ever been on one."

"Well, you're about to go on one now. Fetch your seabag, Newt."

While the crew watched in surprise, Riordan caught hold of the rigging and swung himself from the rail of the *Undaunted* to the rail of the *Sea Challenge,* dropping his seabag on deck. "Come on, Newt," he called to the old man. "You and I have just become part of the Lambert family. At least until we reach London."

When the old sailor followed suit, Ambrosia greeted them with her hands on her hips, her eyes flashing fire. "What do you two think you're doing?"

''We're joining the family, Seaman Lambert.'' Riordan was smiling broadly. ''For a little holiday aboard ship.''

Ambrosia saw the laughter dancing in her sisters' eyes. Her own grew stormy. ''There's but one captain's cabin, and that's been given over to Grandpapa.''

Riordan ignored her anger. ''Where are you and the other ladies sleeping?''

''In hammocks strung belowdecks in the crew's quarters.''

''Newt and I have slept in plenty of hammocks on ships too numerous to count. We'll be just fine.''

He turned and waved to the crew of the *Undaunted* as the two ships began drifting apart. Then he turned to her grandfather. ''Seamen Spencer and Findlay reporting for duty, Captain.''

The old man was positively beaming. ''Welcome aboard, mates. Stow your gear and let's get the ship under way.''

''Aye, Captain.'' Riordan winked at Newton and the two men carried their seabags below. Seeing the five hammocks side by side, the two men strung theirs on the far side of the crew's quarters, with the cargo between them, allowing the women as much privacy as possible.

As he looked around at the tight quarters, Riordan found himself hoping this journey ended quickly. Otherwise, his nights spent watching Ambrosia sleep could become an agony of temptation.

Riordan stood at the wheel of the little ship, enjoying the way she handled the pull of the waves. He had elected to take the night watch, so that the others could sleep. He glanced up at the canopy of stars and felt, as he always did on such a night, that he'd chosen the best of all possible worlds.

The moon was full and round, with a few soft, feathery clouds scudding past. The stars looked close enough to touch. The wind was gentle, just strong enough to fill the sails. What more could a man want?

As if in answer to his silent question, he saw a shadow flit across the deck. He watched as Ambrosia paused at the rail to breathe in the sea air. Then she turned and their gazes met and held. For the space of a heartbeat she gripped the rail. Then she stepped toward him.

"I couldn't sleep."

"I know the feeling." Riordan studied her as she moved closer, feeling, as he always did, the thrill that went through him at the mere sight of her. She was tall. Taller than most women, and even some men, so that her head came nearly to his chin. She was reed slim, with a tiny waist and softly rounded hips and breasts. The mere thought of pressing that lithe young body to his had him reacting in a purely male fashion. "It's the excitement of not knowing what lies ahead."

"Is it the same for you?"

"Aye." He nodded. "And has been from the first time I boarded a ship. It's the curse of a sailor. Once you've heard the siren song of the sea, there's no cure."

"I thought…" She looked away. "I thought it was because I was so long denied the chance to sail. But when I asked my brother, he said it was the same for him."

"We talked about it, James and I." Riordan kept his hands lightly on the wheel. "We both agreed that we'd rather die young at sea than live to be old men confined to the land."

"I wish…" She paused to close her eyes.

"What do you wish, Ambrosia?"

She met his look. "I wish that I hadn't wasted so much time resenting James. When he'd return from a voyage, I would pester him for days to tell me everything he'd seen and heard. Every place he'd visited. Every new food he'd tasted. And then I would go off and nurse my resentment at his freedom to do the things I'd never be allowed to do. I was so busy being jealous, I never told him how much I loved him. Or how proud I was of the things he'd accomplished."

"He knew, Ambrosia."

Her head came up. "How would you know that?"

"You were all he spoke of. You and Bethany and Darcy. He adored you. He was as proud of you as you were of him."

"He said so?"

"Aye. A hundred times or more."

He saw the tears spring to her eyes before she turned away to hide them. Without thinking, he reached out and drew her into the circle of his arms.

Her words were muffled against his chest. "I can't help thinking that it was my wish that sent him to a watery grave. But I never wanted this. I never wanted James to die so that I could have my chance. And if I could, I'd give up everything in my life to have my brother back."

"Shh." Riordan pressed his lips to her temple. "Don't ever think you brought this about. It's just the way life is. We live. We die. And we never know the time or place of our death. But know this. James died the way he wanted. Doing what he most loved. How many men can make that claim?"

As his words sank in, she looked up at him in surprise. "I hadn't thought of that." She sniffed and swallowed back the rest of her tears. "That's a comfort, Riordan.

And I thank you for it. But I'm saddened that he had to die so young. He left no wife. No children to carry on his name.''

The same thought had occurred to Riordan. Especially now that he was holding Ambrosia in his arms. No woman had ever made him ache like this. When he was close to her he found himself thinking about things that had never before held any appeal. Things like planting roots. Making a home. Living the respectable life of a landowner.

Foolishness, he knew. He was a man born for the sea. From his first taste of it he'd known. Still, he reminded himself, John Lambert had found a way to have it all. A home that looked out over the dark Atlantic. A wife, children and the respect of those in Land's End who knew him. From the attendance at his funeral, he'd been fully accepted by landowners, even though he was unquestionably a man of the sea.

That experience had had a profound impact on Riordan. Ever since, he'd been wondering if it could be possible to do the same.

''Don't grieve for what wasn't, Ambrosia.'' His hand tightened on her shoulder. ''Just celebrate who James was, and what he did with his young life.''

''He made so many friends.'' She lifted her face to stare up into Riordan's eyes. ''Especially you.''

He found himself gazing at her mouth with naked hunger. He knew he ought to resist the desire to kiss her. But she was too close. And his need too great.

''Ambrosia.'' He touched a hand to her cheek and she moved against it. His eyes narrowed as he lowered his face to hers. And then there was no need for words as he lost himself in the wild, sweet taste of her.

He'd known, from the first time he'd sampled her lips,

that once would never be enough. With each kiss, each taste, he'd want more until there was nothing to do but have it all. And now, as he filled himself with her, he found his head spinning, his hands tightening, his lips devouring.

Ambrosia couldn't move. She hadn't the will to resist. Because in truth, she'd wanted this. Wanted desperately for him to kiss her. Wanted to feel the heat and flash and fire. But as she melted against him, she realized that this kiss was different from all the others. Always before they'd come together in anger. But this time was softer, sweeter. The feelings flowing between them spoke of shared pain. And healing. And tenderness. And need. A need so long denied.

"You know I want you, Ambrosia." His hands framed her face and he pressed soft kisses to her temple, her cheek, her jaw.

How could she think, when he was bringing her such pleasure? "And I want…" She closed her eyes. "Oh, I don't know what I want, Riordan. I've never felt like this before. But I know one thing. I don't want you to stop doing what you're doing."

He laughed, low and deep in his throat. But the laughter became a growl of pleasure mixed with pain as he ran openmouthed kisses down her throat. He nibbled the sensitive hollow between her neck and shoulder and felt her tremble.

He could have her if he so desired. The thought jolted through him, leaving him stunned and dazed. He could take her. But he had no right. She was so sweet. So good. And he…

His life had brought shame to his family. He'd chosen a life of secrets. Of clandestine meetings and high state secrets, and even, God help him, assassinations. He was a man without roots. And she was firmly rooted in home, family, community.

He abruptly lifted his head. "Go belowdecks now and get some sleep."

"I don't want to leave you, Riordan."

His tone was rougher than he intended. "Go. Quickly. Before we both do something we'll later regret."

She heard the urgency in his tone and looked up to see his eyes hot and fierce. A little thrill shot through her. But was it a thrill of excitement? she wondered. Or fear?

She sensed something hot and smoldering in him. A slow, simmering heat that, if fueled, could blaze out of control. It excited her even while it frightened her.

Reluctantly she turned away. "Good night, Riordan." At the steps leading to the lower cabins she turned for one last look. His hands were on the wheel. Hands that could make her tremble with need.

She dragged in a deep breath before stepping belowdecks. Leaving him alone. Alone to face thoughts that were as dark as the midnight sky. And as distressing as the storm clouds that were blowing far out on the distant horizon.

Chapter Twelve

Riordan trimmed the sails and glanced over to see Ambrosia take the wheel from her grandfather. The old man mopped at his forehead before taking a seat under the canopy they'd hoisted on deck. The housekeeper and nurse, looking as fresh as they always looked at MaryCastle, had already settled themselves under the canopy and were enjoying the air.

It was a perfect summer day, the breeze fresh, the sun glorious. Riordan calculated that if they had no delays, they might make London within two days. He glanced over to admire the sight of Ambrosia, dressed in sailor's garb, handling the wheel with the ease of one born to the sea.

"Ship on the port side," Bethany shouted. "Bearing down fast."

At once Ambrosia called for Newton to take the wheel while she and the women went belowdecks.

Riordan studied the approaching craft through his spyglass. It was as small and sleek as the *Sea Challenge*. He felt himself relax. Not a rogue, but a gentleman's craft, flying an English flag.

By the time the two ships were close enough to shout

a greeting, the three Lambert sisters had come on deck. They'd changed into proper gowns, their hair arranged beneath bonnets. Ambrosia was all in white, Bethany in green and Darcy in pink.

Mistress Coffey had hurried to prepare a lunch, so that they would appear like any other family out on holiday. Winifred Mellon, dressed in a frilly white frock, walked on deck carrying a white parasol to ward off the sun.

The three young women helped their grandfather into his jacket, then took their seats around him.

Riordan handled the wheel, while Newton lowered the sails. The two craft slowed to a crawl.

On the deck of the second ship a man and woman stood by the rail. The woman cupped a hand to her mouth. "Ambrosia. Bethany. Darcy. Is that you?"

Ambrosia groaned as she recognized the high, shrill voice. "Sweet heaven, it's the village gossip, Edwina Cannon."

"Oh, what a grand surprise," Edwina called. "With your permission, Mama and Silas and I will come aboard."

Ambrosia fixed a smile on her face. "Aye. Newton, will you help the ladies aboard?" Under her breath she muttered, "If we're lucky, they both might fall in."

"Hush, Ambrosia," Winifred said with alarm. "That's no way for a fine lady to talk."

"Aye, Winnie. But as you have seen, your fine ladies are something quite different than you'd thought."

"You are, indeed." Their old nurse looked around at the three sisters, relieved that they had chosen proper attire.

Newton scrambled over the rail and secured the two boats with rope, so that they couldn't pull apart. Then he offered his hand to Edwina and helped her over the rail, then did the same for her mother.

Behind them, Silas leapt easily across the distance, landing on the deck. He glanced around, surveying the scene. "A bit far from home, aren't you, Miss Lambert?"

Ambrosia put a hand on her grandfather's shoulder. "Grandpapa misses the sea. We try to take him sailing as often as possible. Especially when the weather is so pleasant."

"Aye. It is." Silas turned to Riordan at the wheel. "What are you doing here, Spencer? I'd heard that you were captain of the *Undaunted* now."

"Did you?"

"Aye. I was told she put into port yesterday, then left within hours on another mysterious voyage. I would have thought you'd be aboard."

"As you can see, you were mistaken." Riordan kept his smile in place. "It would seem that you've been given a great deal of misinformation lately."

Silas gave an exaggerated shrug of his shoulders. "The sailors talk when they're tipping a few at the tavern."

"So it seems." Instead of offering an excuse, Riordan changed tactics. "What are you doing in these waters, Silas?"

Edwina put a hand on his arm in a possessive manner. "Silas is taking Mama and me to London." She smiled up into his eyes. "Mama was scandalized at first when he suggested it, knowing how dangerous these waters can be. But when Silas assured her that no one would dare accost him, and that he could actually get us an audience with the king, Mama relented. After all, how many of us living in Cornwall would ever get the opportunity to see the king?"

"Sing?" Geoffrey Lambert leaned forward, cupping his ear. "That's fine, lass. Sing us a tune."

She wrinkled her nose. "Nay, Captain Lambert. The king. I want to see the king."

"A ring?" The old man caught her hand and frowned as he studied her fingers. "I don't see it."

She pulled her hand free and turned to her mother, rolling her eyes. The two women turned away, ignoring him as if he were addled. With a smile he closed his eyes.

Edwina leveled a look on Ambrosia and her sisters. "It's such a pity you three can't come up to London with us. Silas is so important. He said he sees the king often. In fact, he's expecting that he will soon be given a very important position in the king's council." She sighed. "Ah well. I'll tell you all about it when next we meet."

"I'm sure you will." Ambrosia began filling cups. "Tea, Edwina? Mistress Cannon?"

The two ladies accepted a cup and helped themselves to biscuits slathered with fruit conserve.

"Tea, Lord Fenwick? Or would you prefer ale?"

"Ale." He accepted a goblet from Ambrosia's hand, and felt the way she flinched as he deliberately tangled his fingers with hers. He gave a smug smile. So, it would seem the fearless Ambrosia Lambert wasn't quite so fearless after all. There were some things that could still make her uncomfortable. He'd remember that in the future. Especially since she had gone to so much trouble to snub him.

She poured a second goblet for Riordan, who had turned the wheel over to Newton. The old man held it steady as the two ships bobbed on the gentle waves.

While he sipped his ale Silas studied Riordan carefully.

"I can't believe you'd allow the *Undaunted* to sail without you. Especially in such treacherous times as these."

"You're presuming that the villagers are correct and the *Undaunted* has actually set sail, Silas."

Riordan was rewarded by a narrowing of the other man's eyes. "We sailed past the cove where the *Undaunted* usually sits at anchor. There was no sign of her."

He'd taken the time to check on the *Undaunted*. That knowledge made Riordan uncomfortable. He studied the number of sailors aboard Silas's ship. "That's quite a large crew for such a simple journey."

Silas smiled. "Don't tell me you haven't heard the tales of rogue ships in the area."

"Aye." Riordan returned the smile. "I've heard of them. But I doubt they'd be interested in craft as small as these. We'd have nothing of interest to pirates."

The implication struck Silas with the force of a blow. For a moment he looked around as though seeing this ship for the first time. "You're a clever one, aren't you, Captain Spencer?" He drained his ale quickly, then turned to Ambrosia and her sisters. "The *Sea Challenge* is a fine sleek craft. Would you mind if I take a look at her?"

"Not at all." Ambrosia smiled and offered him a biscuit. "But wouldn't you care for some lunch first, Lord Fenwick?"

"The ale was quite enough." He walked around the deck, looking over the rigging, the sails. A short time later he started down the steps leading belowdecks.

Ambrosia cast a horrified look at Riordan, who quickly set aside his ale and followed.

Riordan watched as Silas opened the door to the captain's cabin, glanced around, then closed the door and moved on to the crew's quarters. "Are you looking for something in particular, Lord Fenwick?"

Silas spun around. "I just wondered how many can comfortably sleep aboard a craft of this size."

"We're about as comfortable as you are aboard the *Sea Devil*. The captain's cabin is occupied by Geoffrey Lambert. As you can see, there is ample room for the rest of us in here."

Silas took note of the five hammocks on one side of the cabin, and two on the other.

He started toward the quilt-covered mounds between them. "What's this?"

"Trunks." Riordan stepped in front of the first, before Silas could pull aside the quilt. "You know how it is with five women aboard." He gave an easy, conspiratorial smile. "I don't know how many trunks Edwina and her mother brought for their voyage to London, but I believe the Lambert sisters and their elderly companions brought half their wardrobe for this simple picnic."

"Trunks? They look too big for…" Silas started to nudge him aside. Just then they heard the sound of hurried footsteps.

Ambrosia came to a halt in the doorway. Riordan's eyes widened when he caught the glint of light at her waist and realized that her dagger, tucked into her waistband, had pulled loose and was clearly visible.

He coughed. Annoyed, Ambrosia looked at him. He stared pointedly at her waist. For the space of a heartbeat she couldn't grasp his meaning. Then, as the truth dawned, she covered her lapse by crossing her hands over her middle, effectively hiding the hilt of her dagger.

"Forgive me, Lord Fenwick." Her breathy tone was made even more pronounced by the fact that she'd barreled down the steps, nearly tripping in her haste. "I realized that my sisters and I may have left some…delicate clothing lying about in plain sight.''

She moved from one hammock to the next, praying she could find something that would justify her words. Just then her hand encountered something soft, and she lifted up a delicately embroidered chemise.

''Just as I feared,'' she said aloud. ''Miss Mellon would be horrified at our lack of dignity.''

She silently counted to five, permitting both men a chance to view it before clasping her hands behind her and backing toward one of the quilt-covered mounds.

While Riordan and Silas watched, she lifted a corner of the quilt and slid the chemise underneath. Then she stared at the floor, avoiding their eyes. She even managed to blush before saying, ''I hope you won't judge us too harshly by this, my lord.''

''Certainly not.'' Silas studied the color that rode high on her cheeks, and the way she avoided looking at him. Perhaps she actually was this modest. Or perhaps, as he believed, she had something to hide. ''Forgive me, Miss Lambert. I fear I've invaded your privacy. I'll leave you to it.''

He walked from the room. As Riordan turned to follow, he could see the little gleam of triumph in those dark depths. Swallowing back his own misgivings, he managed a smile and a wink before trailing Silas from the cabin and up the stairs to the deck.

Bethany and Darcy were doing their best to look interested as Edwina and her mother regaled them with plans for the wedding, while Mistress Coffey and Miss Mellon hung on every word. Geoffrey Lambert was dozing in the shade of the canopy. Newton held the wheel steady and was staring off into the distance.

Silas seemed in a hurry as he crossed the deck and

paused at the circle of women. "Come, Edwina. Mistress Cannon. It's time we were off."

He accepted Bethany's hand, then Darcy's, brushing his lips over their knuckles. "Thank you for the lovely respite, ladies."

"It was our pleasure, Lord Fenwick."

Darcy gritted her teeth and forced herself to hug Edwina. "I do hope you get your audience with the king."

Edwina giggled, then allowed Silas to lead her to the rail. There he paused and shook hands with Riordan before lifting Ambrosia's hand to his lips.

Once again he held it a moment longer than necessary, and felt the way she flinched. It gave him real pleasure to know that he had the ability to disturb her sense of calm. He was about to disturb her a great deal more when he left here. "I look forward to seeing you when we return to Cornwall, Miss Lambert."

"And I you, Lord Fenwick." She snatched her hand away.

"Miss Lambert…"

"Aye?"

"Your secret is safe with me. I won't tell a soul that you left a…delicate item of clothing in plain view."

"Thank you, Lord Fenwick. Your discretion is greatly appreciated."

Silas lifted Edwina and helped her across the rail, then did the same for her mother, before leaping easily to join them.

As the two ships separated, then began drifting apart, the three stood calling out.

"Goodbye." Ambrosia waved happily. "Safe journey."

When they were far enough away that they could no longer overhear what was being said, Riordan turned to

Ambrosia with a look of admiration. "Well done. That was quick thinking belowdecks."

She smiled. "I overheard you saying the quilt-covered mounds were our trunks. I'm just grateful that I managed to snag an article of clothing. We'd dressed in such a hurry, after spotting their ship, I was hopeful there would be one or two things we'd overlooked."

Riordan gave her a long, lingering glance. "You're an amazingly quick-witted woman, Ambrosia. Especially when things aren't going well. But I shouldn't be surprised. You come from an amazing and bright family."

He glanced over at Geoffrey Lambert, who was now fully awake and watching the other ship drift off their starboard side. "Exceedingly dull women," he was saying to his granddaughters. "I don't believe there's much under those fancy bonnets except hair."

"Captain Lambert." Mistress Coffey's mouth turned down in a frown of disapproval. "I'm shocked and appalled that you would say such things about two of Land's End's most important citizens."

"Useless twits," he muttered in reply.

"Was that what put you to sleep, Grandpapa?" Ambrosia called.

He gave her a mischievous smile. "I wasn't sleeping, child. I was merely escaping their annoying chatter."

Riordan threw back his head and roared. Aye. An amazing family. Even the old man wasn't at all what he appeared. Deaf indeed. Riordan began to wonder if there was anything at all the old man missed. Not much, he'd wager. Not much at all.

Still, as he watched the *Sea Devil* veer off course, he couldn't shake the feeling that Silas Fenwick hadn't been fooled by their clever scheme. And if that were true, their picnic could turn into a disaster.

* * *

Aboard the *Sea Devil,* Silas Fenwick gave his ship's captain an order. "We're changing course, Captain Barrow. I wish to put into port at Cairn."

Edwina and her mother shot him matching looks of surprise.

"I must insist, Lord Fenwick, that you consider the danger to my daughter and me. I've heard that Cairn is a treacherous place. That it's nothing more than a haven for pirates and cutthroats."

Silas smiled. "Aye. I've heard that, as well. But you have no need to fear, Mistress Cannon. As long as you're with me, you'll be safe. It's a colorful place. No voyage to London is complete without the chance to walk through the town and perhaps tip an ale in one of the taverns beside a pirate." He turned to her daughter. "Would you like that, my sweet?"

Edwina looked up into his dark, enigmatic eyes and gave him one of her brightest smiles. "I can't wait to go back to Land's End and tell my friends that I actually visited the town where pirates live and work. Come, Mama. We must put on our best bonnets. And we'll need parasols as we stroll the streets. You heard Silas. We need have no fear as long as we're with him."

They walked away. The moment they disappeared below deck, Silas's smile disappeared. His eyes darkened with simmering anger.

"Aye," he muttered. "We'll be safe enough. Though I can't say the same for a certain family who thinks they've outwitted me. Oh, how those fools shall pay."

Ambrosia tossed and turned in her hammock, aware of the man who slept just a short distance away. Even the fresh sea air and the rhythmic slap of waves against the hull of the *Sea Challenge* couldn't lull her to sleep.

Feeling too restless to settle down, she draped a blanket around her shoulders and climbed topside.

Newton stood at the wheel, gazing into the darkness. Without turning his head he called, "Can't sleep, lass?"

"How did you know I was here, Newt?"

"Ye have a way of walking, lass. Soft, like a kitten. What's wrong? Ye should be resting for the morrow."

"I can't, Newt." She prowled the deck, running her hand along the rail, pausing to catch hold of the rigging, before giving a sigh of impatience. She turned to him and blurted, "What do you think of Riordan?"

So that's how it was for the lass. He should have known. She was caught in the throes of first love. At least she'd chosen well.

The old sailor thought a moment. "He's short on patience. Doesn't suffer fools. Nor does he talk unless he has something to say. But he's steady. He's a man of honor. And if I had to go up against a rogue ship, I'd want him by my side." The old man turned and fixed her with a look. "Riordan Spencer's a man who will always steer a straight course through rocks and shallows, lass."

She knew that Newton wasn't speaking of sailing now. He had just paid Riordan the highest of compliments. Touched by her old friend's honesty, she nodded thoughtfully and walked away.

The old man watched as she settled herself by the rail to stare up at the stars. Then he drifted back in his mind to a time when he'd been young and confused and wildly in love. Such a long time ago. But there had been a lass with sunlight in her hair and moonlight in her eyes. And though he'd already been around the world, and had faced storms and battles and sharks, nothing had ever terrified him as much as that one small female, who'd held his heart in her hands. And had left it so shattered, he'd feared it might never mend.

Love was such a fearsome thing. It had the power to hurt. The power to heal. He hoped, for the sake of these two fine young people, they used the power wisely.

Chapter Thirteen

It was past midnight when Riordan came topside to take the wheel.

"Any sign of trouble, Newt?" Riordan's voice was hushed in the darkness.

"No sign of pirates, Cap'n. But I'd say you might have a bit of trouble to deal with." The old man glanced to the spot where Ambrosia sat, as still as a statue, staring at the round, full moon.

He heard Riordan mutter an oath.

"I'll say good-night now, Cap'n." The old man was smiling as he strolled across the deck and disappeared below.

Riordan studied the way Ambrosia looked. Like a beautiful painting he'd seen in Paris. Her eyes dark and unfathomable. Her mood pensive as she stared out over a sea gilded in moonlight.

The night was calm. Not a hint of a breeze rippled the waves. They could have been floating on a sea of gold. There was the barest hint of motion as the small craft drifted on the current.

He had no need to hold the wheel, but his fingers

curled tightly around it as he saw Ambrosia get to her feet.

She clutched the blanket around her shoulders as she walked toward him, moving with fluid, sensuous grace. His throat went dry at the sight of her coming closer, then closer still. A mist swirled around the deck, around her ankles, adding to her ethereal look.

There was something different about her tonight, though he couldn't decide what it was. Perhaps the way her hips moved. Or perhaps the shy, yet bold look of a woman—a look that hadn't been there before.

"Riordan." She paused in front of him and the blanket dropped to the deck at their feet. She smiled up at him. She was wearing the white gown she'd worn earlier in the day. Like a bride, he thought. A beautiful, virginal bride. Needs, sharp and swift, slammed into him with all the force of a lightning bolt.

His tone was gruff. "You ought to be asleep, Ambrosia."

"I can't sleep." She put her hand over his on the wheel, and he was forced to absorb a fierce rush of heat. "And you know why."

He kept his tone casual. "You're thinking about London tomorrow?"

"If you believe that, you're a fool, Riordan Spencer. And I've come to realize that you're no fool." She leaned against the ship's wheel and stared up into his eyes. "I can't sleep because of you."

"Don't worry. When this is over you'll soon enough be rid of me."

"I don't want to be rid of you." She ran her hands up his arms and pressed herself against him. "Kiss me, Riordan."

Though his body reacted in a purely male fashion, he

managed a step back. He even mustered a dismissive smile. "I don't think that would be wise."

"I don't want to be wise. I want to be wild. Kiss me."

He put his hand on her shoulders, to hold her at bay. A mistake, he realized at once. He had to struggle against the desire to drag her into his arms and savage her with kisses.

"You think you can just ask me to pleasure you for a little while, until you tire of it, or grow frightened, and then order me to walk away like a good lad." His tone hardened. "Well, I'm not a lad and I'm not good. And I haven't been either in many years."

She felt a wave of frustration. Why was he being so difficult? She'd been prepared to throw herself into his arms and have him devour her. Instead, he was rejecting her offer. Rejecting her.

"I don't want a lad. I want a man. I want you."

His eyes narrowed. The hands at her shoulders tightened. "I hear the words you're saying. You want. Aye, you want. But what about what I want? Have you thought about that, Ambrosia? Or is this just some game you're playing?"

She pushed back so that she could see his eyes. "It's no game, Riordan. I've thought this over very carefully."

As had he. From the first time he'd seen her. Love and lust and longing were all twisting inside him, and had been, from the moment they'd met. But he'd finally managed to convince himself that she was too innocent for the likes of him. Her kisses too chaste. Her heart too pure. He had no right to sully her reputation for his own gratification.

"And you want me, Riordan. Admit it."

Though it was an effort, he managed to keep her at

arm's length. "I admit only this. What you're feeling is the first stirring of a woman's heart."

She smiled. "Aye." Without warning she caught his hand and pressed it to her heart. "Feel how it pounds when you're near."

Desire rushed through him at the first contact with her breast. He pulled his hand away as though burned. But it was too late. All the blood had drained from his head to another part of his anatomy. His heartbeat was hammering at his temples. Needs, so long denied, were clawing to be free.

"This isn't love, Ambrosia." He had to deny what he was feeling. Otherwise, he'd have no willpower left.

"What is it then?"

He dragged in a breath. "It's lust, pure and simple."

He saw the pain that his words caused, and felt a wave of remorse. But he was doing this for her own good. "If it were love it wouldn't be mulled over like a chess game. In fact, love shouldn't be thought about at all. It can't be planned. Or plotted. Or schemed. True love doesn't make any sense. It isn't convenient. In fact, it's often inconvenient. Now…" He took another deep breath, determined to plunge the dagger, if that's what it took. "It's time you went belowdecks and got some sleep. We have serious business to see to on the morrow. There's no more time for this nonsense."

"Nonsense?" She reacted as though he'd slapped her. She took a step back, staring into his eyes.

"Aye. Nonsense. Now go to bed." He looked away, into the darkness. Out of the corner of his eye he saw her bend and retrieve the blanket. He heard the sound of her footsteps as she made her way across the deck. Then there was only the gentle slap of the waves against the hull of the *Sea Challenge*. And the occasional call of a seabird.

Though he knew he'd done the honorable thing, he'd never felt so miserable in his life.

Holding the blanket around her, Ambrosia started down the stairs, then turned for one last glance at the man who had just broken her heart.

He had rejected her. Rejected her offer of love. Had even demeaned it by calling it nothing more than lust. She wanted to hate him for it. But even now, even after his callous disregard for her feelings, she couldn't. She loved him.

She studied his hard, tight profile as he glanced skyward. If possible, he looked even more miserable than she felt. That ought to give her some measure of satisfaction. But as she watched, the truth dawned.

Now that he thought he was alone, he was able to let his guard down. And his face reflected his true feelings. That wasn't happiness, but sheer misery. Was it possible that his heart felt as bruised and battered as hers?

If that were true, it could only mean that everything he'd just said and done had been an act. For her benefit?

Of course. He'd done it for her. Because he truly cared about her.

She took a deep breath and started toward him. As she did, her heart turned a series of somersaults in her chest. She was about to risk everything, even further rejection, for the sake of love.

She lifted her chin. Hadn't she always lived for a challenge? It was time for the true test of her strength.

"Riordan." She touched a hand to his shoulder. Just a hand, but he reacted as though he'd just seen a ghostly specter. He stepped back, his arms at his sides.

"Ambrosia." His eyes narrowed. "I thought I sent you to bed."

"Aye. Like a naughty child. But I'm not a child, Riordan. In case you haven't noticed, I'm a woman."

"I'd have to be a blind man not to have noticed."

"I'm glad you admit that much." She smiled and laid her other hand on his arm. "I'm a woman, Riordan. A woman who wants to be held, and touched, and kissed."

He couldn't catch his breath. The mere touch of her had all the air leaving his lungs. "You've come to the wrong man."

"Nay. You're the right man for me, Riordan. You told me that love isn't convenient. That's probably the only honest thing you've said tonight."

"Are you accusing me of lying?"

"Aye. Oh, for the most honorable of reasons, I suppose. You thought you'd save me from my foolish heart. But it's my heart. And it yearns for you." She wrapped her arms around his neck and pressed herself to the length of him. "Kiss me, Riordan."

He reached up to remove her arms from his neck. But the moment he touched her, he felt his resolve beginning to slip. "Don't do this, Ambrosia. You're bound to be hurt."

"If I am, it'll be my choice. What about you? Do you want this? Do you want me?"

His intention was to peel her away from him and force her, if need be, to leave. Instead his hands fisted in her hair. He pulled her head back roughly. His eyes stayed steady on hers, hot and fierce. "I want you more than anything in this world. And have, since the first time I saw you."

She felt a thrill of triumph. "Are you afraid we won't be good for each other?"

"Good? You're so good it frightens me." He gave a sound of disgust. "But there's nothing good about me, Ambrosia. You could find a hundred men better for you."

"I don't want a hundred others, Riordan. I want you."

"And God help me, I want you." His next words had the smile fading on her lips. "But I can't be the gentle lover you deserve, Ambrosia. I'll not settle for chaste kisses or a few whispered words. If you don't walk away now, I can't promise I won't hurt you. In fact, I'll probably take you like a savage. Is that what you want?"

She clutched the front of his shirt, dragging him close. "Kiss me, Riordan. Touch me. Before I die from wanting you."

His mouth covered hers in a kiss so hot, so hungry, it poured between them, draining them, then filling them.

With his lips against hers he whispered, "Do you know how many long, lonely nights I've dreamed of you? Of this?"

"Tell me. I need to hear the words."

"Too many." He took the kiss deeper, nearly devouring her with his hunger. "I've thought of every way I'd love you."

"Show me, Riordan. Teach me." She clutched his head, her fingers tangling through the hair that spilled in wild disarray.

And then there was no need for words as he kissed her until they were both breathless and gasping for air. He feasted on her lips, lingering over them like a man starved for the taste of her. And all the while he kept his eyes open, watching the play of emotions on her expressive face. Her skin became flushed with desire. Her lashes fluttered, then closed, as he took the kiss deeper.

When at last he lifted his head, it was to run quick

kisses down her neck to the hollow of her throat. While his mouth fed on her skin, his hands moved along her back, weaving a magic all their own. She couldn't hold in the sigh of pleasure as his fingers trailed her spine, then moved slowly upward along her sides until they encountered the swell of her breasts. He covered her mouth with his and swallowed back her little gasp of surprise as his work-roughened thumbs stroked her nipples until she thought she'd go mad.

"Riordan." She pushed against him, dragging in deep drafts of air.

"Afraid?" She could see his eyes gleaming in the moonlight.

She lifted her chin. "Of course not."

"Liar." He dragged her close, and before she could protest, he brought his mouth to her breast. Ignoring the barrier of her gown, he nibbled and suckled until she was nearly mad with need.

Suddenly he lifted his head. Before she could realize what he was doing, he took hold of her gown and tore it away, leaving it to pool at her feet. As he untied the ribbons of her chemise he kept his eyes steady on hers.

"The last time I undressed you, I was consumed with worry. This time I mean to savor the moment." He slipped the fabric from her shoulders and felt his throat go dry at the vision. "Ah, Ambrosia, you're so lovely you take my breath away."

And then there was no need to speak. With hands and lips and tongue he told her all that he was thinking. His kisses spoke of loneliness. And hunger. And need.

She had a desperate need to touch him the way he was touching her. She slid his shirt from his shoulders and reached for the fasteners at his waist. When her fingers fumbled, he helped her, until his clothes joined hers at their feet. And then she was free to run her hands over those hard, sculpted muscles of his back and shoulders. Muscles that she'd seen glistening in the sunlight as he'd worked on the *Undaunted.* How she'd wanted to touch him. To feel that strength surrounding her. As she trailed her fingertips along the contours of his arms she felt wonderfully, gloriously free. To touch. To feel. To take.

Their kisses became more urgent. Their sighs more frequent. And as he brought his mouth to her breast, she felt her legs tremble. Sensing her weakness, he drew her down to the blanket.

Moonlight played over her, turning her skin to gold. Her hair gleamed blue-black in the darkness. Her eyes, large and luminous, were focused on him. She smelled as clean and fresh as the sea. Somewhere nearby a night bird called, and its mate gave a distant response. But neither Riordan nor Ambrosia heard. All they could see was each other. All they could hear was the sound of their shallow breathing. And the wild beating of two hearts as they lost themselves in the wonder of each other.

Riordan struggled to hold back the need to take her like a savage. He'd wanted her for so long. But he was determined to go slowly. Not just for himself, but for her sake. If this was all he could give her, he would make it as special as possible. And so he forced himself to linger over her lips. To draw out every taste. Every flavor.

Ambrosia began to relax in his arms. She responded to this gentle side of his lovemaking with a sweetness of her own. Now she was free to trace the outline of his lips with her finger. To press soft, moist kisses to his throat until she heard his moan of pleasure. Emboldened, she brought her lips lower, to his hair-roughened chest.

He responded by dragging her upward to trace his lips

across her cheek to her jaw, then lower to her throat. He heard her little purr of pleasure and smiled, before moving lower to her breast.

In the space of a heartbeat the pleasure became so intense, she could hardly bear it. The heat that had been flowing pleasantly between them was suddenly an inferno. Even the night air couldn't cool the fire that clogged their throats, threatening to choke them.

Riordan thrilled to the change in her. The passion that had been slumbering for so long was now unleashed, and ready to devour her. Need, so long denied, was now demanding to be set free. He could see it in her eyes. Eyes that burned hotly. He could taste it on her lips. A hunger that demanded to be fed.

He framed her face with his big hands and stared deeply into her eyes, loving the look of desire that gleamed in their depths. "This was how I wanted you, Ambrosia. Naked and desperate. And mine. Only mine."

With lips and tongue and fingertips he moved over her body, touching, tasting, drawing out every pleasure until she begged for release. Instead, he drove her even higher, until she nearly wept with need.

Following his lead she wrapped her arms around his waist and buried her lips in his throat. Hearing his little moan of pleasure, she grew bolder, exploring his body as he had explored hers, drawing out every sensation.

Riordan had thought he could go slowly. To make this night last forever, so that it would be one she would remember for a lifetime. But now, teetering on the brink of madness, he could no longer wait.

He moved down her body, taking her higher with each touch of his fingers and tongue.

Ambrosia lay helpless, her whole body straining, her heart stuttering, her mind begging for release. The danger of their journey no longer mattered. The only thing that was real was this man. His work-roughened hands. His enticing tongue. His clever mouth. And the need for more.

He heard her little cry as she reached the first crest. He gave her no time to recover as he moved along her body and took her on another wild ride.

Her mind reeling, her eyes dark with pleasure, she reached for him, needing to hold him.

"Riordan, please. I need you. Only you."

Her words added to the frenzy that held him in its grip. He seemed to be looking at her through a blazing mist that clouded his vision.

He wanted to be gentle, but the control was gone. Now all he could think of was having her. Her body. Her heart. Her soul. He took her like a madman. But instead of pulling away, she wrapped herself around him, even more deeply aroused. Incredibly, she began to move with him. Climb with him. Matching him strength for strength.

"Do you know how much I love you, my beautiful Ambrosia?" He whispered her name like a prayer as he began to climb higher, then higher still. There were no more words as the demons inside fought their way free.

And then they were soaring, shattering into little pieces before settling back to earth.

"Did I...hurt you?" Riordan lay on top of her, his face buried against her throat.

"Nay. I'm...fine." Such an inadequate word, she thought. She should feel bruised and battered from the storm she'd survived. But all she felt was...fine. There was this amazing sense of calm. Of peace. As though the whole world had somehow changed. And all because of her love for this man.

Love. It was true. She loved him. Desperately. And he loved her.

She reached up to brush a lock of damp hair from his eye. "You said you love me."

"Did I?"

"You don't remember?"

"I...seem to recall it. I guess I was...otherwise occupied. "

She laughed, then caught her breath.

"I'm too heavy." He rolled to one side, then pulled her into the circle of his arms. "Is that better?"

"Aye. Much." She snuggled close and he wrapped the blanket around them both.

"While I was...otherwise occupied, did you tell me you loved me, too?"

She shook her head. "I don't recall."

"Well?" He stared into her eyes.

"What?" She felt suddenly so lighthearted. The imp inside her took over. She couldn't help teasing.

"Do you?" His eyes narrowed slightly. "Love me?"

"You don't make it easy." She sat up, unmindful of her nakedness. Her hair swirled around her shoulders like a dark veil.

"And what is that supposed to mean?" He tugged on a lock of her hair.

"You have a nasty temper, Riordan."

"I do?" He started to grin. "I'm considered the most generous and kind-hearted of sea captains. Ask any of my crew. They'll tell you the same."

"Then perhaps that temper only rears its head when you're around me."

"That could be." His smile grew. "You do have a way of bringing out the passionate side of me...in more ways than one."

She trailed a finger through the mat of dark hair on his chest. "I'm intrigued by that...passionate side of you."

"Careful." He caught her finger to stop the torment. "Do you know what your touch does to me?"

"I thought..." She looked into his eyes. "I thought once we'd finished loving, the passion would be gone."

He chuckled, and the sound drifted over her senses like honey. "Oh, Ambrosia. The passion isn't gone. It's only spent. But a simple touch can call it back."

"You mean you could...we could...?"

"Aye. But you haven't answered my question yet."

"What question?"

"Do you love me?"

She waited for the space of a heartbeat before smiling. "Aye. Desperately."

"Ah." He let out a long, slow breath. "Next time, don't make me wait so long for your answer. It's apt to stop my heart."

She splayed her hands on his chest and could feel the thundering of his heartbeat, which mirrored her own. "There's been no damage. I can feel it. Beating quite loudly, I'm afraid."

"You do that to me. Set my heart to pounding, my palms to sweating. Any time you get too close, I have these strange reactions."

"How long has this been going on?"

"Since the first time I saw you." He drew her down and pressed his lips to her temple. "In fact, it started before I met you."

"What do you mean, Riordan? How could that be?"

He ran a finger along her arm, loving the soft, porcelain look of her skin in the moonlight. "The more James spoke of you, the more I found myself wanting to know you. You became, in my mind, the perfect woman. You were the woman I dreamed of on all those long, lonely nights at sea. And when I met you, I realized you were even sweeter than the woman in my dreams.''

She shook her head, suddenly overcome with emotion.

''What's this, love? Tears?''

''Oh, Riordan. I don't deserve your love.''

''And I don't deserve you. Maybe nobody ever deserves the good things that come into their lives. But for now, Ambrosia, let's just savor it.'' He drew her down into his arms and covered her mouth with his.

And then, with soft sighs and whispered words, they embarked on another long, slow journey of love.

Chapter Fourteen

It was that silent hour between darkness and dawn. A faint lavender mist danced across the water and swirled around the deck of the *Sea Challenge*.

Ambrosia and Riordan lay curled in the blanket, their arms around each other. There had been little time for sleep. They had spent the night lost in the wonder of their newfound love.

At times Ambrosia had seen the dark side of Riordan's passion. A darkness that excited her, even while it frightened her. But there had been an unexpectedly tender side to him as well. A tenderness that could bring a sudden lump to her throat, or a tear to her eye.

She sighed in her sleep, then opened her eyes to find him watching her.

"Riordan." She touched a hand to his cheek and he caught it, pressing her palm to his lips. "What are you doing?"

"I love watching you sleep. You're so peaceful. Like a child."

"I'm not a child." She started to sit up.

"I know." He pulled her back down and brushed soft kisses over her cheek, her eyelid, the tip of her nose. "As you like to remind me, you're a woman.'' He pressed his mouth to her ear and growled, ''My woman.''

She shivered. ''I like the sound of that.''

''Good. Because you're going to hear it often.'' He traced the outline of her mouth with his tongue and felt the familiar rush of heat. Even after a night of loving, he wanted more. He would never have enough of this amazing woman.

''I've told you so much about myself all night. My childhood. My adventures with James and my sisters.''

He nodded. ''I loved hearing about the things you did. Yours is a…colorful family, my love.''

They shared a laugh.

''But you've told me nothing about yourself, Riordan. About your childhood. Your family. Your life before I met you.''

She could sense his reluctance to talk about it. ''My childhood was one of wealth and privilege.'' He looked away, into the distance, as though going back in his mind. ''My brother, Prescott, and I learned to ride and fight and sail with Charles and James.''

She caught a breath. ''Charles, our king? And James, the duke of York?''

''Aye. We were best friends.''

''And all that gossip that Silas Fenwick told Edwina was a lie?''

For a moment he went very quiet, and Ambrosia wished she could take back the question. But it was too late. The words had been spoken.

''My father disapproved of the life I chose. My inheritance has been given over to Prescott.''

''I don't understand. You are disinherited because you chose a life at sea?''

''There is more to it, Ambrosia. There are things I

can't share with you." He thought of the dangerous missions he'd undertaken at the behest of the king. Political intrigue. Religious zealots bent on assassination. Warmongers who hoped to draw their monarch into battles that couldn't be won. "Secrets that only the king knows. Secrets that will go to the grave with me. I can't ask you to understand. But I ask you to accept me as I am."

She saw the remorse in his eyes, and knew that this was a man who would never betray a confidence. Even for the sake of love.

She wrapped her arms around him, pressing her lips to his throat. "I do, Riordan Spencer. I accept you just as you are. Now…" She started to roll aside. "I'd better slip below and get dressed before the others wake up."

"Umm." Instead of releasing her he drew her closer. "Stay just a few more minutes."

"Riordan." She laughed as he began moving his hands up her back, along her sides. "You know what will happen if I stay."

"You mean…this?" He covered her mouth with his, kissing her until they were both breathless.

"Aye." She came up for air and felt her head spinning. He was the only man who had ever made her feel this way. The only one who ever would.

"All right. Three more minutes. Then I'll let you go." He dragged her even closer and kissed her again.

And then, as the kiss deepened, they forgot about the time. Forgot about the secrets that could never be shared. Forgot about everything except each other. And the wonder of this love that had found them when they'd least expected it.

Ambrosia yawned, stretched and…froze. She had fallen back asleep. Now she could hear sounds belowdecks. The others were up and about. Where was her gown? Her chemise? "Riordan." She nudged him awake.

He drew her down for a slow, leisurely kiss.

"Riordan." She pressed a hand to his chest. "The others are awake. We must hurry and dress."

"Aye, love." He smiled. And drew her back for yet another kiss.

"They'll be topside any minute now. And my gown…"

He reached behind her and held it up. In two pieces.

Her eyes widened. "I can't wear that rag. Whatever will I do?"

"Didn't you bring another?"

"Aye. But it's below. And so are my sisters and my grandfather. Mistress Coffey and Winnie." Especially prim, stern Winnie, she thought with alarm. "How am I to face them?"

"I'll draw their attention." With a chuckle he handed her the blanket. "Just don't forget to bring this back when you've finished dressing."

"Why?"

"I'll be in need of it." Completely unconcerned about his nakedness, he strolled toward the rail and plunged into the sea.

Minutes later, as the others came topside to see who was splashing in the water, Ambrosia hurried belowdecks and dressed. When she returned to the deck, she carried the blanket over her arm.

"Good morrow," she called as casually as she could manage. "Newt, you might want to give this to Riordan when he finishes his swim."

"Aye." The old man gave her a steady look, and she

turned away with a flush before joining the others around the brazier, where they were preparing a morning meal.

"Good morrow, Ambrosia." Bethany studied her older sister's flushed cheeks. "Are you feeling feverish?"

"I feel fine. Why do you ask?"

"You look…" Winifred Mellon watched as Riordan pulled himself over the rail, draped in a blanket. For the space of a heartbeat he and Ambrosia exchanged a most intimate, knowing look. Then, dripping water, he crossed the deck and disappeared down the stairs. "You look a bit warm, Ambrosia. But then, it was a warm night. Don't you agree?"

"Aye." Ambrosia ducked her head, missing the smiles exchanged between Bethany and Darcy.

"I woke once through the night." Darcy poured tea. "You weren't in your hammock, Ambrosia."

"I…came topside for some air."

"Ah. Air." Darcy grinned. "The night air is so much sweeter on deck, don't you think?"

"Aye." Ambrosia saw that the others were studying her a little too carefully. Even her grandfather was staring.

She set aside her cup and escaped to where Newton was standing at the wheel, guiding the ship. "I'll relieve you, Newt, so that you can break your fast."

"I thank ye, lass." He swallowed back his smile. Judging by the cheerful mood of the cap'n this morn, the night had gone well for both of the lovers. Poor Ambrosia thought she was hiding her feelings from the others. What she didn't realize was that her heart was there in her eyes for all to see. And such a fine, warm, generous heart it was. He only hoped it wouldn't be broken.

Riordan stood at the helm of the *Sea Challenge* and watched as Ambrosia, Bethany and Darcy climbed the rigging with a grace that would put dancers to shame. Watching beside him, their grandfather lifted a hand to shade the sun from his eyes.

"You have remarkable granddaughters, Geoffrey."

The old man smiled. "They can do anything a man can do aboard ship."

"I'm sure you had a hand in their teaching."

"Aye. It eased some of the pain when I had to give up going to sea. But it may have been a blessing in disguise. If I were still a ship's captain, I would never have had all this time to spend with them. And I'd never have had the chance to know what wonderful young women my granddaughters are." He watched as the sails billowed, and the three young women chatted and giggled while they worked high above. Then he turned and stared directly at Riordan. "I've been around sailors all my life. I know how the long nights spent aboard ship can sharpen a man's appetite. I know, too, how life at sea can make a man forget the rules of civility on land."

"Aye." Riordan tore his gaze from Ambrosia to meet the old man's look directly.

"I'd not blame a man for losing his heart to one of my granddaughters." Geoffrey Lambert kept his tone low, reasonable. But Riordan recognized the thread of steel beneath the softly spoken words. "I'd even understand how a man might forget his common sense where one of my granddaughters was concerned. But if a man were to break the heart of one of them, I'd be as unforgiving as the shark that took old Newton's leg."

Riordan nodded. "I'd expect no less."

The old man's smile returned as he headed toward the shelter of the canopy across the deck, where the two old women sat watching the activities of the three young ones high above them.

As the old man walked away, it occurred to Riordan that Geoffrey Lambert hadn't missed a single word he'd spoken. That slippery old man was as sharp as a barracuda's tooth.

"A ship off the port, Riordan." Darcy's voice echoed from the rigging. "A ship with no flag."

The others turned in alarm to Riordan, who stood at the wheel.

"Until they're closer, and we see what we're up against, we'll do as before," he said. "Behave like a family out for a day's sail."

"But if they're pirates, we haven't a chance without our weapons, Riordan." Ambrosia turned to her two sisters, who nodded agreement.

"If they're pirates, we haven't a chance anyway," he said patiently. "We have no choice but to play out the charade. There's no place to hide."

When the women went belowdecks to change, he turned to Newton. "Take the wheel, Newt."

"Aye, Cap'n."

The old sailor did as he was told, while Riordan went in search of weapons. Though he couldn't risk wearing a sword, he did manage to conceal a knife below the waist of his breeches, and another in his boot.

One by one Ambrosia and her sisters returned to the deck wearing frilly gowns and bonnets. This day Ambrosia was dressed in violet, Bethany in blue and Darcy in yellow. They looked like lovely flowers in a summer garden as they helped their grandfather into his proper gentleman's coat and settled themselves around him under the canopy. Mistress Coffey prepared tea, and Miss Mellon, all in white, sat beside her.

Riordan lifted his spyglass to his eye to watch the ship's progress as it bore closer. It seemed to be a fairly new craft, larger than the *Undaunted*. Twice the size of the *Sea Challenge*. And from the number of sailors moving about the deck, they would be outnumbered by nearly ten to one.

As they drew close enough to make out the figures on deck, Riordan felt his blood turn to ice.

Seeing his sudden reaction, Ambrosia hurried to his side. "What is it, Riordan? What do you see?"

His tone was angrier than she'd ever heard. There was a note of such fury, it frightened her. "The face of someone I see nightly in my sleep. The face of the man who killed your father and brother. The pirate, Eli Sledge."

For the space of several minutes no one moved.

Finally Riordan began barking commands. "We can't outrun them. And we're badly outnumbered. But you and your family might have a chance to escape in the skiff."

When he turned toward the afterdeck, it was Geoffrey Lambert who stopped him. "Nay, Captain. We'll not run and leave you and Newton to face these scoundrels alone. We stand or fall together." He turned to his granddaughter. "Ambrosia, take Mistress Coffey and Miss Mellon belowdecks and fetch our weapons."

"Aye, Grandpapa." But when Ambrosia turned to the old women, they stood their ground.

"We'll not hide in our cabin below, while our family is facing danger." The housekeeper straightened her shoulders. "We've come this far together. We'll see it through."

Beside her, Winifred Mellon, looking absolutely terrified, nodded in agreement.

Ambrosia turned to her grandfather. "Aye," he muttered. "Stay then. Ambrosia, fetch our weapons."

She hurried belowdecks and returned carrying an armload of swords, knives and pistols.

"Quickly now," the old man said. "Take up your weapons and your positions."

Riordan was shaking his head. "This is madness." But even as he shouted the words, he realized the futility of his argument.

Like a well-trained militia, each of the Lambert sisters took a different location at the rail of the ship, with their grandfather in the middle. The two old women were given ammunition for the dueling pistols, and positioned between the others.

"All right," Riordan called. "Before we fight, we'll try to evade. Stand steady. And be prepared to be thrown about."

As the pirate ship pulled alongside, the men on board saw the three women in their finery, holding aloft their weapons, and threw back their heads in laughter.

"Ahoy," came a man's raspy voice from the larger ship. "This is Captain Eli Sledge of the pirate ship the *Skull*." He grinned, knowing such words always threw fear into the hearts of those who heard them. "Throw down your weapons, or prepare to die."

In reply, Riordan signaled to Newton, who turned the wheel sharply, sending the *Sea Challenge* ramming into the side of the *Skull*. Because they'd been given prior warning, those aboard the *Sea Challenge* remained upright, clinging to the rail. The men aboard the *Skull* weren't so fortunate. The unexpected collision sent sailors tumbling about the deck. Those closest to the rail were tossed overboard, where they floundered about in the waves churned up by the two craft.

Riordan grabbed the wheel and shouted to Newton, "Hoist the topsail. We need all the wind we can find now."

"Aye, Cap'n." The old man scrambled up the rigging, hauling the sail to the highest point, where it caught a breeze and began to turn the *Sea Challenge* away from its enemy.

"Lower your sails," came an order from the *Skull*. "Or we'll destroy your ship."

Riordan held the wheel steady, hoping to catch enough breeze to put some distance between the two craft. But as the smaller ship turned, there was the smell of gunpowder and the terrible roar of cannon. The *Sea Challenge* shuddered as she took a hit from close range.

Newton raced to his side, and the two men struggled to hold the ship on course. But the damage was too great. The *Sea Challenge* was listing so badly that, if she weren't hauled to shore quickly, she would sink.

"They're coming, Riordan," Ambrosia shouted.

The *Skull* moved closer. As soon as the two ships were side by side, the pirates began tossing their lines and landing on the deck of the *Sea Challenge*.

"Look, Eli," one of the pirates called. "Females, waiting to greet us with kisses, I'll wager."

That was followed by a roar of laughter. But as Ambrosia engaged first one, and then another pirate, and relieved them of their swords, the laughter turned to grunts of surprise and pain.

"Here's a comely wench," one of the pirates called as he pointed the tip of his sword at Bethany's chest.

Instead of the weeping and wailing he'd anticipated, she merely lifted her hand from behind her skirt to reveal a dueling pistol. Taking careful aim, she fired and watched as he fell to the deck with a look of utter astonishment. Then she turned to the two old women, who calmly handed her more gunpowder.

"And who's this pretty little thing?" another pirate jeered as he challenged Darcy.

Without a word she lifted her hand and tossed a small, deadly knife. It landed with a thud in the man's chest. As he fell to the deck, she pulled the knife away and stepped over him. Seeing her grandfather holding several swordsmen at bay, she joined him, hoping to even the odds.

Riordan fought off a score of pirates, all the while struggling to keep Eli Sledge in his line of vision. Sledge was the key. If the pirate captain could be stopped, the others might lose their will to fight.

"Behind you, Riordan."

At Ambrosia's shout, he turned and faced two menacing pirates who came at him from opposite sides. Though he was able to disarm the first, the second brought his sword up in a slashing motion, laying open Riordan's arm. At once, Mistress Coffey and Miss Mellon picked up pieces of the shattered ship's rail and attacked the sailor, sending him toppling into the water. For a moment the two old ladies looked at each other with matching looks of horror. Then, realizing they'd been victorious, they leapt into another fight with a pirate, sending him into the water as well.

Riordan could see the blood spilling from his wound, and could feel the warmth of it. But the pain didn't register as he saw, across the deck, four swordsmen advancing on Ambrosia. For a moment his heart nearly stopped. Then, leaping to her defense, he was able to eliminate one, then another.

Ambrosia dropped the other two men where they stood, then raced the length of the deck to fight alongside her grandfather, who was holding several more pirates at bay.

The old man was still able to defend himself, but he was beginning to tire. The sound of his heavy breathing had Ambrosia more worried than she cared to admit. She shot him a quick glance. He winked, then ran one of the sailors through with his sword. As the man dropped, he turned to face three more. Just then, the housekeeper and nurse stepped in, swinging wildly with their wooden weapons. Two more sailors went into the water.

Ambrosia felt a sting of pain in her arm and looked down to realize she'd been wounded. Out of the corner of her eye she caught the flash of a blade and knew that someone was attacking. Before she could turn she heard the sound of a pistol shot and looked up to see Bethany holding a smoking pistol. The man who had been about to run Ambrosia through fell instead at her feet. She mouthed a silent word of thanks to her sister, then turned.

By the rail of the ship Riordan was fighting several men, and easily winning. But just as Ambrosia was about to turn away, she saw a man sneaking up behind him, holding aloft a club.

"Riordan." Though she shouted at the top of her lungs, she realized he hadn't heard her. The words had been snatched away by the wind. And then, as she watched, she saw the club come crashing down on Riordan's head. Saw him go limp. And then two sailors lifted him and tossed him over the rail and into the churning water between the two ships.

"Nay!" With a cry of desperation she began running. Her sword slipped from her fingers and clattered on the deck.

She scrambled over the rail and, without a thought to her own safety, jumped into the foaming waves. Again and again, looking for a sign of Riordan, she dived beneath the bodies that floated on the surface. Finally, knowing each second lost brought him closer to death, she caught her breath and swam beneath the hull of the *Sea Challenge.*

Though the water was murky from the cannon fire, she spotted him, facedown, lying motionless. She wasted precious moments struggling to free his sword, which had become entangled in his sleeve and was weighing him down. Then, with one last burst of strength, she pulled him from beneath the ship and began swimming toward the surface. Her lungs were straining, and for one terrible moment she feared she wouldn't make it. Then she broke water and dragged precious air into her lungs, before clutching at his head.

"Breathe, Riordan. Please breathe," she sobbed.

He gasped, then opened his eyes. "Ambrosia. How…?"

"It doesn't matter, love. You're alive."

"The others?"

She looked up to the deck of the *Sea Challenge* and her heart nearly stopped. The little ship was tilted almost on its side. Flames enveloped the deck.

"Grandpapa. My sisters. Those sweet old people." She felt tears spring to her eyes.

"There." Riordan pointed. As she watched, she saw her family and old Newton standing on the deck of the *Skull,* being held at swordpoint against the railing. Sailors were hauling the last of the cargo from the *Sea Challenge* to the *Skull.* And a small skiff was already heading in their direction to pick them up.

"You didn't escape." Riordan swore fiercely.

"Nay, Riordan. But we're alive. You're alive. And we're together."

Rough hands lifted her from the water and she was tossed into a corner of the skiff. As soon as Riordan was hauled aboard, the little boat returned to the *Skull*.

"Now, isn't this cozy?" Eli Sledge stared boldly at the young woman whose wet gown clung to her like a second skin.

He was a big man who used his size to intimidate. Though his face may have been handsome in his youth, it was now marred by a scar that ran from his cheek to the base of his throat. His skin was ruddy from his years at sea. Thick black hair hung down his back. Over his breeches and boots he wore a tunic that was stained with blood. In his hand was a coiled whip, which he used to punctuate his words. And just to assure that his prisoners understood he knew how to use it, he uncoiled it and drew his hand back, then brought it down with such force it sounded like cannon fire as it hit the deck.

He stood, feet apart, hands on hips, staring down his nose at the people who now crowded together for mutual protection and comfort.

With a laugh he turned to his men, who were grinning like fools. "It was everything our benefactor promised. A king's ransom in gold. Wenches, three of them young and easy to look at. He said that when we get to Cairn we can do with them what we choose. I say we kill all but the young females. And those who die must do so slowly, to make up for the pain and suffering they caused us. As for these three, our benefactor didn't say what was to be done with them, but I've decided that we'll keep them alive awhile. At least until we tire of them. So let's head for port, lads. There'll be ale for all tonight. And then we'll…'' he gave a crude laugh as he looked the three young women up and down ''…enjoy the rest of our bounty.''

Chapter Fifteen

"Bethany. Darcy," Ambrosia whispered fiercely. "Give me your petticoats." While the pirates stood guard over them, she knelt beside Riordan, who lay on the deck, bleeding profusely. His arm had been slashed from shoulder to elbow, and he'd lost considerable blood while in the water.

With the aid of her nurse and housekeeper, she tied a tourniquet to stem the flow of blood, then began wrapping the wound.

As Ambrosia and the women huddled around him, he opened his eyes, fighting to remain conscious. But the pain of his wound and the blow to his head were threatening to take him down into a well of darkness.

"Listen to me, Ambrosia." His fingers gripped her wrist so tightly she nearly cried out. "My life no longer matters. I'm already a dead man. You heard what Eli Sledge said."

"Aye. He intends to kill all but the three of us. But I intend to stop him."

"What can you do against a score of hard-bitten pirates? You have to forget about everything except finding a means of escape."

"Not without the rest of you."

"Don't you understand?" He glanced from her to her sisters, and then to the two stoic old women, hoping to convince them. "These men will have their sport with you. Death would be far more welcome than what they intend."

Ambrosia gritted her teeth and continued wrapping his wound. When she was through she cradled his face in both her hands and stared deeply into his eyes. "Now you listen to me, Riordan Spencer. I've just found the man I love." She heard Mistress Coffey and Winifred Mellon suck in their breath, and realized she'd revealed more than she'd intended. It no longer mattered. Aloud she said, "I have no intention of losing you to this pack of cutthroats. We'll find a way to escape. A way that works for all of us. Or we'll all die together. Is that clear?"

There was something else he wanted to warn her about. Something that hovered on the edges of his mind. But the pain was too great, and the darkness was closing in. He struggled to hold on to the thread of thought.

"There's another enemy. More dangerous than Sledge. The…benefactor. It has to be…" His voice trailed off. The darkness swallowed him.

Ambrosia watched as the *Skull*'s anchor was lowered. Just beyond was the town of Cairn, long rumored to be home to some of the toughest pirates to sail the ocean.

"I'll take the prisoners ashore," Eli Sledge called to his men. "And then return for the cargo."

At the point of a sword they were herded aboard a skiff. Two sailors dumped Riordan in a heap, then took up their oars and rowed to the docks. From there they were taken to the upper room of a tavern that reeked of ale and unwashed bodies. Several filthy pallets were strewn about the equally filthy floor.

As soon as the door was slammed and the lock thrown, Ambrosia and Newton helped Riordan to one pallet, while Bethany and Darcy guided their weary grandfather and the old women to others. While they rested, Ambrosia looked around.

One small window overlooked the docks. She rushed across the room to stare out the window, hoping to find a means of escape. Her heart fell when she saw an armed sailor standing below.

"Sledge has posted a guard."

Her two sisters came alongside her and peered down.

"I'd feared as much," Bethany muttered. "What are we to do?"

"I don't know." Ambrosia's eyes narrowed. "I have a knife in my boot. Knowing Riordan, he'll have one as well."

"As do I," Bethany said.

"And I." Darcy smiled for the first time. "We're not helpless, are we, Ambrosia?"

"Nay. Nor are we brainless. We'll do as Papa taught us. We'll watch and listen. We'll endure. And when the time is right, we'll escape."

"You have the gold?" Silas stood in the shadows of the tavern, watching the movements of the serving wench across the room. He'd been too long without a woman. But he'd been careful not to despoil any of the precious maidens of Land's End. That would ruin his plans.

"Aye." Eli Sledge was elated. "'Twas a clever ruse to hide it in three tea casks."

"Our enemies become more cunning with each shipment. That's why they must be destroyed, if the king is

to be toppled from the throne. Have your men load two
of the casks aboard my ship. The other is yours, to keep
as payment.'' Silas couldn't keep the glitter of greed from
his eyes. ''What about the family aboard the *Sea Challenge*?''

''Upstairs.'' Sledge grinned. ''I'll send a sailor to dis-
pose of them after dark. My crew is eager for the young
women.''

''I've seen them. A pity they have to be wasted. Three
more comely wenches I've yet to meet.'' Silas sighed
and drained his tumbler of ale. ''It can't be helped. What
we do, we do for England.''

Sledge saw the way his companion's eyes followed the
movement of the serving wench. ''Would you like one
of them before you leave?''

''What I wouldn't give…'' He caught himself before
he said more. ''I must leave for London. I'm taking my
betrothed to see the king.''

''You're to be wed?''

''Nay. I fear an accident will have to befall the lovely
lass before the nuptials. But she suited my purpose. There
were certain…things I needed to see to in her village.
She was the perfect foil.''

''Ah. You were using her.'' Sledge drained his own
goblet and ordered another by pounding it down on the
table. The serving wench hurried over and filled it, then
glanced toward his companion.

Silas looked her over, lingering on the full breasts beneath the simple gown. ''Perhaps I have time for another.'' He held out his tumbler, then added, ''But I'd
like it served in the back room.''

Sledge threw back his head and roared as Silas caught
the wench by the wrist and dragged her from the room.

Then he drank his ale and thought about all the ways he'd spend the gold that had just come into his possession.

Riordan opened his eyes and winced. His head was pounding, his arm throbbing. Across the room Ambrosia and her sisters were huddled around Newton, their voices little more than a whisper.

Despite the pain, he forced himself to sit up. For a moment the room spun in dizzying circles. Then it stopped, and he got to his feet.

"Riordan. You mustn't push yourself." Ambrosia hurried to his side and caught his arm when he stumbled.

"How long have I been unconscious?"

"Two hours or more."

He glanced at the old people on their pallets. "And the others?"

"At least as long."

Just then they began to roll over and open their eyes. "Grandpapa. Mistress Coffey. Winnie." The three young women gathered around them. "Are any of you harmed?"

"I was just weary. The swordfight drained me." Geoffrey Lambert clasped his granddaughters' hands. "Have any of Sledge's men been here?"

Ambrosia shook her head. "We've heard voices below in the tavern. I'd guess, from the sound of their laughter, they're drinking great quantities of ale."

Riordan exchanged a worried look with the others. "That's what I feared. Once they're drunk, they'll become even more dangerous."

"Not necessarily." Ambrosia nodded toward her sisters. "We've been discussing what we'll do when they come for us."

Riordan's eyes narrowed. "What you'll do is stay over

there, as far from the door as possible. Your grandfather and Newt and I will be the first line of defense. They'll have to go through us to get to the rest of you."

"Which shouldn't take them more than a few minutes." Ambrosia touched a hand to his arm, bound tightly against his chest. "Think, Riordan. How long can you fend them off?"

"I'll die trying."

"Aye. As will Newt and Grandpapa. But we want you alive. All of you. Let us try our way first."

"You have a plan?"

She nodded. "Ofttimes the best defense is surprise. I think…" She looked up at the sound of booted feet climbing the stairs. "There's no time to explain. Please, Grandpapa and Riordan, Mistress Coffey and Winnie. Lie down and pretend to be dead. Newton will be hidden beneath one pallet."

When Riordan started to protest, she begged, "Please trust me."

"Newt?" He glanced at the old sailor, who appeared as undecided as he.

Newton shrugged. "I haven't a better plan at the moment, Cap'n."

"Nor I," Geoffrey Lambert said in a tired voice.

"I trust my girls," Miss Mellon said with great dignity. "After all, I taught them to use their minds."

"Very well." As the others lay down, Riordan settled himself on the pallet, using his body to hide Newton. But he decided to keep one eye open. Just in case.

Ambrosia and her sisters listened as the footsteps halted outside the door. Linking arms, they stood together as the brace was thrown and the door opened.

A bearded pirate stood on the threshold. "I've come

for the others," he announced. "Captain Sledge ordered me to kill them before my mates come for the three of you."

"You're too late." Ambrosia indicated the pallets. "Captain Spencer's wounds were too grave. As for the others, their poor old hearts couldn't take the strain."

The pirate seemed actually annoyed that he'd been deprived of the chance to kill. Seeing that only stiffened Ambrosia's resolve. She'd thought only to wound him. Now she would have to see that he didn't live to call out a warning to the others.

His eyes narrowed as he glanced around. "What of the old sailor?"

"Gone." Bethany's lips trembled. She even managed a tear. "He slipped out the window and fled like a coward."

"He couldn't have. Sledge posted a guard."

"The coward took some of our gold to use as a bribe."

"You have gold?" The pirate stepped closer.

"Aye." Darcy tossed her golden curls. "More than we could ever spend. Did you not see the gold we carried aboard our ship?"

"Aye. But we weren't told 'twas yours. Only that it was bound for the king."

Bethany laughed. "Perhaps Sledge hopes to keep it all for himself."

"That's not the way of a pirate. We share the bounty."

"How would you know?" Ambrosia asked slyly. "Do you and the other men watch each time casks are opened and gold counted?"

"Nay. But we're given a share."

"An equal share?" Ambrosia's brow arched. "Or just enough to keep you content, while your captain grows rich?"

They could see that the pirate was mulling this over.

Ambrosia decided it was time to make the offer. "Perhaps you'd like to be as rich as Sledge."

"How?" The man's eyes narrowed.

"We have no man to protect us." Bethany blinked away another tear. "If you were to become our protector, we'd be ever so grateful."

The time at sea had been long, the nights lonely. The pirate was staggered by the helplessness of these three maidens. Hadn't he fought the king's own sailors countless times and won? Why couldn't he fight off his own mates if necessary? The rewards would be worth any sacrifice. Gold. Enough to live like a monarch. And the gratitude of three beautiful ladies, who would be his for as long as he wanted.

Filled with his own importance, the pirate swept past them. "First I'll have to make certain these others are dead."

As he bent to the first pallet, he felt a sudden shaft of searing pain. He tried to straighten, and found that his body wouldn't obey his command. He reached a hand to his back and felt the hilt of a knife buried deep.

With a gasp, he gave up his life and dropped forward, falling on top of Riordan.

The three young women rolled him aside, while Riordan and Newton scrambled to their feet. Beside them, Geoffrey sat up, looking at his granddaughters in disbelief, while the housekeeper and nurse averted their gaze, refusing to look at the dead man.

"Come," Ambrosia called urgently. "We must flee before the others come for us. There's not a minute to waste."

As they hurried from the room and started down the

stairs, they heard the sound of footsteps climbing toward them.

"Tell me." Riordan stopped in his tracks and turned back. "Have you another plan, Ambrosia?"

She shook her head. "I believe I'm all out of plans. But I'll…" She swallowed. "I'll think of something." She glanced around, then pointed toward a small ladder. "Quickly," she whispered. "We'll climb to the roof."

Newton climbed first, shoving open a small trap door that led to the roof of the tavern. Next came the two old women, then Bethany and her grandfather, then Darcy and Ambrosia, with Riordan following.

"We'll have only a few minutes," Riordan told them. "Once they sound the alarm, the building and the street below will be swarming with Sledge's men."

Ambrosia looked at the line of pitched roofs, outlined in the fading light of evening. Then she hiked up her skirts, cursing the fact that they would make her and her sisters clumsy. How she longed for a pair of breeches. "We come from a long line of seamen who've been climbing rigging since we could walk. We can certainly leap a few rooftops, if that's what it takes to gain our freedom."

Geoffrey Lambert chuckled. "That's my girl." He turned to Riordan, who was looking at them as if they were all addled. "Come on, lad. What have we got to lose?"

"Just our lives," Riordan muttered as he followed the three women to the very edge of the roof. "What about Mistress Coffey and Miss Mellon?"

"I was considered quite athletic in my youth," Winifred Mellon said haughtily. "I should think a few rooftops wouldn't be much of a challenge."

"And you, Mistress Coffey?" Riordan asked.

Her face had turned a shade pale. But she lifted her skirts, determined to keep up. "If Miss Mellon can jump rooftops, I shall do the same."

"Where will we go if we become separated?" Darcy whispered.

The others paused and glanced toward Riordan. Without hesitation he said, "The *Sea Challenge*'s at the bottom of the ocean by now. What's say we take Sledge's ship, the *Skull*?"

"Aye." Ambrosia clenched a fist by her side. "It seems only fair."

"It's agreed then." Bethany clasped her sister's hand. "We run to the docks and swim to the *Skull*."

"Aye. And we must set sail before dawn." Riordan glanced at the others, to make certain they understood. "Else we'll never get out of this harbor alive. So we must all agree to leave before dawn, even if some of our party doesn't make it. Do you swear?"

"Aye," the others called in unison.

Through the small window of the upper room they heard the shouts and oaths of the pirates as they discovered the body of their comrade, and realized the prisoners had escaped.

"Now," Riordan called. "There's no time to waste."

They raced to the edge of the building and leapt to the next rooftop. Then, running until their breath burned their lungs, they leapt from rooftop to rooftop, determined to outrun their captors.

"Where's Ambrosia?" Riordan clung to the edge of a steep roof and peered ahead through the gathering shadows. Night was falling quickly. It was both a blessing and a curse. It sheltered them from their pursuers, but it also hindered them from seeing obstacles in their path.

"Up ahead, Cap'n." Newton pointed to a skirt just disappearing around a chimney. "She's sticking close to her grandfather and the old women, in case they should grow weary."

"Keep up with them, Newt. I'd hate for them to walk into danger."

"Aye, Cap'n. What about you?"

"I'll be fine." As Newton raced ahead, Riordan shook his head in wonder. Half the town was chasing through the streets below, searching for them. Pirates as angry as hornets trailed behind them, brandishing swords. And this amazing family showed no fear as they continued on, showing no sign of the weariness that must be plaguing them.

For Riordan, the pain was almost overwhelming. With each step, his head swam and his eyes misted. His arm throbbed like the fire of hell. What kept him going was the knowledge that once they reached the pirate ship, they would be safe.

He felt responsible for them. All of them. And he wouldn't rest until he had them safely away from this hellhole.

He saw another rooftop looming before him and set his teeth against the pain as he made the leap. He landed, catching hold of the chimney with his good arm. For a moment he staggered and nearly fell. Then, as his vision cleared, he saw the others running ahead.

Soon, he told himself. Soon they'd be safe. And he could rest. It was the last coherent thought he had before his vision swam and the world went dark. And he felt himself falling through space.

"Hold on, Grandpapa." Ambrosia helped the old man scramble across yet another rooftop. "We're almost there."

"I can take care of myself."

She smiled in the darkness. "I know you can. I'm so proud of you, Grandpapa."

"And I'm proud of you, lass. But save your words. We aren't there yet."

"Aye." She led him toward the edge of the roof and could see the docks looming straight ahead. "Look, Grandpapa. Only one more."

She waited until he'd made the leap, then she followed. When they'd crossed the roof, they paused at the edge to peer down. Newton and Bethany followed, with the two old women between them.

"Where's Darcy and Riordan?" Ambrosia looked around.

"Right behind us," Bethany said. "Now, how do we get down?"

"Stay here." Newton began circling the rooftop. "I'll see what I can find."

Minutes later he beckoned them to the far side, where a ladder rested against the wall.

They scrambled down and began running toward the docks. By the time they got to the edge of the wharf, Darcy had joined them.

Ambrosia glanced beyond her. "Where's Riordan?"

"I'm sure he'll be along. He was right behind me."

Newton pointed toward the ship in the distance. "We have no time to lose."

"Aye." Bethany peeled off her gown and Darcy did the same.

For a moment the two old women paused. Though they'd survived a battle, and had escaped by leaping over rooftops, shedding their proper gowns seemed the most daring by far. Finally, grateful for the cover of darkness,

Winnie and Mistress Coffey tossed aside their gowns and stepped out of their petticoats.

Bethany and Darcy jumped into the water, then waited until the two old ladies and their grandfather joined them.

Newton turned to Ambrosia. "Are ye coming, lass?"

"Aye. But I'll just wait a moment for Riordan."

"Ye shouldn't wait, lass. He'll be along. He sent me ahead to see that ye were all kept safe."

"I'll be fine. We both will." She nodded. "Go now, Newt. We'll be right behind you."

The old sailor jumped in and started swimming.

Ambrosia watched, then turned and peered through the darkness toward the lights of the town, torn between her desire to run and her need to find Riordan. In the end, her worry over Riordan won out. She couldn't leave him. Couldn't be safe unless she knew he was, too.

She turned and began to run, ducking behind buildings whenever she saw the light of a torch moving toward her. She was just racing past another darkened building when she saw something lying on the ground. As she moved closer she heard the moan, and realized it was Riordan.

"Oh, my darling." She knelt in the grass and touched a hand to his throat. There was a pulse. Feeble, thready, but at least he was still alive. "Can you stand?"

"Go." The word was torn from a throat so dry he could barely swallow. "Leave me. I…order…"

"I'll go to the ship and get the others."

"Nay. I forbid…"

"Shh. I'll be right back, love."

She got to her feet and started to run. And as she rounded a corner, slammed into a solid wall of chest.

Strong hands gripped her shoulders. And a deep, raspy

voice said, ''Well, now. Isn't this cozy. You decided to come back and pleasure me and my men.''

Ambrosia found herself looking into the cruel, mocking eyes of Eli Sledge.

Chapter Sixteen

Ambrosia tried desperately to pull free of the pirate's arms. But she was no match for his strength.

"Where are the others hiding?" he demanded.

"They're gone." She prayed he wouldn't spot Riordan lying in the grass just around the side of the building. And then another thought struck her. If Riordan were to moan, he'd give himself away. Determined to save him at all cost, she found an incredible strength within herself. She bolted and started to run in the opposite direction.

Out of the darkness she heard the whistle of the whip as it snaked out and coiled around her neck. She was jolted backward with such force all the wind was knocked out of her lungs. What was worse, she couldn't breathe. Though she clawed desperately at the rope around her throat, she couldn't pry it loose. She could feel herself beginning to fade as spots danced in front of her eyes. And then, just when she thought she couldn't bear it another second, the whip was suddenly loosened, and she dragged in a series of deep, shuddering breaths. Thin lines of blood trickled down the front of her gown.

"Let that be a lesson, woman. Don't you ever try to run away from Eli Sledge. Or my trusty little friend here will flog the life out of you." He gave her a kick with the toe of his boot. "You hear?"

"Aye." It was the only word she could manage through a throat left so raw it was nearly impossible to swallow.

"Come on, woman." He hauled her to her feet and started dragging her back toward the tavern.

As he passed a companion he called, "Tell the others I've found one of them. A female. And if she's the only one left, she's going to have to pay double the price for those who got away."

Ambrosia wouldn't let herself think about what fate awaited her at the tavern. For now, it was enough to know that she'd drawn his attention away from Riordan's hiding place. Now if only he could find the strength to make it to the ship, where the others awaited him.

Despite her pain and weariness, Ambrosia forced herself to put one foot in front of the other and continue walking. She couldn't let this pirate see her fear. If so, he would use it against her. Papa said that's what bullies always did.

When she stumbled, he yanked her roughly against him, allowing his hand to find her breast. She flinched, then cursed herself for it. He mustn't see any weakness. Stiffening her spine, she continued walking toward the lights of the tavern.

He led her around to a small room at the side of the tavern and gave her a shove, causing her to stumble inside. Holding a stick to the fireplace, he lit a torch and stuck it in a sconce along the wall. Then he left her standing while he sat down and lifted the lid of a tea cask. Inside she caught the gleam of gold as he grabbed a handful of coins.

He held them up. "See this, woman? This is my reward for ridding the world of the likes of you."

"I thought you did it for the sheer pleasure of inflicting pain."

He laughed. "That, too. I enjoy my work. But I enjoy it a lot more when there's gold involved. With this much gold, I can buy all the women and ale I want."

"Is that all it's good for?"

"It's all I crave out of life. That and a fast ship when my enemies are after me."

"I'm sure you have a lot of them."

"Aye." He threw back his head and roared. "And that suits me just fine. I have no use for people. I'd as soon kill them as look at them." He thrust the gold into his pocket. Then he lowered the lid and grabbed her arm, shoving her roughly ahead of him toward the larger room of the tavern.

Inside, the raucous voices and laughter faded when the pirates caught sight of Eli stepping through the doorway with his prisoner.

"Look what I've found, mates." Sledge gave a rumble of laughter. "Her friends deserted her. But I'm sure we can find a way to cheer her up. What say you, mates?"

"I don't know how cheery she'll be when I'm through with her." A hulking pirate with stringy gray hair and yellow teeth stepped forward. "But I'll be feeling a whole lot better for it, Captain."

"Why should Seton get her first?" another pirate complained. "I want a chance with her."

"Let's draw lots," another called. "It's only fair, since we all want her."

"Aye. You can draw lots. But nobody gets her until I've had her first." The pirate captain stared around at the others, daring them to argue.

An uneasy silence fell over the room.

"That's better." Sledge's smile returned. "Drinks for everyone. And while we're slaking our thirst, we'll have the woman entertain us." He shoved her forward. "Dance for us, wench."

"Aye. Dance for us." The men laughed and clapped and pounded their tankards on the tables.

Dazed, Ambrosia stumbled a few feet, then righted herself. At first all she could see was a blur of leering faces. But as they came into sharper focus, she began to really look at them. Could she read any compassion in their eyes? Any pity? Was there even one among them who might come to her aid? As she stared about, she was faced with a terrible truth. These men had long ago discarded any vestige of humanity. They'd stopped caring about anyone but themselves.

The chorus of shouting and laughing increased as the ale flowed and the men emptied their tankards and demanded more. Some of them grabbed at Ambrosia as she moved past, pinching her flesh until she was bruised and humiliated. Others laughed and jeered. One kicked her, causing her to fall.

"I said dance, woman."

At Sledge's command, Ambrosia picked herself up and began to sway and weave among the tables. As she did, an old man reached over and lifted her skirt. She slapped his hand away and the crowd roared with laughter.

Her eyes narrowed as she realized that she had the full attention of every man in this room. If she could keep them watching, and drinking, perhaps she could seize an opportunity to escape. She would try it, no matter how painful or dangerous. For she already knew the fate that awaited her here. She would rather die than continue to suffer this pain and humiliation. And this was only the beginning.

She lifted her skirt, revealing her ankles, and began to circle the room. The men went wild, some even standing on the tables for a better view.

As she dipped and twirled, Ambrosia noted the doors, and the men who stood guard at each. One of them held a knife in his hand, his gaze scanning the room. Another had his hand down the gown of a serving wench. That might bode well. Especially if he and the wench decided to seek their pleasure elsewhere. Ambrosia kept the man in her line of vision as she continued circling the room.

She was suddenly jolted out of her reverie when an old man stepped in front of her and hauled her into his arms, kissing her full on the mouth. Stunned, she could only stare at him as the men shouted their approval. Then, without a thought to what she was doing, Ambrosia took the tankard from his hand and poured the contents over his head.

Out of the corner of her eye she saw Eli Sledge uncoil his whip, and she steeled herself for what was to come.

Instead, she looked around to find the entire crowd on their feet, laughing and clapping.

''Good one, lass,'' one of the pirates shouted.

''Give 'im 'ell, lass,'' another called.

Ambrosia glanced back at Eli Sledge. Though his dark scowl remained, he was staring around, surprised by the reaction of the others. Slowly he began to coil his whip around his arm. She swallowed her fear and continued weaving her way through the crowded tables. For the moment, at least, she'd won a reprieve.

Riordan stumbled through the darkness. The blow to the head during the fight aboard ship had left his vision blurred. His arm was bleeding again. The blood had already soaked through his dressings and stained his shirt and breeches. He mopped at his face, and left it bloodstained as well. But he wasn't finished yet, he reminded himself. He had two good legs, and one hand that still worked. A hand that now held the knife he'd carried in his boot.

What kept him going, what gave him his supernatural strength, was the voice he'd heard in the darkness. The voice of the man whose vision had tormented him since that terrible night when John and James Lambert had given their lives. Eli Sledge couldn't be allowed to harm another Lambert.

Ambrosia. Riordan felt the blood pounding in his temples as he drew near the tavern. His own life meant nothing to him. For if the woman he loved should die at the hands of that hated pirate, he couldn't bear to go on living.

He crept toward the small window and peered inside. What he saw had his blood running cold.

The young pirate was drunk and wild-eyed. He'd lost an ear and half of a once-handsome face to a seaman's sword. Now he stood, barring Ambrosia's path, holding a dueling pistol to her head.

"Let 'er go, Griff," a man shouted.

"Nay. Look at her. She's too pretty." The hand holding the pistol trembled violently. "Nobody deserves to be this pretty. Especially not when my Becky lies in the cold ground."

"She didn't kill yer Becky," another shouted.

"But it was one like her. A pretty one." He pressed the pistol against her cheek, and Ambrosia could smell the gunpowder. Fear rose in her throat, threatening to choke her.

"Put away the pistol, Griff." Eli Sledge's voice was deadly soft.

"Let me kill her, Captain."

"And spoil my fun?" The voice grew firmer. "Take out the gunpowder, Griff. At once. Or I'll have to kill you."

Ambrosia could feel the way the sailor trembled as he fought the urge to pull the trigger. But in the end, his fear of the pirate captain was greater than the madness that had caused him to aim his pistol at her.

The young sailor turned the pistol over, spilling gunpowder all over Ambrosia's hair and neck and shoulders. While the men laughed, she shook it into her pockets and stood perfectly still, fighting the panic that had rendered her speechless.

She'd never before been that close to madness. She had been trying desperately to prepare herself for a violent death.

Now, pushed and poked by the men around her, she was forced to keep moving.

While all around him his men grew louder and more raucous, Eli Sledge sat alone at a table, watching and brooding. Each time his tankard was empty, a serving wench filled it quickly, for his temper was legendary. No one wanted to risk the sting of that whip.

"Bring the woman," he shouted.

The laughter died. A half dozen pirates caught hold of Ambrosia and hauled her across the room.

"Dance for me, woman." He pointed with his whip. "On my table."

Strong arms lifted her onto his table, where she stood, hands on hips, staring at him.

It occurred to Ambrosia that she'd just lost her best chance to run. She'd almost made it to the door. And now this. The men formed a circle around the table and began clapping and shouting.

When she didn't move, Eli began uncoiling his whip. "Maybe you need prodding."

She shot him a hateful look and began to move slowly around the table.

"Faster. Show me your legs." He drained his tankard. "Such long, lovely legs."

A serving wench hurried over with a pitcher of ale while Ambrosia lifted her skirts and began to spin around and around. At that the men began keeping time with their hands, clapping in rhythm.

"Lift the skirt higher," Sledge commanded.

Ambrosia gritted her teeth and hiked her skirts up, all the while watching his face. He was still scowling. But there was an intensity that hadn't been there before. A darkness in his eyes. A tightening of his jaw. It was the most lustful look she'd ever seen, and it frightened her more than the young sailor's madness.

She swallowed the knot of fear that was threatening to choke her. She had to be strong. To be alert to everything that was going on around the room. To be ready to run. And if that possibility was denied her, she had to be ready to defend herself, or die trying. She would plunge her dagger into her own heart before she'd let this monster have his way with her.

"Come here, woman." He held up a hand.

At once the clapping stopped. The men who only moments ago had been laughing and calling out good-naturedly grew silent. An expectant hush fell over the room.

From her position atop the table, Ambrosia was able

to see over the heads of the men who ringed the room. When she spotted the bloody face at the window, she nearly cried out. Then, biting back her words, she realized that it was Riordan. Her own beloved Riordan.

The slightest change in her looks or demeanor would give him away.

"Woman. I said come here."

Ambrosia knew that she needed to keep everyone's attention riveted on her, if Riordan were to survive. Striking a seductive pose, her hands on her hips, she sauntered across the table toward Eli Sledge.

Halfway across, she paused. Forcing a smile to her lips, she taunted, "If you want me, you have to come and get me."

"Why you…" He was on his feet and uncoiling his whip.

The men, their blood heated by the ale and the thought of the woman they would soon be allowed to ravish, began cheering him on.

"Teach 'er a lesson, Captain."

"Take her. And then it'll be our turn."

"Aye, Captain. Hurry. Take 'er now."

Sledge shoved back his chair, sending it crashing against the wall, then leapt onto the table, facing Ambrosia. On his lips was a smile of pure evil. "Now, woman, I'm going to teach you a lesson you won't soon forget."

Ambrosia saw Riordan drag himself through the narrow window. The sight of all that blood had her heart turning over in her chest. The pain must be unbearable. But he'd come back for her. And she mustn't fail him now.

She could see that he needed time to get to his feet and take aim with his knife. And that meant that she needed to keep the pirates' attention focused on her.

"You keep calling me woman. Wouldn't you like to know my name?"

Eli's eyes narrowed. "Why should that matter to me?"

"Because you know my family. My father." She absorbed the first sudden burst of pain and forced herself to speak, even though her heart was breaking. "My brother."

"I know them?"

"Aye. My name is Ambrosia Lambert. You killed my father, John, and my brother, James."

"Lambert." Eli Sledge raised his arm and snapped back the whip. "Oh, this is perfect. I enjoyed killing Captain John Lambert and his son. Loyal to the bloody king, they were. But I'm going to especially enjoy what I do to you. By the time I'm through with you, you'll be begging me—"

His words ended abruptly. His eyes went wide. His body stiffened, before slumping over and toppling to the floor.

It took several seconds before the shocked onlookers realized that he had a knife protruding from his back.

In the confusion, Ambrosia leapt from table to table, over the heads of the crowd that had gathered around their captain. When she reached Riordan's side, he was leaning weakly against the wall. It had taken all of his strength and concentration to aim the knife and toss it with such accuracy.

"Come, love." Though he was barely hanging on, he caught her hand and yanked her through a doorway.

"Nay." She stopped and turned back.

"What are you doing? Don't you understand that at any moment that angry mob will be coming for us?"

"Aye. But I'm not finished with them yet."

She picked up a torch from along the wall and held it

to a wooden table. She was rewarded by a thin flame dancing along the tabletop, flaring into bursts of fire whenever it encountered spilled spirits. In no time the fire was spreading from table to table, and picking up speed as it did.

She reached into the pocket of her gown and tossed a handful of gunpowder, adding to the display.

"Fire!" someone shouted.

As the shouts went up, the tavern became a place of pandemonium.

"Now we must run," Riordan called, catching her hand.

But once again Ambrosia defied him. "Nay. There's one more thing we must do, love."

Outside the tavern he leaned weakly against the trunk of a tree, wondering how much longer he could remain conscious. "And what is that, Ambrosia?"

"The gold." Before he could stop her, she dashed through a doorway, returning a few minutes later dragging the heavy cask.

"How do you intend to get that to the ship?"

"I'll find a way." She disappeared into the darkness, returning minutes later leading a horse and cart.

It took both of them, struggling beneath the weight of it, to load the cask aboard the cart. As soon as it was secure, she helped Riordan into the back, then climbed up and flicked the reins. The horse started off at a slow trot.

The streets of Cairn were filled with people rushing to put out the fire in the tavern before it spread to other buildings. No one noticed a horse and cart heading toward the harbor.

Once there, Ambrosia ran off in search of a skiff. Spying one on the beach, she raced toward it, only to see that a man was seated inside.

Before she could duck out of sight the man spotted her. She saw him stand up. In his hand was something shiny. She braced herself for what was to come.

Instead she was surprised to hear a familiar voice call, "Ambrosia. Is that ye, lass?"

"Newton." She let out a long, slow breath. "Oh, Newton, praise heaven."

She caught his hand and led him to where Riordan lay in the back of the cart, his breathing shallow, his body bathed in sweat.

"We must get him into the skiff at once, Newt."

"Aye, lass." The old sailor eased Riordan from the cart, then helped him across the beach until he was lying in the skiff.

When he turned he saw Ambrosia dragging the cask across the sand.

"What's this, lass?"

"The gold, Newt. Now we must hurry. They'll be on us in no time."

Nerves had them fumbling as they struggled to load the cask aboard the skiff. As the old man picked up the oars and began rowing, they could hear the sound of voices coming closer. The voices of an angry mob.

"How long have you been there, Newt?" Riordan asked.

"All night, Cap'n. I knew I'd have to leave ye if ye and the lass weren't here by dawn. But until then, I was determined to wait and watch." And pray, he thought. In the long, lonely hours of the night, he'd prayed as he'd never prayed before.

He was grateful that he'd never have to find out

whether or not he'd have had the courage to leave without them.

By the time they reached the *Skull*, the others were there to help them aboard. And as boats were being launched from the harbor by angry pirates, Ambrosia and her sisters hoisted the *Skull*'s sails and watched from the rigging as flames seemed to engulf the entire town of Cairn.

Chapter Seventeen

Ambrosia stood by the rail of the *Skull,* watching the feverish activity on shore. It was obvious that the pirates were torn between their need to battle the fires that engulfed the town and their need to go after the thieves who had stolen their ship. Some had already launched smaller boats and were trailing the wake of the *Skull.* They could be spotted easily by the long line of torches that marked their progress in the predawn mist.

Geoffrey Lambert turned to Riordan. "Setting fire to the town was an inspired move, lad."

Riordan managed a smile, despite his pain. "It wasn't my doing, Geoffrey. It was your granddaughter's decision."

"I should have known." The old man drew an arm around Ambrosia and pressed a kiss to her forehead. "I've never known you to do things by half measure, Ambrosia. Now tell us where you've been and how you came by the pirates' gold."

"I will, Grandpapa." She turned to Riordan, who was clinging to the rail with a death grip, as though afraid he might fall if he let go for even a moment. "But first, we must see to these wounds."

"And what about yours?" Her grandfather touched a finger to the angry red welts around her throat and saw her wince.

"Aye. I'll see to these as well."

Geoffrey turned to Newton. "We'll take them below to the captain's cabin."

"But that's yours, Grandpapa."

"Hush, lass." He gave her a tender smile. "I'd much prefer to sleep in a hammock, the way I did when I was a lad. I'm feeling that way now. Like a young lad, out on my first adventure at sea." He breathed deeply. "Now that we're safely aboard ship, I'm finding this...invigorating."

He put a hand beneath Riordan's elbow and assisted him belowdecks. Then he opened the cabin door and stepped aside. "See to your wounds, and then you and the lass must get some sleep."

Before they could offer a protest, he was gone. Humming a sailor's tune he'd learned as a lad.

Riordan crossed to the bunk and sat, drawing Ambrosia down beside him.

She touched a hand to his fevered brow. "You need an opiate for the pain, Riordan."

He shook his head. "You're all the opiate I need, love. To think that you risked everything to come back for me." He shook his head in wonder. "And then, when I thought I'd lost you to that monster..." He stopped for a moment and waited for his heartbeat to settle. "It was the hardest thing I've ever endured, to watch you in that den of cutthroats, alone. It tore at my heart to see what you had to go through. I knew then that I'd find a way to save you, or die trying." He framed her face with his hands and stared deeply into her eyes. "Do you know how truly amazing you are? Ambrosia, my love, you simply take my breath away. I've never known a woman like you. I feel so…'' He couldn't find the words. And so he drew her gently into his arms and told her, with the softest of kisses, all that was in his heart.

She started to pull back. ''Riordan, your wounds—''

''Shh. This is more important.'' He lay down and gathered her against him. And without another word, they fell into an exhausted sleep.

It was late afternoon when Ambrosia and Riordan made their way topside. They had bathed away the blood and grime, and had changed into fresh clothes.

''Well now.'' Geoffrey looked up from the wheel. ''You two are looking almost human again.''

''And feeling the same way,'' Riordan said with a smile. He glanced around. ''How many ships are trailing us?''

''Three or four that we've counted,'' Mistress Coffey said.

''But they're much smaller than this pirate vessel, and not nearly as well fortified,'' Winifred Mellon put in. ''Did you know there are four cannons aboard, as well as an arsenal of swords and dueling pistols?''

''Aye.'' Riordan couldn't help smiling at the note of enthusiasm in both women's voices. As though they were thoroughly enjoying themselves. ''As you'll recall, Miss Mellon, the poor *Sea Challenge* felt the full force of those cannons.''

Geoffrey Lambert gave a relaxed smile. ''I doubt those boats following us can overtake us. Especially now that we've got a fresh wind behind us. We should make London by nightfall.''

''Will the king be terribly disappointed in us for losing most of the gold to those pirates?'' Darcy asked.

Riordan smiled at the lass. She and her sisters had been through so much. But like their grandfather, they seemed to be thriving on the danger. As were their two elderly companions. "King Charles will be angry, but not at us. We did our best against the invaders. And, thanks to your sister, we still have one cask of gold."

"However did you manage that, Ambrosia?" Bethany asked.

"I don't know." She shook her head, sending dark curls tumbling around her face in a most appealing way. "I was so angry. I didn't think it was at all proper that those cutthroats should be rewarded for their cruelty. I think it was my anger that gave me the strength to do those things. Setting the fire. Retrieving the gold. Stealing a horse and cart."

"You did all that?" Bethany asked with sudden attention. "I wish I'd have been there."

"Aye." Darcy clapped her hands. "You must tell us everything, Ambrosia."

Her grandfather nodded. "I quite agree. You've a tale to tell, and we want to hear every detail of it."

"I will. I promise." She kissed his cheek. "Perhaps this evening. When we take our meal on deck. For now, I intend to climb the rigging and check on the boats that follow us."

With her sisters right behind her, Ambrosia made her way to the very top of the rigging, where she studied the horizon.

Below, Geoffrey Lambert studied the young man beside him, seeing a look on his face that left no doubt of his true feelings.

"You have an amazing granddaughter, Geoffrey."

"Aye, lad."

"I wouldn't be here if it weren't for her."

"According to Ambrosia, you saved her life as well."
He offered his hand. "And for that, I am forever in your
debt."

The two men shook hands solemnly. Then Riordan
crossed the deck and relieved Newton at the wheel. As
he faced into the breeze, and felt the deck of the ship
beneath his feet, he found himself thinking of what he'd
nearly lost. And of all he'd gained.

He glanced skyward and watched Ambrosia and her
sisters laughing as they worked among the rigging. Then
he turned to where two old men leaned on the rail and
talked of younger days and seagoing adventures. Seated
nearby were two elderly women, heads bent close, reliv-
ing every moment of their hair-raising escape with a
sense of pride and accomplishment.

This day was truly a gift. A gift to be savored. And
this night, if all went well, they would be in London.

"Oh." Ambrosia pricked her finger with a needle, and
frowned as a tiny drop of blood stained the cloth on
which she and her sisters were frantically sewing. Then
she jumped up. "You know I'm no good at needlework,
Winnie. I always hated it."

"Aye, my girl. That you did. But when it came to
climbing and jumping, you were a most apt pupil."

Bethany tossed aside the cloth she'd been working on
and stomped her foot in frustration. "Why are we bothering with this? Nobody will recognize it anyway."

"Why are we bothering? Because this is a pirate
ship." Winifred Mellon reverted to her stern nursemaid's
tone that she'd used with such effect throughout her lifetime. "Do you want someone in London to shoot at us?"

Riordan strolled on deck and paused to peer over her
shoulder. "What's this?"

"The English flag." Ambrosia caught the doubtful look on his face. "At least that's what we were trying to sew. But none of us has any skill in needlework except Winnie."

"Did you hope to fly that?" He shot her an incredulous look.

"Aye. It's only right." The old woman began correcting the mistakes of her pupils. Before she was finished, it would, by heaven, resemble a proper English flag. "We're approaching London with cargo bound for the king. If we don't fly our colors, we'll not be welcome. In fact, we could be the object of cannon fire. After all, this is a pirate ship."

Riordan swallowed back his smile and left them to their work. It wouldn't do to tell them that he carried a flag from King Charles himself. A flag that would open any door in London.

As daylight drifted into evening, and the *Skull* floated up the Thames, they could see the lights of the city looming ahead. The sight of it stirred their hearts. For though they loved their home in Cornwall more than anywhere on earth, this was a special place. The king of England was in residence here. And all loyal subjects felt the honor of his presence.

Ambrosia turned from the rail. "How will you know where to go when we dock, Riordan? The king has so many palaces."

"Aye. But his favorites are Hampton Court and St. James Palace. I know that he ofttimes keeps his mistresses at Whitehall, but that palace has such sad memories for him, since it was there that his father, Charles I, stepped to the scaffold to be hanged."

Ambrosia thought of the death of her own father, and felt a kinship with the king. He'd been a mere lad when he was forced to watch his father's hanging. What would that do to the child, and to the man he'd become?

A short time later, as the *Skull* moved up the Thames, Riordan pointed. "Seeing no banners here, I'm inclined to believe the king is in residence at Hampton Court."

Ambrosia gazed into the distance. "And you'll have to go there and explain how we lost the cargo bound for him."

"Aye." He closed his hand over hers at the rail as the sails were lowered and Newton smoothly guided the ship to its mooring.

"Must you go to him right away?"

"As quickly as possible. But first, I'll take you to my town house in London."

"You have a home here?" It occurred to her that Riordan had never spoken of his possessions. Except for Edwina's gossip, which he had admitted was true, she knew nothing of his past. He was a man of complete mystery. But there was no time for further questions as they engaged in the activities of disembarking.

Riordan led the way from the boat and hired a carriage. While they were being seated, he handed several scrolled missives to a messenger and handed him some money. Then he pulled himself up to sit beside Ambrosia. As they rolled through the streets, they found themselves staring at a vast array of fascinating people. Elegant carriages bearing beautifully dressed ladies and their equally well-dressed gentlemen. Vendors haggling with ladies' maids and housekeepers. Beggars on street corners calling for alms from those who hurried by. There were shopgirls in long dark skirts and shirtwaists, and dandies in satin breeches and brightly plumed hats. And dark-skinned men who wore ornate headdresses, and their exotic women in slender, body-skimming gowns. There were visitors from India, Spain and even the Orient.

"I haven't been in London since I was a girl," Miss Mellon said wistfully. "I'd forgotten how fascinating it is."

"Aye." Mistress Coffey breathed in the fragrances of tea and spices brought by ships from far-off lands. "And how exotic it can be."

"And how dirty." Geoffrey wrinkled his nose at the mass of humanity and animals crowded together in the streets, all fighting for the right to move.

Ambrosia felt the press of Riordan's shoulder to hers. There had been so little time to be alone. "Will you wait until morning to go to the king? Or will you see him tonight?"

"Tonight. As soon as I've had time to bathe and dress. Speaking of dressing…" He looked down at himself, in tattered breeches and a stained coat. "Do you think I ought to change before visiting the king?"

"I should certainly hope so." Miss Mellon wrinkled her nose with disdain.

Ambrosia saw the quick smile on Riordan's face and knew that he'd been having fun with them. He shouted orders to their driver to stop in Bond Street.

Outside a shop they waited while Riordan stepped inside, inviting Geoffrey and Newton to join him. A short time later a young clerk walked out and lashed several bulging packages to the back of the carriage.

When the three men returned to the carriage, they were grinning like conspirators. But all Riordan said was, "I suppose you ladies would like to buy some clothes, since all your trunks were lost aboard the *Sea Challenge*."

"But we brought no money," Ambrosia protested.

He arched a brow. "We could help ourselves to some of the king's gold."

"We couldn't." The women looked outraged at his suggestion.

Riordan burst into laughter. "Put your mind at ease, ladies. My credit is still good in London."

They made several more stops, at dressmakers' and milliners', adding more packages to the growing pile, before leaving the bustling city behind.

Soon they entered a lovely green park and rolled to a stop before a graceful manor house. Ambrosia glanced at Riordan's face. If he felt any pleasure at being home, he gave no sign.

They were helped from the carriage and welcomed by a housekeeper named Mistress Davis, who sent a team of servants scurrying in every direction, preparing rooms and baths, tea for the ladies, ale for the gentlemen.

"What about a meal, Captain Spencer?" Mistress Davis asked.

Ambrosia spoke for all of them. "It's so late, and we're so weary, we would rather bathe and retire, if you don't mind, Riordan."

At his nod of agreement, the housekeeper hurried away, relieved that she wouldn't have to see to a meal in the formal dining room. Instead, trays were dispatched to the various rooms and suites. Within the hour, the house had grown quiet, and many of the servants retired, knowing their guests were already tucked into their beds.

In her room Ambrosia sat by the fire, feeling warm and content. The only thing that would have made the night perfect would have been Riordan by her side. But the thought of him supping with the king had her smiling dreamily. What would he and the king talk about? How could anyone actually talk to the king of England? She tried to picture in her mind the Riordan Spencer she knew, visiting with the king.

The Riordan Spencer she knew. That made no sense. For she didn't know him. Not really. All she knew was that he was good and kind and decent, and that he had seen her and her family through a difficult time, without once entertaining a thought of deserting them.

She heard the door open, and turned, expecting to see the maid. Instead, Riordan closed the door, then leaned against it, looking at her in a way that had her heart stuttering.

He was dressed all in black. An elegant black waist-coat. Black breeches tucked into black boots. His dark hair still glistening with droplets of water from his bath. He looked as she'd first seen him. A dark, mysterious stranger.

She got to her feet and took a step toward him. "I thought you were with the king."

"I must leave for the palace now. But I had to see you before I left." He remained where he was, drinking in the sight of her. Her hair had been washed and scented, and hung down her back in a riot of damp tangles. She was wearing one of the ivory nightshifts purchased at a dressmaker's. The soft fabric revealed every line and curve of her body in a way that had his throat going dry. "You looked so pensive when I came in. What were you thinking, Ambrosia?"

She smiled shyly. "That I know so little about you, Riordan."

"You know that I love you. Isn't that enough?"

"Oh, aye." She walked closer, and the hem of her nightgown fluttered around her ankles.

He remembered the first time he'd seen her bare toes peeking from beneath the hem of her nightshift. She'd been on her way to her room. And he'd wanted, more than anything in the world, to take her into his arms and ravish her. He wanted the same thing now.

"How long will you have to stay with the king?"

"That is entirely up to Charles. Whether an hour, a day or a week, his wish is my command."

A week? The thought struck fear in her heart. She and her family couldn't possibly remain in London for a week. They would have to start home to Cornwall within a day or two. Would she get to see him again before she left?

She forced the thought aside.

She touched a hand to his cheek in a gesture so sweet, he sucked in a breath. "I'll miss you, Riordan."

"And I'll miss you. I wish…"

When he paused, she looked up at him. "What do you wish?"

"That I could just stay here and love you all night. And all through tomorrow. And tomorrow night…"

She laughed. "But would we get any sleep?"

"Nay. None. But what we would have would be far more healing than sleep." He gathered her against him and pressed his lips to a tangle of hair at her temple. "Oh, Ambrosia. Do you know how afraid I was when I saw you in that tavern?"

"Aye. As frightened as I was when you were sent into the sea, wounded and unconscious. I thought my poor heart would never beat again."

"Promise me you'll never put me through that again, love."

She drew a little away, staring up into his eyes. "Only if you'll make me the same promise."

He gave a long, slow sigh that might have been anger or despair. Then he caught her by the chin and lifted her

face for his kiss. His gaze swept her, taking in the spill
of dark hair, the haughty upturned nose, the pouting lips.
And then he caught sight of the huge discolored welts
that marred her beautiful throat.

"Oh, love. I can't bear the thought of the pain this
must have caused." The words were torn from his lips
as he pressed soft, tender kisses to each bruise.

"It's all right, Riordan. Now that we're safe, I've already forgotten the pain."

But he never would forget, he vowed. Not until all
those guilty of inflicting this pain were punished.

The anger dissipated as he found her lips, and heat
spread through his veins. He lingered over her mouth,
loving the sweet, clean taste of her. Then he dragged her
closer and kissed her until they were both trembling.

"I wish I didn't have to go, but I must. You understand, don't you?"

"Aye." She took a deep, steadying breath.

They heard the sound of a carriage, and the call of the
housekeeper belowstairs.

"One minute more," he whispered, gathering Ambrosia tightly in his arms and brushing her lips with his. The
heat grew, spread, until it threatened to become an inferno.

He lifted his head. "Now I really must go. The king
awaits me."

"Aye. You must, Riordan."

He turned away, then swore and turned back, kissing
her again. This time he allowed his hands to move along
her back, lighting fires with every touch.

Their breathing grew harsh and ragged.

"Captain Spencer." Mistress Davis shouted from the
foot of the stairs. "Your carriage is here."

He swore. And kissed Ambrosia one last time. Then

he turned and opened the door, striding out before he could change his mind.

The door was firmly closed. His footsteps sounded on the stairs.

Ambrosia rushed across the room to the window and watched as Riordan stepped into the carriage. As it pulled away he glanced up to her window and lifted a hand in a salute.

And then he was gone. There was only silence as Ambrosia made her way to her bed. And as she climbed between the covers, she could still taste him on her lips. But what she wanted, more than anything else, was to have him here in her arms. In her bed. In her life.

Chapter Eighteen

"Good morrow." Ambrosia walked into the dining room of Riordan's town house, where the others had assembled to break their fast.

They were all there, looking refreshed, and none the worse for their recent ordeal.

"How did you sleep, my dear?" Geoffrey Lambert stood and kissed her cheek, then held her chair.

"Quite well. Though I must admit, I missed the swaying of the hammock."

The old man caught Newton's eye. "Spoken like a true seaman, eh, Newt?"

"Aye, sir."

Ambrosia didn't bother to add that she'd missed Riordan even more. Somehow she'd hoped he would return during the night and slip into her room. But she'd awoken this morning to find herself alone. And so lonely.

Riordan's housekeeper, Mistress Davis, bustled in, followed by several servants, who began to serve the meal.

"Have you heard from Captain Spencer?" Ambrosia asked her.

"Nay. But then, it's quite common for the captain to be gone for months at a time without leaving word."

Ambrosia clasped her hands together in her lap, trying not to think about the implications of what she'd just heard. Months. She couldn't bear the thought of not seeing Riordan for days. What would it be like to be without him for months?

Hearing a knock on the door, the housekeeper hurried off to answer it.

Minutes later she returned, holding out a scroll. "This missive came for you, Miss Lambert."

"It…bears the royal seal." Ambrosia stared at it for several minutes before she could summon the courage to unroll it.

When she'd finished reading she looked up. "We have been summoned to Hampton Court Palace, to visit the king."

The others stared at her in disbelief.

She handed it to her old nurse. "Go ahead, Winnie. Read it for yourself."

Miss Mellon read, then nodded toward the others. "It is as Ambrosia said. We're…" She burst into tears. "Oh, dear heaven. We're invited to visit the king."

The town house was the scene of chaos, as five women prepared for the most amazing day of their lives.

There were gowns to decide upon, as well as shawls, gossamer petticoats, dainty kid boots and bonnets. They fretted over their hair, their skin, especially their faces, which were no longer pale as English roses, but instead had caught the bloom of the sun and wind on their voyage. They worried over what they would say, how they would curtsy, whether or not they would embarrass themselves in front of the vast assembly that was part of the king's daily life.

While the others walked around in a daze, Ambrosia

was infused with new energy. She would see Riordan. Nothing else mattered. Not even the thought of seeing the king. Besides, she told herself, they would be lost in a sea of faces. From what she'd heard, there were often as many as two and three hundred people gathered in the public rooms of the palace. Who would notice them?

When the five women finally gathered in the parlor, they were delighted to find Geoffrey Lambert looking like the most distinguished gentleman they'd ever seen in fashionable satin breeches and a dark waistcoat.

Even Newton was fitted out in a waistcoat and dark breeches. But though he was dressed like a gentleman, he still moved like one who had spent his life aboard ship. And though he'd been offered a new pair of shoes, he refused, saying that since he had only one foot, it would be a waste of good money.

By the time the carriage arrived for the journey to Hampton Court, nerves were at a fever pitch.

Mistress Coffey was wearing a fashionable gown of black, with a lovely lace shawl embroidered with flowers and leaves on a black background.

Miss Mellon was dressed all in white. White gown, white shawl, her white hair looking as soft as down. Even her skin was as pale as a ghost, and they all feared she might take one of her spells.

Bethany, with her fiery hair and green eyes, had chosen a gown of emerald satin, with a daringly low neckline and long tapered sleeves, guaranteed to draw the attention of every man in the palace from four to four score.

Darcy had chosen watered silk, the color of sapphires to match her eyes. The gown was simple, with a rounded neckline that fell off the shoulders, and puffed sleeves inset with lace. The look was as innocent and demure as the young lady who wore it.

Ambrosia's gown was red velvet with a high, ruffled neckline that hid the angry welts still marring her throat. The skirt was full, the sleeves long and tapered, with points that fluttered over the backs of her hands. With her dark ringlets swept to one side, spilling over her breast, she looked every bit a fashionable London lady.

Seeing their high spirits, Geoffrey Lambert cleared his throat. "My dear ladies, I feel very fortunate to be accompanying the loveliest of England's flowers to visit their king."

"Oh, Grandpapa." His granddaughters smiled and twisted their hands in their laps, eager for the carriage ride to end.

But one among them was even more anxious than the rest, Geoffrey thought as he watched Ambrosia. And he had a pretty good idea why. She was missing her sea captain. He hoped Riordan Spencer was missing her as well.

The carriage started up the long, curving road that led to Hampton Court Palace. The roadway was lined with the king's own soldiers, resplendent in their crimson-and-gold tunics, their swords at the ready.

Everywhere they looked, their party saw signs of regal splendor. The gardens, bursting with color. The fountains. The palace itself, which was favored by the king not only for its beauty and parklike setting, but for its country air.

As they came to a halt, a liveried aide stepped forward to assist them from their carriage. They were led inside, past milling throngs of people.

Ambrosia and the others could only stare at the titled men and their ladies who filled the halls.

"So many," Darcy said, slipping her hand into Ambrosia's for courage.

"Aye. Who are they, Grandpapa?"

"People here to petition the king for a favor. People here to redress a wrong. And many more, I suspect, who simply want an opportunity to see the king and be seen by others." He winked. "After all, where can the titled nobility of England go to display their power except where all the other titled nobility will see them?"

"You mean they simply spend all day standing about, hoping to be seen by others, Grandpapa?" Darcy's mouth dropped open.

"I would think so. At least whenever the king is in residence. And it looks as though we'll no doubt do the same."

No sooner were the words out of his mouth than they heard a shrill voice behind them.

"However did you get in here?" Edwina Cannon and her mother hurried over, looking more than a little flustered to find their country neighbors from Land's End in such a grand place.

Before any of them could answer her, she beckoned to Silas Fenwick, who stood to one side, talking in hushed tones to several other important-looking gentlemen. "Silas. Come quickly. Look who's here."

When he caught sight of the Lambert family, his eyes widened. He turned away from the others and hurried over. "How did your day of sailing become a journey to London?" Though his words were spoken softly enough, there was frost in his eyes.

"We were having such a grand time." Geoffrey Lambert smiled. "It seemed a shame to turn back until we'd seen London. And once here, we were summoned to the palace."

Edwina turned to Silas with a pout. "I thought you said only the titled could enjoy the privilege of seeing the king."

"Aye." He patted her hand. But his gaze was fixed on Ambrosia, who stood beside her grandfather. "And it's true. Except in special cases." He turned to Geoffrey. "Perhaps you're in some trouble, Captain Lambert. You were summoned, you say?"

When the old man nodded, Silas's smile grew. "The king enjoys humiliating his enemies in front of the crowds. It makes a fine spectacle."

He saw that his words had the desired effect. Ambrosia closed a hand around the old man's arm. Her sisters crowded closer together. The two old ladies looked as though they would drop in a faint at any moment.

"I have considerable influence with Charles. Perhaps, if he is grievously offended, I may be able to temper his justice, which is ofttimes harsh." Silas offered one arm to Edwina, the other to her mother. "Come, ladies. As special guests of His Majesty, we have seats in the gallery."

As he led them off, Edwina turned for a last glimpse of Ambrosia and her sisters. Then she gave a triumphant little laugh and tossed her head as she moved away.

"I'd like to strangle that little twit," Ambrosia muttered.

"You must stop that," Winifred Mellon whispered fiercely. "I raised you to hold your tongue and behave like a lady."

"Aye, Winnie. You did. But you also taught me it wasn't possible to make a rose from a thorn."

Ambrosia caught her grandfather's arm. "Please, Grandpapa. Can't we leave before we're called upon for public humiliation?"

"Nay, child. We'll simply have to show these people that Lamberts can take whatever life hands them. Even at the hands of our beloved king. Now stand tall and proud, and show them what we're made of."

Just then a hush fell over the room as a dozen or more robed figures entered the great hall and took their places on a raised dais. A moment later another robed figure pounded a staff on the floor and announced the arrival of the king.

Every man in the room bowed his head, while every woman curtsied. They kept their gazes averted until the king ascended the throne. But even when they straightened, nobody spoke. Nobody coughed. Not a sound could be heard throughout the great hall.

Ambrosia felt herself trembling. It didn't seem possible that she was actually here, in the presence of the king. As she glanced at the others, she knew their reaction was the same. Her sisters were staring at the regal figure, afraid to even blink. Mistress Coffey had a glazed look in her eyes, as though she was in a daze. And poor old Winnie was weeping into her handkerchief, she was so overcome.

The king whispered to one of his aides, who straightened and called in a loud voice, "Will Captain Geoffrey Lambert and his party step forward."

"Grand...Grandpapa." Ambrosia was clutching his arm so tightly she was nearly cutting off his circulation. But he gently patted her hand, then led her and the others forward.

As she passed Edwina, she heard her giggle and whisper loudly, "Now they'll wish they'd stayed in Cornwall where they belong."

Ambrosia caught sight of Silas Fenwick's face. He had the satisfied smile of the devil himself.

Geoffrey Lambert and his party paused.

"I am Captain Lambert," he said in a loud, clear voice.

"Come forward and pay homage to your king."

With halting steps the entire party moved toward the figure seated on the throne.

The closer they got, the more regal he appeared. King Charles was younger than Ambrosia had anticipated. And far more dashing, with a handsome, poet's face, swarthy complexion and long dark hair curling over the crimson tunic and the lush crimson cloak he'd tossed rakishly over one shoulder.

When they reached the steps to the dais, they paused. While Geoffrey and old Newton bowed, the women curtsied.

"Arise, Captain Lambert." The king's voice was deep and commanding. "I would meet your family."

"Aye, Majesty." Geoffrey stepped back, allowing his three granddaughters to stand alone. "These are my granddaughters. Ambrosia, Bethany and Darcy."

As the three young women curtsied and blushed, the king studied them carefully, his gaze lingering a moment longer on the dark-haired beauty in the scarlet gown.

"This is their nurse, Miss Winifred Mellon. And our housekeeper, Mistress Mary Coffey. And this is Newton Findlay, my first mate when I sailed the Atlantic."

"So." The king stared around the room, seeing the way the crowd seemed to be holding its collective breath.

He so loved the pomp and ceremony. The drama. Because it had been snatched from him at an early age, with the public execution of his father, and he'd been forced to spend half his life in exile, it seemed all the sweeter now. He savored the power. And so he drew out the moment, until he could almost feel the tension vibrating in the great hall.

His voice rang out, reaching even the farthest corners of the room. ''There was a certain cargo aboard the *Dover,* which was transferred to the *Undaunted.* A ship that belongs to your family, does it not, Captain Lambert?''

''Aye, Majesty.'' Geoffrey felt Ambrosia's hand slip into his.

''That cargo was later transferred to another of your ships, the *Sea Challenge.* Is that not so, Captain?''

''Aye, Majesty.'' He looked down to see Ambrosia's fingers squeezing his so tightly he had to pry them loose to get the feeling back.

''I am told the *Sea Challenge* was attacked by pirates, who captured all of this assembled family, and claimed that cargo for themselves.''

A murmur went up from the crowd, and many of the people strained to catch a better look at the people who had actually tasted the wrath of pirates.

King Charles lifted his voice, causing the crowd to grow silent once more. ''I am told further that, at great peril to your own lives, you not only escaped the pirates, but reclaimed as much of the cargo as you could carry, and escaped in the pirates' own ship.''

The murmur of voices grew louder. Many in the crowd got to their feet to stare at this remarkable family. Among them Edwina and her mother, and Silas, who watched and listened in brooding silence.

''Captain Lambert.'' For the first time Charles smiled. ''You will bring your family up here.''

''Up…?'' The old man couldn't seem to find any words as several armed guards came forward to assist them up the steps of the dais.

To the amazement of the entire crowd, the king

touched each of them on the shoulder as they stepped toward him and kissed his hand. Then he turned to the assembled and said loudly, "A grateful king thanks these noble people for the sacrifices they made on behalf of their country."

There was a moment's hesitation as the words sank in. Then the king's council began pounding their staffs on the wooden dais, and the people joined in with deafening applause.

Ambrosia turned to her grandfather and saw the look of stunned disbelief on his face. Tears welled in her eyes as she thought of the price he had paid for his country. He'd been injured a score of times, until he'd been forced to give up his great love—sailing. And then he'd made the ultimate sacrifice. He'd given a son and a grandson. Had been robbed of all his hopes for the future. But for this one bright shining moment, he could bask in the glow of love and gratitude from king and countrymen.

Ambrosia looked at the others and saw that they, too, were moved to tears. Bethany and Darcy were smiling and weeping. Mistress Coffey was biting hard on a trembling lower lip. Winnie was sobbing into her handkerchief. And even old Newt seemed to be struggling to hold back the flood of emotions.

The king allowed the outpouring of affection to continue for several thunderous minutes. Finally he held up his hands, signaling for silence.

"These good people will remain at my side, so that all might look upon the faces of those who have a grateful king's favor."

At once his councillors began making room for the Lambert family to be seated around him.

Charles caught Ambrosia's hand and leaned close to

whisper, "There is one who sends his regrets that he cannot be here to witness your proud moment."

"Riordan." Her eyes widened. "Where is he, Majesty?"

"That I cannot tell you. But this I can." He smiled. "I can see how such a rogue could lose his heart to you, my lady."

"He...told you that, Majesty?"

His laughter was quick and deep. "He did not have to. I could see it in his eyes. Just as I see it in yours."

She blushed and lowered her head. But then, just when her heart felt overflowing with happiness, he added, "I should warn you, Miss Lambert. Some rogues were never meant to put down roots. They thrive on danger. And would wither and die without it. I believe Riordan Spencer is such a man. Even now, without a word of protest, he has accepted a mission from his king that could cost him his life."

Ambrosia sat through the rest of the afternoon in a state of shock. She neither saw nor heard the parade of petitioners who appeared before the king and his council. She was oblivious to the pomp and ceremony that surrounded the throne. She neither saw nor cared about the fact that Silas had left the hall in a rage, leaving Edwina and her mother alone.

All she could think of was Riordan, putting himself once more in danger.

He could be dead, and she would never have the opportunity to tell him all the things that were in her heart.

Dead. She shook off the attack of nerves that shuddered through her. Nay. He wasn't dead. She would know it. Her heart would somehow sense it. It wouldn't be possible to calmly sit here, feeling nothing, if Riordan

Spencer were dead. For surely her own heart would cease beating as well.

Ambrosia glanced around in a daze and noted that everyone was on their feet, bowing, curtsying, as the king swept from the room.

"Come, Ambrosia." Her grandfather offered his arm.

"Where, Grandpapa?"

He smiled. "Where have you been, lass? The king has invited us to join him in his private chambers. It is the highest of honors that he could have bestowed upon us. We are to sup with the king of England."

She saw the way her sisters were giggling and the two old women were beaming.

And then another thought struck. Perhaps Riordan would return to join them. And if not, perhaps the king could be persuaded to tell her where Riordan had gone.

Aye. If she could find her voice when in the presence of the king, she would dare to ask. For the sake of her poor, aching heart.

Chapter Nineteen

Ambrosia put on her brightest smile as a liveried gentleman said, "Would you follow me, please?"

They were taken to a withdrawing room, where a fire burned on the hearth, and elegant chairs were drawn up in a circle around it.

A servant entered, offering tea or ale and a tray of pastries and cheese.

Eventually others began to enter. Elegant lords and their ladies. A Frenchman and a Spaniard, who seemed to switch from English to their native tongues without catching a breath. A cardinal and his assistant. Several of the king's council. And all came up to congratulate Geoffrey Lambert and his family on their extraordinary adventure.

Each time the door opened, Ambrosia's head came up and she stared hungrily until, catching sight of another stranger, disappointment would wash over her and she would return her attention to her tea.

Seeing her distress, Newton leaned close. "Ye mustn't worry, lass. He'll be along."

She tried to smile, but her lips trembled. "The king said he has sent Riordan on a dangerous mission."

"It wouldn't be the first, I'd wager." He patted her hand. "Nor will it be the last."

"But I can't bear worrying about him, Newt."

"That's part of loving, lass. Worrying. Wondering."

With sudden insight she gave him a long, speculative look. His words had been spoken with the intensity of one who knew of such things from personal experience. "Who was she, Newt?"

After a moment's hesitation he said, "A Welsh lass. The prettiest thing I'd ever seen. Sweet, she was. And a maiden when I met her. Her family were fishermen."

"Why didn't you marry?"

"She wanted me to give up sailing the world. She couldn't take the worry of it. She begged me to join her family as a fisherman. But I couldn't take the sameness of it."

"And just like that, you parted?"

"Aye. My ship was ready to sail. I wasn't about to be left behind."

"Did you ever see her again?"

"Once." He looked away. "After that same voyage, when I tangled with a shark and returned without my leg. I came to tell her I was ready to be a fisherman. But it was too late."

Ambrosia's voice lowered to a whisper. "You mean she wouldn't marry you because you'd lost a leg?"

"Nay, lass." He turned to her, and she saw the bleakness in his eyes. "If that had been the case, I could have accepted it. But it was worse. She admitted she still loved me. But she'd wed another. And was carrying his child."

"Oh, Newt." Ambrosia touched a hand to his arm.

"Remember this, lass." His voice was a fierce whisper. "Such love comes along but once. And if we waste the moment worrying about what the future might hold, we could have a lifetime to regret it.'' The old sailor lifted his ale and drained it, then went off to fetch another.

It was the first time he'd ever spoken aloud of his pain to anyone. And it still had the power to crush him. But if it helped the lass through this time, he figured it was worth it.

Rows of long wooden tables ran the length of the great serving hall. Long lines of people filed in and were led to their places at table according to their rank and importance. There were members of the royal family. Titled noblemen and their ladies. Foreign ambassadors, hoping to curry favor with the king. Men of the church. There was color and pageantry and spectacle. All the things Charles enjoyed.

Whenever the king was in residence, dinner at Hampton Court Palace was a splendid affair. What made it even more memorable for the Lambert party was the fact that the king insisted that they sit at his table, which was a level above all the others, so that everyone in the great hall could see and be seen by their monarch. That meant, of course, that they could also see every honored guest invited to sit with him.

''You'll sit on one side of me, Captain Lambert.'' The king turned to Ambrosia. ''And you'll sit on the other, Miss Lambert.''

''Aye, Majesty.'' Astonished to be singled out, she settled herself beside the king. Because she was feeling slightly overwhelmed, she kept her eyes downcast and spoke only when he spoke to her.

Keeping his voice low, Charles said, ''I should not have been surprised to hear of your family's heroism, my lady. For your father was one of my most loyal subjects.

What did surprise me was the missive signed by you and your sisters, offering to continue the work of your father.''

"You received our missive, Majesty?''

"Aye. And I was moved by it. I have never known a female privateer, let alone three. And each of you as lovely as the next. I was considering rejecting your kind offer, until I heard of your brave actions. Someone who…knows your family well assures me that you are all capable of serving your king. I feel I have no choice but to accept your kind offer.''

"Majesty.'' Ambrosia's eyes lit with pleasure. "You make us proud that we can serve you as our father before us.''

"Nay, my lady.'' He lifted her hand to his lips. "It is I who am proud yet humbled by your love and devotion.''

"Majesty.'' At the familiar voice Ambrosia looked up to see Silas Fenwick bowing before the king.

"Aye, Lord Fenwick.'' Charles looked annoyed. "What is it?''

Silas gave his best smile. "Since my betrothed and her mother are also from Cornwall, and are, in fact, dear friends of the Lambert family, I thought we might be invited to join them at your table.''

Charles, always one to admire a pretty face, looked at the young woman clinging to Fenwick's arm. "Aye, Lord Fenwick. Please join us.''

Edwina and her mother dropped a curtsy before being seated across from Ambrosia and the king, with Silas between them.

"So. You know each other?'' Charles smiled at Edwina.

"Oh, since we were children.'' Edwina's nerves had

her voice even higher than usual, making it sound like the bleating of a lamb. She blushed and giggled, and curled her fingers around Silas Fenwick's arm with a death grip that had him wincing.

The king turned to Ambrosia. "And you are best friends?"

Ambrosia glanced at Winifred Mellon and, seeing her warning look, gritted her teeth and tried an evasive tactic. "We all live in Land's End. Do you know it, Majesty?"

"Aye. I am most fond of Cornwall, even though its citizens often consider themselves other than English."

"We are fiercely English, Majesty." Ambrosia couldn't curb her tongue, even though she knew it was considered very improper to correct the king. "And fiercely loyal to Your Majesty. You will find no more loving subjects in all of England."

At her vehemence he smiled and placed a hand over hers, surprising the others around them. "It does your king's heart good to hear of such love and devotion, my dear. For so many years I was denied the love of my people after the…untimely death of my father."

"My sisters and I grieve your loss, Majesty. For we lost our father on his last voyage. As well as our beloved brother."

"I am aware of your loss, my dear." He looked into her eyes and felt a jolt. Unlike so many who mouthed the words, this young woman's pain, as well as her sympathy, were genuine, and deeply felt. He was more moved than he cared to admit.

"We are loyal to you, as well, Majesty." Edwina's high-pitched voice broke through his thoughts.

"I thank you, madam." He turned to study the young woman beside Silas. She seemed not at all his type. But perhaps Silas was growing weary of his wenching, and had decided to choose a woman more for her ability to give him offspring than for her ability to please him. Still, the thought of more than one with a voice like hers had him shuddering. Silas could find himself with a house full of shrill-voiced harpies.

Charles turned back to the woman beside him. Now this was a woman who would turn a man's head. His friend, Riordan Spencer, had chosen well. And, if he was correct, had fallen hard.

"Majesty." Silas leaned forward, hoping to hold the king's attention. "If I could speak of a matter that seems on everyone's mind these days."

"Aye. Speak, Lord Fenwick."

"It would seem that the pirates operating in England's waters are growing bolder. Attacking even those ships under Your Majesty's protection. Perhaps it is time to consider appointing a lord admiral, who would determine what ships would be permitted to carry cargo deemed necessary for the Crown."

"A lord admiral?" The king studied him. "And you think you should be lord admiral?"

"I have knowledge of shipping and cargo, Majesty."

"Ah yes. You inherited your grandfather's import company, I believe, Lord Fenwick."

"Aye, Majesty. And I can state with pride that the ships under my command have never lost a cargo to pirates." His tone deepened. "The same cannot be said by those privateers who claim to be Your Majesty's loyal friends."

Geoffrey Lambert's eyes flashed. "My son and grandson gave up their lives in service to their king. Do you demean the sacrifice they made, Lord Fenwick?"

"Nay." Though his lips curved in a smile, it didn't reach his eyes. "I am simply saying that England can no longer afford to lose precious cargo, especially when it is bound for the king's own purse. As lord admiral, I would take it upon myself to see that England's waters are purged of pirates. We would no longer have need of privateers who, though they see to the safety of England's seas, selfishly keep their bounty for themselves.''

The king appeared interested. ''I will consider what you have said. Then I shall arrange a meeting between you and my council, so that we may discuss this further, Lord Fenwick.'' He smiled. ''Or should I say, Lord Admiral?''

''I am most humbly grateful, Majesty.'' Silas looked smugly around the table. The deed was as good as done. And once he was put in charge, change would come swiftly. And the rest of his plan would fall into place.

His smile froze when he caught sight of the tall figure striding across the room.

''Riordan.'' Ambrosia's face was alight with excitement.

He looked so dashing. So handsome, he nearly took her breath away. For the space of a moment their gazes met and held.

Then he tore his gaze from Ambrosia and bowed deeply before the king. ''Forgive my tardiness, Majesty.''

''Not at all, my friend. I'm certain it couldn't be helped.'' Charles glanced around the table. ''Do you know everyone here?''

''Aye.'' Riordan's smile dissolved when he saw Silas seated across from the king. ''Forgive me, Majesty. But I have urgent news that must be shared with you immediately. In the privacy of your chambers.''

Charles gave a sigh and turned to Ambrosia. ''As you can see, a monarch's work is never done.'' He lifted her hand to his lips, then smiled at the others before pushing away from the table.

At once there was a great commotion as the crowd shoved back their chairs and got to their feet, bowing and curtsying as the king strode from the room, followed by a thoughtful, distracted Riordan Spencer.

As soon as they left the hall, the crowd grew more relaxed and more raucous. Except for Silas Fenwick, who suddenly slumped in his seat and wore a worried frown.

"It all fits, Majesty." When they reached the king's private chambers, Riordan was too restless to sit. And so he paced while the king settled himself in a comfortable chair and watched as a liveried servant poured two goblets of ale.

When the servant departed, Riordan turned. "I felt certain that no one else could have alerted the pirates about our cargo. But now I have the proof."

"You went to Cairn?"

"Nay. I couldn't show my face there." He smiled. "Not after the way Ambrosia decimated the town."

"Miss Lambert?"

"Aye." His smile grew. "Before taking her leave, she retrieved the cask of gold and burned down the tavern. And that in turn caused nearly half the town to burn as well."

Charles shook his head. "Who would have thought it of that gentle lady?"

"Gentle?" Riordan burst into laughter. "There is nothing gentle about Ambrosia. She can sail a ship better than any seaman I've ever seen. She can best most men in a swordfight. And woe to the man who tries to win an argument with her."

"I take it you've tried?"

"Aye. And lost miserably."

The two men chuckled.

"You've lost something else, I'd wager."

Riordan picked up his tumbler and looked at him.

"Your heart, my friend."

There was a moment's silence before Riordan nodded. "Completely."

Charles laughed. Then his laughter faded. "You're not thinking of something…permanent? Like marriage?"

"I am indeed," Riordan admitted. "God help me. Ever since I've met Ambrosia Lambert, I've been bewitched and befuddled."

Charles shook his head. "And to think I told the lass that you weren't the type to put down roots."

"You told her that?" Riordan's own smile faded. "Why?"

"Because the friend I've known for a lifetime would have never considered giving up his wandering ways for the sake of a woman. Any woman."

"Ambrosia isn't any woman. She's…" He shook his head in turn, lost for words. "She's simply the most amazing woman I've ever met."

"And you intend to marry her."

"Aye. If she'll have me."

Charles studied him with a look of astonishment. Then he set down his tankard. "Now about this other matter."

"Aye. I've looked into Silas Fenwick's financial affairs. The business he inherited is failing miserably. But more important than that is the fact that he has aligned himself with your cousin, Earl Humphrey Buckingham."

"Buckingham? Who covets the throne?"

"The same."

"You have proof?"

"Aye. I paid a call on your cousin." Riordan smiled.

"I had only to draw my sword, and he was eager to tell me anything I wanted to know."

"The sniveling little coward."

"Aye. He admitted plotting against the throne. He said that both he and Lord Fenwick were in need of a fresh infusion of gold, and quickly. What better way to acquire it than to steal it from the king, and then use it against him? It was Silas who murdered your representative in Land's End, in order to learn the name of the ship carrying the casks of gold."

Charles leaned forward. "And what better way to steal all the gold bound for England than to be the one in charge of assigning the cargo and the ships that will carry it."

"What are you saying?"

"Lord Fenwick very nearly persuaded me to appoint him lord admiral. He's a clever fellow. More clever than I'd given him credit for."

The two men fell silent.

Charles sighed. "I'll have him brought before the council on charges."

Riordan nodded. "You may want to move quickly. Once he hears that your cousin has admitted his guilt, he'll be eager to escape. My thought is that he'll seek refuge in France, since they have so little love for England's king."

Charles stood and clasped Riordan's hand. "Once again you've been a good and faithful friend. I cannot count the number of times you've saved my royal hide. Not to mention the throne. Do you know how grateful I am, Riordan?"

"Grateful enough that you're going to buy me a very expensive present for my wedding."

Charles threw back his head and roared with laughter.

"You'll have it. I'll give you something so extravagant that all of Cornwall will talk of nothing else for years to come." He sighed. "Go now. And kiss that lovely lady who has stolen your heart."

It was all the invitation Riordan needed. He drained his tankard and set it on the table. With a quick grin, he was gone.

Ambrosia lay in her bed, listening as the sounds of activity in the town house slowly settled into silence. She was relieved to finally be alone in her bedroom.

The excitement of Hampton Court had remained with their family for hours, keeping them talking and laughing long after they'd returned. For simple country people this had been an extraordinary day. One they would never forget.

Now, finally, their energy was beginning to drain away, leaving them eager to sleep. All except Ambrosia.

She was too keyed up to think about sleep. The sight of Riordan had stirred her heart as nothing else possibly could, not even dinner with the king.

Riordan would come to her, she knew. Whenever he finished his important discussion with the king, he would come. And she would be here waiting. No matter how late the hour. She closed her eyes. Not to sleep, she promised herself. Just to rest a few moments.

It was her last conscious thought before she drifted on a lovely cloud of contentment.

Ambrosia was dreaming. Riordan was coming for her. She could hear the faint crunch of carriage wheels on the path. Heard the sound of the door open and close, and the muted footfall on the stair.

She was smiling when the hand covered her mouth.

Dazed, confused, she struggled to sit up, but something sharp was pressed to her tender throat. She couldn't swallow. Couldn't breathe.

Her eyes flew open and she found herself staring up into the cruel eyes of Silas Fenwick. She clawed at the hand he held to her mouth, but it wouldn't budge.

"Not a word," he whispered. "Or I'll slit your pretty throat. Do you understand?"

Eyes wide with fear, she nodded.

Very carefully he removed his hand.

"What—" She started to speak, but he moved with lightning speed, pressing the knife to her throat until it drew blood.

She hissed in a breath.

"I told you not a word. You don't speak. You listen. And obey. Do you understand?"

She nodded.

"Get up out of bed."

She complied, feeling sullied by the way he studied her in her nightshift.

"Take this." He tossed a shawl at her.

She reacted instinctively. Instead of merely catching it, she tossed it into his face. Caught off guard, he wasn't prepared when she snatched up her pillow and heaved it at him, nearly knocking him over. As he regained his footing, she was already at the window, trying to climb out. He dragged her back, but she held on to the curtain, tearing it off the sash.

His hand swung out in a wide arc and he slapped her so hard her head snapped to one side. For a moment she saw stars. Then she bent and picked up one of her boots and caught him in the temple.

Enraged, he came at her. She reached for the gown and petticoats on a nearby chair and tossed them, cov-

ering his head. In his surprise he dropped the knife, and
she fell to the floor, hoping to retrieve it. The two scrambled and he gave a hiss of pain when she caught him in
his eye with an elbow. But before she could grasp the
knife, he wrapped an arm around her throat and began
choking her.

She rolled around the floor, dragging him with her. Desperate now, she struggled to breathe, but could feel herself
fading. Spots danced in front of her eyes, and she remembered the feel of Sledge's whip, wrapped around her
throat, squeezing the life from her. She stopped fighting.

In one smooth movement Silas released her and
snatched up the knife, while she lay panting, every breath
a fresh stab of pain.

"Now." He got to his feet. "You'll do as I tell you.
Or you'll die here, where your lover can find you." He
stood over her, his voice triumphant. "Get up. Without
a word."

Ambrosia struggled to her knees, then got slowly to
her feet.

"After that little scene, there'll be no shawl to ward
off the night's chill." He caught her by the arm and
dropped a scroll in the middle of the bed.

"A note for your lover," he said with a laugh as he
hauled her toward the door.

There were no servants around to see them. No family
members to hear them as they left. There was only the
silence of the house. And the rush of cool night air as
they made their way to his waiting carriage.

The town house was dark. That fact had Riordan smiling as he let himself in. He wouldn't have to bother with
polite talk, or Ambrosia's family, or dealing with servants. He could go directly to Ambrosia's room.

He unbuttoned his coat as he took the stairs two at a time. The thought of what awaited him had him nearly groaning with frustration.

He paused outside her door, then decided to dispense with knocking. She was probably asleep. He'd wake her gently. And they would make slow, delicious love all night long.

He opened the door and stepped into her room, closing it firmly behind him. The room was in darkness. The fire on the grate had burned to embers.

As he started across the room he stepped on something that nearly tripped him. Swearing softly, he peered through the darkness. It looked to be a boot. He stopped and touched it. Aye. A fine kid boot. One of Ambrosia's.

He glanced toward the bed. The bedcovers had been stripped away. The pillows were scattered, one at the foot of the bed, the other on the floor nearby.

Alarmed, he held a taper to the hot coals, then held it aloft and stared around the room. Clothes were scattered everywhere. The window curtain had been torn from the sash and lay in tatters on the floor.

He walked to the bed and lifted the taper. In the middle of the bed was a scrolled missive. He read the words and felt his blood freeze.

I have your woman. You can exchange
your life for hers. Come alone. S.F.

In a rage, Riordan crumpled the scroll in his fist and tossed it against the wall. Then, as he turned, he saw something that made his heart stop.

Blood. Drops of blood on the bedcovers.

Sweet heaven. Ambrosia was hurt. And in the clutches of a madman.

Chapter Twenty

Ambrosia was trembling violently. But she couldn't tell if it was from the night air or the fear of what was to come. Silas Fenwick whipped the team of horses and the carriage raced through the darkened streets of London.

Suddenly they veered from the street onto a curving ribbon of road that led to a magnificent estate. When they halted at the main entrance, Silas turned the team over to a sleepy-eyed stable lad and hauled Ambrosia roughly toward the door.

It was opened by an elderly butler who showed absolutely no emotion at the sight of his master holding tightly to the arm of a young lady clad in night clothes.

"You must help me," she shouted to the old man.

"Powell, you may go to bed now. I have no further need of your services this night."

"Aye, my lord." The old man refused to look at Ambrosia as he hastily turned away and shuffled up the stairs.

Silas had hold of her arm with such force it had gone numb. Now he dragged her toward a room down the hall, where he flung her, sending her sprawling. While she struggled to her feet, he closed and latched the door, then leaned against it and stood facing her.

"Why have you brought me here, Silas? What is this about?"

"It's about power, my dear Miss Lambert. And about revenge."

"I...don't understand."

"You and your family thought you were so clever, using your little scheme to transport the king's gold. Did you really think I wouldn't see through your simple ruse?"

"You?" She thought back to that moment before Riordan had lost consciousness. He'd been trying to warn her about something. "It was you who sent the pirate, Eli Sledge, after us?" She'd been so intent upon the battle, she'd overlooked the obvious.

Silas clenched his teeth. "The fool Sledge deserved to die if he couldn't even contain a party of old men and helpless women." His eyes narrowed. "And Captain Riordan Spencer."

Hearing the venom in his tone, she asked, "Why do you hate Riordan so?"

"Why? Because he represents everything I would have had, if my plan had succeeded."

"Your plan?"

"Aye. To replace Charles with his cousin, the earl of Buckingham. Then I would have been to the new king as Spencer is to Charles."

"As Riordan is to the king?" Ambrosia's eyes widened. "Are you saying that Riordan is not just a privateer?"

Fenwick threw back his head and laughed. "Is that what you think? That Riordan Spencer is a mere ship's captain? He is, by all accounts, one of the most powerful men in England. Without him, Charles would have never achieved his dream of becoming king." His voice lowered. "And Charles is extremely generous in his gratitude. I've heard it said that he's offered his friend vast estates throughout the kingdom, which Spencer has steadfastly refused. If he chooses, he could be one of the richest men in the realm."

"And you covet what he refuses."

"Aye. That and more. Riordan Spencer, with his meddling, has ruined all my carefully laid plans. The coward Buckingham has admitted his guilt, and even now is in the Tower. By morning the king's soldiers will be coming for me as well. But I'll be far from England by then."

Ambrosia lifted her head. "Where do I fit into your plans, Silas? Why have you brought me here?"

"Because I have discovered the fearless Captain Spencer's only weakness. You, my dear Miss Lambert. Where you go, Spencer will follow. And it's Spencer I want. I won't rest until he's as dead as the pirate, Sledge."

"You know he won't be foolish enough to do as you bid, Silas."

"Ah, but he will. Love turns men into fools. The noble Riordan Spencer will be unable to resist this last chance to impress the woman he loves."

He unsheathed his sword and started toward her. "Now, Miss Lambert, you can sit in that chair and allow me to bind your wrists and ankles, or you can try to fight me again. In which case I'll be happy to slice off your hands or your feet, or whatever it takes to subdue you. And when your lover arrives, he can have what's left of you."

She braced herself for a fight. But when she looked into his eyes, she saw a determination born of madness.

And as he advanced, sword at the ready, she could sense his desperation.

Desperation and madness. A deadly combination. And though it went against every fiber of her being, she knew she had no choice but to yield. For the moment.

Riordan led a horse from the stall and, without bothering to saddle it, leapt onto its back and headed into the darkness.

He knew of Silas Fenwick's estate. It stood in a remote, parklike setting on several acres, far from its nearest neighbor. As he raced toward his destination, he couldn't tear himself from the dark thoughts that had set in. It had been the sight of that blood. A man like Fenwick was capable of any cruelty. Hadn't he sent the pirates after their ship, knowing there were five females and two old men aboard who would pay the price for his greed? A man driven by greed with no conscience was doubly dangerous.

As he entered the gates of Fenwick's estate and stared at the darkened manor house looming before him, Riordan vowed to himself that if Silas Fenwick had harmed Ambrosia in any way, he would fight him to the death.

His own life meant nothing. He no longer cared if he lived or died. The only thing that mattered was Ambrosia. He would do whatever necessary to save the woman he loved.

Winifred Mellon awoke from a sound sleep and gazed at the figure of Mistress Coffey, snoring peacefully in the next bed. She sat up, staring through a gap in the draperies at the stars winking in the night sky. A slow smile spread across her face at the thought of all they'd experienced since leaving Land's End.

Who would have believed it possible? They had been captured by pirates, escaped with the king's gold, arrived safely in London and been singled out by the king himself for praise.

These had been the most truly memorable days of her entire seventy-eight years upon this earth. And all because of the irrepressible Lambert sisters. These three feisty women had been a handful when their mother had died so young. Winnie used to say that she'd have rather raised a score of boys than these three little girls, who broke every rule ever set.

She sighed, thinking of the way they looked aboard ship, climbing the rigging, swabbing the deck, handling the wheel. Perhaps she should have broken a few rules of her own along the way. Certainly she'd felt younger and more alive these past few days than she had since she was a girl in ringlets.

She slipped out of bed and tiptoed across the floor, intending to go belowstairs and quench her thirst with a sip of water.

As she passed Ambrosia's room, she was surprised to see the door open, a candle burning on a night table. In consternation she paused in the doorway and glanced around the room, noting the torn curtain, the spill of clothing and bedcovers across the floor. Almost as if, she thought, there had been a scuffle.

Stepping farther into the room, she saw the blood on the sheets, and the crumpled missive lying on the floor. Smoothing the scroll, she read the words, then with a cry flew out of the room and raced along the hall until she came to Geoffrey Lambert's room.

Without regard for propriety she threw open the door and shouted, ''Captain Lambert. You must wake at once.''

The old man sat up, peering at the figure in the doorway. "What is it, Miss Mellon?"

"It's Ambrosia. She's in grave danger. You must dress at once, Captain, while I wake the others."

Silas touched a hand to his eye, which Ambrosia had battered during their scuffle in her room. It was swollen now and tender to the touch.

He glanced in the mirror and was offended by what he saw. A vain man, he hated anything that would mar his handsome, perfect features.

"You'll have to pay for this," he muttered at her reflection.

"You mean this isn't payment enough for you?" Her wrists and ankles were bound so tightly to the chair, she could feel the cord cutting through her flesh.

He had positioned the chair in front of the open door, so that Riordan would have no trouble seeing her when he forced his way inside the house. While a candle burned on a table beside her, the rest of the room was in darkness. Silas stood across the room, his sword unsheathed and lying on a nearby table. In his hand a knife gleamed.

"How do you intend to explain all of this to Edwina and her mother? Don't you think they'll be a little annoyed that their dear Lord Silas Fenwick permits blood and bodies in his parlor?"

"I care not what those two silly fools think. I've already arranged for their return to Cornwall on the morrow. Their vessel will have a little…accident along the way. Alas, my betrothed and her mother won't survive."

"You intend to kill them?"

"Why do you look so distressed? I can tell you care not about them."

"I may consider Edwina and her mother rather silly, but I wish them no harm. But to kill them? Oh, how can you be so heartless?"

"They've served their purpose."

"Their purpose?"

"I needed an excuse to visit Land's End, so that I could learn the names of the ships' captains who would be carrying the king's secret cargo."

"Barclay Stuart." Ambrosia's eyes widened. "You were the one who murdered him."

"How astute you are, my dear. Like Edwina and her mother, you will also have to be eliminated."

"How many people do you intend to murder before this ends?"

He laughed. "As many as it takes."

"You're mad."

His eyes blazed. "Shut up." He stepped closer and swung his hand, slapping her so hard he left the imprint of his fingers across her cheek. "Unless you hold that tongue, I'll be forced to cut it out." His eyes narrowed on her. "In fact, it would give me pleasure to do so. I've heard all I'll allow from you."

He held up the knife, so that the finely honed blade caught the glint of moonlight from the windows behind them. "When I'm finished with your lover, I'll make you pay."

"I'm not afraid of death, Silas."

"There are many ways to die, my dear Ambrosia." His eyes glittered with madness. "I'll see that yours is slow and painful to you, while extremely satisfying to me."

It wasn't a sound that alerted Ambrosia to Riordan's presence. It was just something she sensed.

When she saw his shadow flit across the doorway, she cried out, "Nay, Riordan. Go back. This is all a trap."

The shadow loomed larger, and he stood on the threshold, his sword lifted. "Has he hurt you, Ambrosia?"

"Please, Riordan. You must go. It's you he wants."

"I know that." He was studying her with a hunger that caused an ache around her heart. "I ask again. Are you hurt, Ambrosia?"

"Nay, Riordan."

For the first time he looked at Silas, standing directly behind Ambrosia. "Let the woman go and I give you my word, I'll lower my weapon and let you have the pleasure of killing me."

"I'll have that pleasure anyway." Silas gave an evil grin as he grabbed a handful of her hair and pulled back her head before pressing the blade of his knife to her throat. "Lower your weapon now, Spencer. Or the woman dies."

When Riordan hesitated, he laughed. "It would be a shame to cut this pretty throat when it's so recently healed." He pressed the knife until she sucked in a breath. "What's the matter, my dear Ambrosia? Am I hurting you?"

"Let her be, Silas." Riordan tossed his sword aside and stepped closer. "It's me you want. Take me."

"With pleasure." In one swift motion Silas picked up his sword and ran it through Riordan's shoulder. He had the satisfaction of watching the color drain from his enemy's face as blood streamed down his tunic.

At Ambrosia's cry he turned with a smile. "Did you think I would end his life quickly? If so, you weren't listening. I told you, my dear Ambrosia, there are many ways to die. I intend to show you and your lover all of them."

When Riordan lunged, Silas neatly sidestepped, then brought the knife to Ambrosia's throat once more. This time he drew blood. ''I warned you, Spencer. You're not to fight me. If you do, I'll simply have to punish you by hurting the lovely lady.''

Riordan froze in his tracks. The sight of Ambrosia, helpless and bleeding, was worse than any pain inflicted by a sword. He squared his shoulders. And prepared himself for the torture to come.

''I've never seen Winnie in such a state.'' Bethany tumbled into the carriage behind her sister, Darcy, as it took off with a lurch. When she got her bearings, she pulled out her pistol and began loading it with gunpowder.

Up front, Newton was driving, with the old nurse beside him, urging him to go faster. Their housekeeper, awakened from a sound sleep, looked befuddled. Beside her, their grandfather was strapping on his scabbard, tucking a knife at his waist and looking very much like the privateer he had been in his youth.

''How will we find Silas Fenwick's home, Grandpapa?'' Darcy asked as she fingered the knife in her hand.

The old man looked up. ''Do we know the way, Newt?''

''Nay, sir. But Miss Mellon believes the king will know.''

''The king?''

Everyone in the carriage went deathly quiet.

It was Bethany who finally spoke. ''We're heading for the palace?''

''Aye.'' Winnie's normally pale cheeks were suffused with color. ''This is no time to be timid. We must do whatever it takes to save our Ambrosia and Captain Spencer.''

Ambrosia bit back a scream as Silas inflicted yet another horrible wound to Riordan. This time it was his arm. Blood streamed from both his shoulders.

"Still standing, Spencer?" Silas gave a shrill laugh. "I'll soon have you on your knees, and begging me to end your life. But it's far too soon for that. I have a great deal more pleasure planned first.''

He strolled to where Ambrosia was seated and lifted the knife to the bodice of her nightshift. With one quick slice, it fell open, revealing the darkened cleft between her breasts. "I'll tempt you with that much now, Spencer. Just to whet your appetite. And mine.''

His laughter grew more shrill. A sound that sent icy shivers along Ambrosia's spine, for she knew now that he was completely mad.

As he walked back toward Riordan, Ambrosia noted that he'd left the knife on the table behind her. For the first time in hours she felt a glimmer of hope. If she could edge her chair backward, there was a chance.

She waited until Silas lifted his sword to inflict more pain on Riordan. As he ran the blade of his sword through Riordan's tunic, she shifted her chair backward. It was only a tiny movement, but she wiggled her fingers around and felt the sting of the blade. Ignoring the pain, she closed her fingers around it and maneuvered it until she could feel it begin to cut through the cord. Keeping her eyes on Silas, she continued to slice until she felt the cord begin to give.

She saw blood ooze from yet another wound on Riordan's body, and prayed for strength. Unless she freed herself quickly, it would be too late.

Tugging against the bonds, she felt the cord drop away. Before it could fall to the floor, she caught it and continued holding her hands behind her, with the cord grasped firmly in her fingers.

She saw Riordan watching her. When he realized what she was doing, he turned to Silas, determined to keep his full attention.

"If you were to drop that sword, I'd show you that I'm still twice the man you are, despite these wounds. Or are you afraid to face me without that weapon?"

"Afraid?" Silas laughed. "You can barely stand up. Why would I be afraid of you?"

"Prove it. Toss aside that sword and face me like a man."

Silas Fenwick's face darkened with fury. "You think to prove yourself a hero to the woman, do you, Spencer?" He tossed aside his sword. "This is going to give me pleasure."

Riordan managed to evade the first blow, but when he tried to raise his fists, he found that his arms were nearly useless. He could barely lift them above his chest.

The second blow caught him on the chin and he fell backward, against the wall. He leaned there a minute, struggling to clear his head. Over Silas's shoulder he saw Ambrosia working feverishly on the cords that bound her ankles. He would do whatever it took to distract Silas until she was free. Then, he prayed, she would have the sense to run to freedom.

He braced himself for the next blow and managed to twist aside so that Silas's fist connected with the wall. But he wasn't so fortunate with the next, as Silas gave him a vicious shove backward, then rammed a fist into his midsection.

Riordan dropped to his knees and waited for his vision

to clear. When it did, he found himself facing the tip of Silas's sword.

"I grow weary of this sport. I've decided to end it. And end your life, Spencer. There's still the woman to deal with. I'd like the energy to steal as much pleasure as possible from her before I send her to join you in death."

Fenwick brought his arm back, ready to plunge his sword through Riordan's heart. But just as he did, he felt something hot pierce his flesh between his shoulders. The sword slipped from his hands. He turned. And saw Ambrosia standing across the room. A room that had begun spinning wildly.

His body refused to obey him, and he dropped to his knees, still struggling to reach the hilt of the knife that protruded from his back. With a gasp he fell forward.

Ambrosia raced across the room just as Riordan's eyes began to close.

"Oh my darling." She wrapped her arms around him and held on. So much blood. His eyes were glazed with pain. His pallor terrified her. "Hang on, Riordan. Don't die, my darling. Oh, please don't die."

That was how the others found them when they arrived minutes later. The king and his soldiers stormed into the manor house through the front door, while Bethany and Darcy, Newton and Geoffrey, Mistress Coffey and Miss Mellon came through the window, prepared for battle.

As they surveyed the bloody room, and realized just how close these two had come to dying, the scene became one of bedlam, with soldiers marching through each room of the house, in search of any more traitors, the king demanding to know exactly what had happened, and Ambrosia's family all talking at once.

But through it all, Ambrosia clung to Riordan, her tears

mingling with his blood, her lips pressed to his temple, urging him not to die. Begging him to stay with her.

They were, he realized as the blackness overtook him, the sweetest words he'd ever heard.

While the others stared around at the violent scene of death, it was proper little Winnie who assessed the needs and began shouting orders.

"Bethany. I want water. At once. Darcy. Fetch some clean cloth to bind Captain Spencer's wounds. Geoffrey and Newton, carry him to that chaise. Now. Mistress Coffey, we'll need disinfectant. And opiates for the pain."

Ambrosia refused to let go of Riordan, even while her grandfather and Newt hauled him to the chaise and laid him gently down.

While the others raced off to do the old nurse's bidding, Edwina Cannon and her mother stepped into the parlor, dressed in their nightclothes and looking completely bewildered by the soldiers marching through the house with drawn swords.

"Silas," Edwina called. "Can you tell Mama and me what's happening?"

She paused, staring around at the grisly scene. Spying Silas lying in a pool of blood, she put a hand to her throat. All the color drained from her face. "Silas, my beloved."

"Your beloved is a traitor," Mistress Coffey said as she returned with disinfectants and opiates.

"A...traitor?" Edwina caught her mother's arm and the two stared at each other in stunned silence.

"Aye. And he was planning to have the two of you murdered before you reached Cornwall," Ambrosia announced.

"This cannot be." Edwina began to weep in her mother's arms. "He...loved me. We planned to be wed."

"He was planning to flee the country," the king said matter-of-factly, repeating what he had just learned from Ambrosia. "And he wanted no one left alive who could tell of his treachery. He was merely using you so that he could visit Cornwall undetected, until he could murder Barclay Stuart and steal the list of ships carrying secret cargo for England."

At that, amidst all the chaos, Edwina and her mother fainted dead away.

Too busy to deal with them, the others walked over them as they hurried to assist Winnie, who was disinfecting and binding Riordan's wounds.

By the time she had finished, Riordan was awake and clenching his teeth at the pain.

The king leaned over the back of the chaise, peering down at his old friend. "Are you alive under all those dressings?"

In reply he got a vicious oath.

"I say. Is that any way to speak to your king?"

Again the muttered oath, this time stronger.

Charles smiled at Ambrosia. "He's going to be fine, my dear. I can tell by his...colorful language. He's endured many more serious wounds than these." He turned to Riordan. "You look bloody terrible. You know, old friend, you really ought to make yourself more presentable for your king."

Riordan gritted his teeth against the pain.

Charles merely smiled as he looked over at Edwina and her mother, still lying on the floor. "If someone can revive those two fallen sparrows, I think we should all return to Hampton Court. Since my royal sleep has been disturbed, and morning is upon us, we'll break our fast, and while we're all being restored, Miss Lambert and my old friend Riordan Spencer can tell us all the fascinating details of this latest adventure. Or should I say misadventure?''

Chapter Twenty-One

It was a strange procession that made its way to the palace. The king had insisted that Ambrosia and Riordan ride in the royal carriage. Two more carriages followed, bearing the rest of the Lambert family, as well as Edwina Cannon and her mother. Alongside rode the king's soldiers, in scarlet and gold, their swords gleaming in the morning light.

Riordan was grateful for the cool air. It helped to clear his mind, though he still seemed to drift in and out at times. He was tucked up in the corner of the carriage, with Ambrosia beside him. The king sat across from them, feeling energized by all the excitement.

"How did you happen to be here?" Riordan leaned his head back, enjoying the movement of the carriage. It made him feel as though he were back on his ship.

Charles smiled, remembering. "The Lambert family barged into the palace, making quite a noise. They demanded to see their king, and my servants almost had them tossed out like beggars. But that feisty little nurse just wouldn't accept anything except that she be allowed to speak personally with her king."

Ambrosia gasped. "Are you talking about Winnie?"

"Winnie, is it? She called herself Miss Mellon, and she insisted that I would lose two of my most loyal subjects unless I sent my soldiers at once to Silas Fenwick's estate."

"Winnie." Ambrosia smiled. "Who would have believed it of that sweet old thing?"

"That sweet old thing was like a dog with a bone. The woman was vicious." Charles smiled again. "And did you see how she took over when she saw Riordan's wounds?"

"Aye. I believe she's becoming absolutely fearless."

"It seems to run in the family." He studied the bruises at Ambrosia's throat, visible beneath the shawl her old nurse had insisted she wear over her torn nightshift.

As they arrived at Hampton Court Palace, half the staff was gathered at attention in the courtyard, awaiting the arrival of their monarch.

Minutes later orders were barked out by a haughty housekeeper, and the servants scattered to see to the comfort of the king's guests. Baths were ordered. Fresh clothing was to be portioned out. And a lavish meal prepared.

Edwina, still looking as pale as a ghost, stared around in astonishment. "You mean, Majesty, we are to be your guests?"

"Aye. Until I can arrange safe passage back to Cornwall."

He turned away, then turned back when Miss Mellon shrieked, "Somebody catch them."

Edwina and her mother had once again fainted. As servants rushed over to carry them inside, the old nurse could be heard muttering, "I always thought Mistress Cannon and her daughter a bit too frail for my taste."

Ambrosia and her sisters had to cover their mouths to keep from laughing aloud.

"Apparently," Ambrosia whispered to the others, "Winnie has forgotten those spells she used to take whenever things got a bit too frantic."

"Aye. Let's not remind her." Bethany caught Darcy's hand, and the two sisters danced up the steps of the palace. "I rather like the new Winnie."

"So does Grandpapa," Darcy whispered.

Her two sisters stopped dead in their tracks.

"Whatever does that mean?" Ambrosia asked.

"See for yourself."

As the three young women watched, Geoffrey Lambert gallantly offered his arm to their old nurse. "Come, Winnie. It's time we refreshed ourselves."

"Thank you, Geoffrey." She placed a hand on his arm and moved easily by his side.

As they walked past, Ambrosia turned to her sisters. "Did I just see a slight flush on those pale white cheeks?"

"You did." Bethany was shaking her head in amazement. "The next thing you know, Winnie will be wearing pink, or blue, or even purple."

"Impossible." Ambrosia put her hands on her hips. "She vowed she would never give up wearing white as long as she remained a virgin."

Bethany arched a brow. "You don't think…she and Grandpapa…"

As the thought struck, they burst into peals of laughter.

"Stranger things have happened," Darcy whispered.

"Come along, ladies," Mistress Coffey sputtered. "I suppose it will have to fall to me to see to those silly Cannon ladies."

As she brushed past, the three sisters collapsed into giggles. Had their dour housekeeper just called the Cannon women silly, after a lifetime of trying to impress them?

Miracles, it would seem, were happening everywhere.

Charles paused outside the royal chambers. "I'll expect a full report, my friend."

Riordan nodded. "You'll have it."

As he started away, the king called, "And you'll have that expensive wedding present you asked for. You've more than earned it."

At that, Riordan turned. His words were clipped. "There'll be no need."

"What say you?" Charles shook his head. "Do you deny you love the lass?"

"I deny nothing. But that little scene with Silas has brought me to my senses. This life I lead would bring nothing but grief to a wife."

"And so you'll just walk away from her?"

"Aye. It's the only decent thing to do. And I've done little enough of that in my lifetime."

Charles dropped a hand on his shoulder. "You're too hard on yourself, my friend. What you've done, you've done for king and country. Without you, I'd not be here. And England would not be free of villains like Silas Fenwick."

"Don't misunderstand. I don't regret what I've done. If I've helped my king and country, then it was worth the cost. But I'll not drag Ambrosia into it. She deserves better."

The king studied his face, seeing the determination, as well as the pain, in his eyes. "You're serious, my friend."

Riordan nodded.

Charles studied him with new interest. "Perhaps you need time to think on this."

"I've made my decision." Riordan bowed. "I'll go now and make myself presentable for my king."

"If you were filthy, and clad in rags, you would be the most welcome sight in the world to your king, my friend."

Charles became lost in thought as he watched his oldest and dearest friend disappear along the hall.

Love, it seemed, was never easy. Even for the strongest and bravest of hearts.

"Ambrosia. Look at you." Bethany and Darcy stopped by their sister's room on the way to the king's private chambers, where they were to break their fast with Charles.

"You think this gown too daring?" Ambrosia drew back.

"Nay." Bethany caught her hands and studied the shimmering gown of scarlet satin with a softly rounded neckline and long, tapered sleeves. "The gown is stunning."

"My hair then." She gestured to the dark locks that spilled down her back in a riot of curls. They were held off her face in a flirtatious manner by mother-of-pearl combs. "Is it too fancy?"

Darcy laughed. "Ambrosia, you look beautiful. Why are you acting so fluttery?"

"I don't know." Ambrosia touched a hand to the length of scarlet fabric she'd tied around her throat, to hide the cuts inflicted by Silas. She wanted nothing to mar this first meeting with Riordan since that horrible scene.

"It wouldn't be because of a certain sea captain, would it?" Bethany asked slyly.

Ambrosia turned several shades of pink, and the two sisters looked at each other with sudden knowledge. This would be the day Riordan Spencer would ask their grandfather's permission to wed. It was no surprise, of course. Only a blind man could miss the feelings these two had for each other.

"Come." Bethany opened the door and fairly danced down the hallway to the king's private chambers.

Beside her Darcy whispered, "Shall we pray for one more miracle?"

"Aye." Bethany caught her hand.

Ambrosia trailed more slowly. She had hoped that Riordan would come to her in her room. When he didn't, she realized that he was, like her, taking more time than usual. Wasn't that what lovers did, when they were hoping to impress each other?

She struggled to calm her frantic pulse beat as she stepped into the magnificent rooms reserved for the king's most honored guests.

This was where Charles ate when he wished to withdraw from the public. A room big enough to accommodate fifty or more people, with elegant wall hangings and comfortable chairs and chaises positioned here and there for conversation. A fire burned on the grate, adding to the soft warm glow. A table in the middle of the room had been set with the finest china, crystal and silver, all gleaming in the glow of hundreds of candles. A regal chair had been set at the head of the table. Beside it stood a liveried servant, awaiting the arrival of his master.

Ambrosia accepted a goblet of hot mulled wine and felt the warmth slip through her veins. But nothing would truly warm her until she was with Riordan.

"Ambrosia." Miss Mellon, who had been standing with Mistress Coffey, Edwina Cannon and her mother, beckoned her over. "Oh, don't you look lovely."

"Thank you, Winnie." Ambrosia smiled. "I see you managed to find a white gown."

"Aren't the dressmakers here at the palace amazing?" Mistress Cannon purred. "They had such an array of lovely things, I didn't know which to choose. I simply couldn't believe I was here, in Hampton Court, about to break my fast with the king. But in the end, I managed to make a choice."

"It was the same for me," Ambrosia admitted.

"You chose well, my dear." The old nurse patted her hand, then looked up with a smile. "Ah, here's your grandfather now, and old Newton." She beckoned them over. "Geoffrey. Newton. Come see how well our Ambrosia has mended."

The two men hurried over.

Geoffrey Lambert pressed a kiss to his granddaughter's cheek. "None the worse for wear, lass?"

"Nay, Grandpapa." She brightened when Riordan entered, followed by the king.

At once they all fell silent. The men bowed, while the women curtsied.

"Well, here we are now." Charles lifted a hand in greeting, then made his way to the head of the table. The others followed, taking the seats indicated by the king's butler. "Riordan, I'd like you on my right hand. Ambrosia on my left."

Geoffrey Lambert was pleased to note that he was to anchor the other end of the table, with Winifred Mellon on one side of him and Mistress Coffey on the other. Old Newton found himself between Bethany and Darcy and whispered, "Nothing like a whale between two minnows." That had the sisters giggling into their hands.

On the other side of the table were Edwina and her mother, who were looking so pale, everyone feared they might embarrass themselves by fainting yet again. Their hands trembled as they sipped their wine, and they refused almost everything being offered by the servants. In the end they picked at crusts of bread, while the others sampled thin slices of roast beef swimming in juice, salmon, mutton, joints of fowl, and biscuits still warm from the oven, offered with fruit conserve. It was indeed a feast fit for the monarch who sat among them, talking and laughing as though he'd known them for a lifetime.

Through it all, Ambrosia kept glancing across the table at Riordan, who seemed preoccupied with the mulled wine in his goblet. He answered only when spoken to, and seemed lost in his own thoughts.

Perhaps that was a good sign, she told herself. After all, a man ought to be nervous about becoming betrothed. Her own father had often told them how, after fighting off pirates, he'd sailed the *Undaunted* through a typhoon, and then had raced through the streets of London, refusing food or sleep until he'd proposed to his beloved Mary.

"…to the two of you."

At the king's words, Ambrosia and Riordan were both pulled from their thoughts. Their heads came up sharply. Their eyes locked on one another. Ambrosia smiled.

Riordan turned to the king. "I beg your pardon, Majesty. I fear I was distracted."

Charles smiled. "I offer a toast to the two of you. To my dear friend Riordan Spencer, and to Ambrosia Lambert and her family and friends. Because of your extraordinary courage, England still sails in smooth waters." He lifted his goblet. "Your grateful king salutes you."

Ambrosia blushed as the others lifted their glasses and sipped.

Charles cleared his throat. "And now, I must bid goodbye to my dear old friend Riordan once again."

"Goodbye?" Ambrosia looked from the king to Riordan.

"I have another…mission I must send him on." Charles saw the look of consternation in Ambrosia's eyes and felt a wave of pity. But Riordan, who never asked anything of him, had requested this favor. He had no choice but to grant it.

When they'd argued in his chambers, Riordan had pointed out that the break must be quick and clean. And if it caused her pain, think how much suffering she would be spared in the future. It had been an eloquent plea, and one that had touched the king's heart.

"You must love her even more than I thought," he'd muttered.

Riordan had made no reply.

Now, seeing the way the others were looking at him, Riordan said, "I am your obedient servant, Majesty. I can be ready to leave at once."

"At once?" Ambrosia set down her goblet with a clatter. "But Riordan, we haven't…you haven't…" She clasped her hands in her lap, struggling with all the emotions churning inside.

Desperate, she turned to the king. "Majesty, perhaps I could go with him. As the others will attest, I'm a fine sailor and can fight with a sword as well as any man."

Charles could feel the tension around the table as Riordan stared straight ahead, and Ambrosia's family gazed from one to the other with looks that ranged from compassion to outright fury, especially in the eyes of her grandfather and old Newton Findlay. Charles feared that if he didn't act quickly, there might be a war right here in the palace.

He turned to Geoffrey Lambert. "I've arranged for a ship to take you back to Cornwall. You'll board within the hour."

"What about the *Skull?*" Newton asked.

"She's a fine ship. It would seem the pirates of Cairn spent a good bit of England's gold to have her built. I've presented her to Riordan, to use in service to the Crown. It will be a fine replacement for the *Warrior,* his ship that went down." Charles stood, cutting off anything more they might have asked. "Your king will bid you goodbye when the carriages are ready to take you to the docks." He turned. "Come, Riordan. We have much to discuss before you set sail."

He swept from the room, with his old friend beside him. Leaving the others to stare after them in stunned silence.

Riordan finished packing his seabag, then walked to the window of the palace and stared out at the elegant gardens. It was the first time he could ever recall preparing for a voyage without that heady feeling of anticipation. Instead a feeling of dread had lodged in his chest, threatening to choke him.

He hated what he'd done to Ambrosia. Hated himself even more. But now it was over. Finished. She would grieve. But at least she would be safe. That was what mattered most to him. To keep her safe.

When the grieving was over, she would move on with her life. That thought had him clenching his fists. She would meet a man whose way of life was normal. A man who could give her a home. Children.

He pressed his forehead to the cool windowpane and struggled with fresh pain. The wounds he'd endured at the hands of Silas Fenwick were nothing compared to this pain in his heart. The thought of Ambrosia in the arms of another man, loving him, bearing his children, was almost more than he could bear.

"Riordan."

At the sound of his name he turned. Standing in the doorway was a vision he thought he would only see in his mind. But there she was. Wearing breeches tucked into tall boots. A colorful shirt with billowing sleeves, her hair tied back with a length of scarf. In her hand was a sword.

Under other circumstances he might have smiled. "Have you come to fight me?"

"That depends."

"On what?"

"On the answer to one question."

He sighed. "I have no time for games, Ambrosia."

"Nor do I. The king's carriage awaits us in the courtyard."

He stiffened his spine. He could get through another minute, before his heart shattered completely. "What is your question?"

"Do you love me, Riordan?"

It was on the tip of his tongue to lie. A simple evasion, and he could send her away, knowing she would hate him for a lifetime. But he owed her the truth. He squared his shoulders. "Aye. With all my heart."

Ambrosia closed her eyes. These had been the longest steps she'd ever taken, from her chambers to his. She'd been terrified of the answer. What if he didn't love her?

What if it had all been a lie? But she'd needed to know. And now she did.

She took a deep breath.

Before she could speak, he turned away. Over his shoulder he said, "But this changes nothing, Ambrosia. I still intend to continue with this dangerous game I play for king and country."

"Then I shall play it with you."

"Nay." He turned, and she saw the fire in his eyes. "I couldn't bear to worry about you again, the way I did when you were in the clutches of Silas Fenwick."

"And I can't bear to see you hurt the way he hurt you. But if that's the choice we have, we must accept it."

"I can't. I can't bring you into such a life. Not after seeing you with your family. In your lovely home. With the affection of the people of Land's End. That's what you deserve, Ambrosia. A husband who will give you a home. Children of your own."

"Wouldn't you like those things, Riordan?"

"Aye. More than anything in this world."

"Then we'll find a way to have it all. But don't cut me out of your life, Riordan. Let me be with you. Sail with you. Fight for king and country."

He shook his head. "The worry and fear will eat at us. And after a while, it'll tear us apart."

"A wise man told me that part of loving is worrying and wondering."

"I love you too much, Ambrosia. I couldn't bear—"

She touched a finger to his lips to silence him. Heat spiraled through him, and he had to fight the overwhelming desire to crush her in his arms. Instead he took a step back.

She faced him, chin jutting as though ready for a fight. "That same wise man said that such love comes along but once in our lives. If we waste the moment worrying about what the future might hold, we could have a lifetime to regret it.''

He kept his hands firmly at his sides, struggling against the need to touch her. ''I can't be a traditional husband, who goes to his shop in the village in the morning and hurries home each night. I can't stop doing what I do for Charles, even if that means sailing to the New World and back.''

''Nor would I ask you to. And I can't be the kind of wife who can mend a tunic or roast a goose.'' She touched a hand to his cheek, and he wondered how much longer he could resist this need to hold her, to kiss her lips. ''But I can sail with the best of men, Riordan. And stand by your side in a fight. Isn't that enough?''

''Enough?'' His voice warmed with unspoken laughter. ''Though you're not the sort of woman a man has in mind when he seeks a wife, I find your offer far too tempting.''

Was the warmth in his tone a sign he was weakening? She couldn't be certain, but she had to try. ''If that isn't enough, there is more.'' Boldly she caught his face between her hands, staring deeply into his eyes with a passion that left him shaken. ''I'll fight for you, Riordan. If you're down, I'll lift you up. If you fall, I'll remain beside you rather than desert you. And best of all I'll love you, Riordan. I'll love you more than any other woman could. And I'll grow old with you,'' she whispered fiercely. ''I'll love you with my last breath and beyond, into eternity.''

''God in heaven, Ambrosia.'' At the intensity of her words, he felt a series of tremors along his spine. He'd thought he could resist her. Could send her away, and go on with the solitary life he'd carved for himself. But with

this fiery woman, resistance was impossible. She would
bully and badger and bother him until he was completely
worn out or won over.

And so he would yield. Like any mere man.

He dragged her into his arms and pressed his lips to
her temple. "I can no longer deny it. I adore you, Ambrosia Lambert. And I intend to love you with every
breath that's in me."

He covered her mouth with his and kissed her long
and slow and deep, until they were both shuddering with
need.

"And we'll marry? And sail together? And fight for
England together?"

"Aye, my love. No matter what the danger, at least
we'll face it together."

Her smile was radiant. "Oh, Riordan. Do you know
how long I've waited to hear you say those words? We
must find my family and tell them the news. Quickly,
before the carriages depart for the ship. And the king.
He'll want to know."

Riordan was laughing now. A rich, joyful sound. His
heart felt lighter than it had in a lifetime. "Aye. Charles
will want to know. And your grandfather, who has probably contemplated a dozen ways to maim the man who
dared bring pain to his beloved granddaughter. And we'll
tell them all. In just a little while. But first, Ambrosia,
stay here and let me love you. It's been so long. Too
long." He kissed her again until they were both breathless.

And as they lost themselves in the wonder of love,
Ambrosia thought about the man her father had sent to
carry the news of his death. Had he known, even then,
that Riordan Spencer would be the man to win her heart?

　Oh, Papa, she thought. You told us to carry on. And we have. We shall.

　With this man, she had no fear of the future. They would chart their own course. Together.

Epilogue

It seemed that all of Cornwall had come to the little church in Land's End for the wedding of Ambrosia Lambert to Captain Riordan Spencer.

Of course, they may have been drawn by the fact that King Charles had decided to travel to Cornwall for the event. His white-and-gold carriage, drawn by a team of six matched white horses, was being admired by all who passed by.

The vicar stood at the door of the church, his young deacon at his side, greeting the congregation. The altar was banked with masses of wildflowers, picked by the bride's sisters just that morning. The church smelled as fragrant as one of the lovely green meadows that dipped and curved along the rocky shore of Land's End.

Ambrosia had wanted to be married aboard the *Undaunted*. Especially since young Randolph had returned the ship unscathed from its voyage in pirate waters. But her family had persuaded her that she should be wed where her father had wed, and his father before him.

Geoffrey Lambert stood proudly in the nave of the church, watching as the pews became ever more crowded. The same people who had come to bid a final farewell to John and James were now here to celebrate Ambrosia's joy.

The circle was complete. From death had come new life. Life, he thought, that was amazing in its complexity. It took such strange twists and turns. He'd thought himself an old man, waiting to die. And suddenly, with the arrival of a stranger, he'd found new life within himself. And strengths he'd long buried.

Winifred Mellon came down from the altar, where she'd been arranging flowers, and started toward him. On her face was the sweetest smile. It elicited a matching smile from him. And old, familiar twinges around his heart that he'd thought long dead.

"Have I told you how fetching you look in that pink frock, Winnie?"

Her cheeks turned a becoming shade of pink as well. "Thank you, Geoffrey. And you look dashing in your captain's coat."

He offered his arm and she accepted, walking with him to the little room where Ambrosia was being helped into her veil by her sisters. At the door they were joined by Mistress Coffey, who had insisted upon helping Ambrosia dress.

Now the three sisters were sharing a few private moments.

"Oh, my." Winnie felt tears spring to her eyes when she saw the three young women standing together.

Bethany was in a gown of emerald green, her red hair piled on top of her head like a crown. She stood to the left of Ambrosia, smiling through her tears.

Darcy was in pale blue, with her golden curls dancing about her shoulders. She clung to Ambrosia's right hand, squeezing gently. Both girls wore sprigs of wildflowers in their hair.

Ambrosia was wearing her mother's wedding gown, a lace so fine it could have been spun by angels. Her dark hair spilled down her back in tangled glory. The veil fell from a jeweled tiara nestled in her hair—an extravagant gift from the king.

"It will never be the same, will it?" Bethany whispered.

"And why not?" Ambrosia demanded.

"Because you'll have Riordan now. He'll come between us."

"Nay. Never." Ambrosia's voice left no doubt of her determination. "We are sisters. Nothing will change that. Ever."

"You mean we'll still sail together?" Darcy dabbed at her tears with a lace handkerchief.

"Aye. And stand together. And fight together. When the three of us are together, who can best us?"

"No one," Bethany said firmly.

"Aye. No one." Darcy caught Bethany's hand, and the three embraced.

Hearing a sound in the doorway, they looked up to see the others watching.

"You are a vision, lass." Geoffrey stepped forward, wrapped his arms around Ambrosia, taking care not to wrinkle her gown, and pressed a kiss to her cheek.

"Thank you, Grandpapa. Have you seen Riordan?"

"Aye." He chuckled. "He looks like a man about to walk the plank."

The others laughed.

"That bad?"

"Aye. But he'll survive, lass. He's survived worse fears. The king is offering him comfort. And a bit of ale, I believe."

Mistress Coffey blinked back tears. "Ambrosia, I wish your father and brother were here to see you."

Ambrosia wrapped an arm around the old woman's shoulders and pressed her smooth cheek to the wrinkled one. "They are here, Mistress Coffey. Of that I have no doubt."

That had both the old women bursting into tears, while her two sisters swallowed back theirs. The pain of their loss, still so fresh, was like a knife wound to the heart.

Geoffrey winked. "I think I'd best take these two out for some fresh air."

"We'll go with you." Bethany caught Darcy's arm. "Since most of Cornwall is here, it might be wise to look over the crop of dashing gentlemen."

"You can look if you please," Darcy said. "And they'll most certainly be looking at you. As for me, I have no intention of giving my heart."

"To anyone but Graham Barton," Bethany whispered.

At the mention of her childhood love, Darcy blushed before giggling in embarrassment. She linked her arm with Bethany's, and with a last kiss for their sister, the two walked away.

Ambrosia saw Newton peeking around the doorway and motioned for him to come in.

"Is it all right, lass? I wouldn't want to intrude on yer last minutes of privacy."

"Oh, Newt." She rushed forward and caught both his hands. "I want you here with me. My, don't you look fine."

He looked down at his waistcoat and breeches with disdain. "Mistress Coffey's doing. She said I wasn't to bring shame on the Lambert family by showing up looking like a weathered old salt. Even made me buy a pair of shoes. A pair." He rolled his eyes.

Ambrosia laughed and hugged him. "I appreciate the sacrifice you're making for my wedding day."

"I'd do anything for ye, lass. Ye know that."

"You've done more than you'll ever know, Newt. It was the advice you gave me at Hampton Court that finally brought Riordan around."

"It wasn't my doing, lass. Ye saw yer chance and seized it. I've no doubt ye'll always live yer life that way." He bent close and pressed a kiss to her cheek. "Be happy, lass."

"Thank you, Newt. I will."

"I leave my bride-to-be alone for a few minutes and find her in the arms of another man."

At the sound of Riordan's voice, they both looked up. Riordan and the king were standing together. They looked not like a monarch and his obedient servant, but rather like two old friends who'd been sharing a few words and more than a few drops of spirits.

Old Newton grinned as he walked up and offered his handshake. "I'm wishing yer bride happiness. And ye, too, Cap'n."

"Thank you, Newt." Riordan clasped the old man's hand in both of his and looked him in the eye. "And thank you for the advice you gave."

The old man winked, then strolled away.

Riordan turned to Ambrosia, and, for the space of several seconds, found himself speechless.

The king seized the opportunity. "I realize this is a joyous time for the two of you. But for me, it's a sad moment. This day I will lose the old friend who drank with me, and gambled with me, and wenched..." He cleared his throat. "We once vowed that neither of us would ever become mired in the muck of matrimony." He saw the way Riordan winced, and added, "Well, perhaps it was I who said that. But I think, looking at the two of you, that I'll not be losing a friend so much as gaining a new one."

"Aye, Majesty. I will be your friend."

Ambrosia started to curtsy, but Charles caught her hands to restrain her. "Nay, my lady. Today I bow to you. You have won the heart of the finest man in England." He glanced at Riordan. "Next to your king, of course." He leaned close and kissed her cheek. "I echo what the old sailor said. Be happy, my lady. For you have already made my friend the happiest man in the world. Now I must go and charm my subjects."

And then he was gone. Striding out of the room and up the aisle, where everyone strained for a glimpse of their king.

In the silence that followed Ambrosia turned to Riordan. "Grandpapa said you looked like a man about to walk the plank. Nerves, my love?"

He laughed. "Aye. Until this moment. Now…" He shook his head. "Now I'm wondering what took me so long." He drew her close and pressed his lips to her temple. "Ambrosia, you take my breath away. I love you so much it frightens me."

As the first notes of the harp sounded, she lifted a hand to his cheek and kept it there, loving the touch of him. "I have no fears, Riordan. Not about this. Nor about our future. Not as long as you love me."

"My fearless little privateer." He pressed his forehead to hers and took in a deep, steadying breath. Then he stepped away and caught her hand. "Come, love. I can't wait for that future to begin."

As she stepped out into the aisle of the church, she saw the wealthy and titled guests seated side by side with sailors and housemaids. She took her grandfather's arm and waited until Riordan had joined the vicar and deacon at the altar. And then, as the notes of the harp swelled, and the crowd held its breath, she started forward. Toward her husband. Her future. Whatever it was, she and Riordan would share it together.

Together. It was, she realized, the most beautiful word she'd ever heard.

And then there was no time to think as, before God and king, before a family that beamed with pride and wiped away tears of joy, they spoke the vows that would make them forever loved. Forever blessed. Forever one.

* * * * *

Praise for a few of Ruth Langan's recent titles

RORY
"Great! Absolutely ROMANTIC! RORY soars with imagery, suspense, plot twists and passionate, sexual tension. This is a must read!"
—*Rendezvous*

BLACKTHORNE
"Ms. Langan has written a tender love story with strong characters and powerful Gothic overtones."
—*Romantic Times Magazine*

THE COURTSHIP OF IZZY MCCREE
"A very tender romance that touches your heartstrings."
—*Romantic Times Magazine*

THE SEA WITCH

Harlequin Historical #523—August 2000

DON'T MISS THESE OTHER TITLES AVAILABLE NOW:

#524 THE PAPER MARRIAGE
Bronwyn Williams

#525 PRINCE OF HEARTS
Katy Cooper

#526 PRAIRIE BRIDE
Julianne MacLean

HARLEQUIN®
Makes any time special ™

HARLEQUIN

Duets™

**Don't miss
an exciting opportunity
to save on the purchase of
Harlequin and Silhouette books!**

Buy any two Harlequin or
Silhouette books and save
$10.00 off future Harlequin
and Silhouette purchases

OR

buy any three
Harlequin or Silhouette books
and save **$20.00 off** future
Harlequin and Silhouette purchases.

*Watch for details
coming in October 2000!*

PHQ400

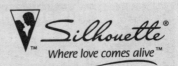

RUTH LANGAN

Award-winning and bestselling author Ruth Langan creates characters that *Affaire de Coeur* magazine has called "so incredibly human the reader will expect them to come over for tea." Four of Ruth's books have been finalists for the Romance Writers of America's (RWA) RITA Award. Over the years, she has given dozens of print, radio and TV interviews, including *Good Morning America* and *CNN News*, and has been quoted in such diverse publications as *The Wall Street Journal*, *Cosmopolitan* and *The Detroit Free Press*. Married to her childhood sweetheart, she has raised five children and lives in Michigan, the state where she was born and raised.

HH523IBC